PRAISE FOR THESE AUTHORS

ELIZABETH BEVARLY

"The very best in love and laughter."
—*Romantic Times BOOKclub*

"Exceptionally engaging!"
—*Publishers Weekly*

TRACY KELLEHER

On *The Truth About Harry*
"Effectively mixes stirring sensuality with sophisticated
humor and light suspense."
—*Romantic Times BOOKclub*

On *It's All About Eve...*
"Well-rounded characters, sizzling love scenes
and witty dialogue."
—*Romantic Times BOOKclub*

MARY LEO

"Warmth, humor, quirky characters—
Mary Leo always writes a winner!"
—Maureen Child, *USA TODAY* bestselling author

"Mary Leo's stories are sort of like wearing Prada with
your circa-70s striped toe socks...classy but fun!"
—Holly Jacobs, 2004 *Romantic Times BOOKclub*
Career Achievement Award Winner

Dear Reader,

It's hard to believe that the Signature Select program is one year old—with seventy-two books already published by top Harlequin and Silhouette authors.

What an exciting and varied lineup we have in the year ahead! In the first quarter of the year, the Signature Spotlight program offers three very different reading experiences. Popular author Marie Ferrarella, well-known for her warm family-centered romances, has gone in quite a different direction to write a story that has been "haunting her" for years. Please check out *Sundays Are for Murder* in January. Hop aboard a Caribbean cruise with Joanne Rock in *The Pleasure Trip* in February, and don't miss a trademark romantic suspense from Debra Webb, *Vows of Silence,* in March.

Our collections in the first quarter of the year explore a variety of contemporary themes. Our Valentine's collection—*Write It Up!*—homes in on the trend of alternative dating in three stories by Elizabeth Bevarly, Tracy Kelleher and Mary Leo. February is awards season, and Barbara Bretton, Isabel Sharpe and Emilie Rose join the fun and glamour in *And the Envelope, Please....* And in March, Leslie Kelly, Heather MacAllister and Cindi Myers have penned novellas about women desperate enough to go to *Bootcamp* to learn how *not* to scare men away!

Three original sagas also come your way in the first quarter of this year. Silhouette author Gina Wilkins spins off her popular FAMILY FOUND miniseries in *Wealth Beyond Riches.* Janice Kay Johnson has written a powerful story of a tortured past in *Dead Wrong,* which is connected to her PATTON'S DAUGHTERS Superromance miniseries, and Kathleen O'Brien gives a haunting story of mysterious murder in *Quiet as the Grave.*

And don't forget there is original bonus material in every single Signature Select book to give you the inside scoop on the creative process of your favorite authors! We hope you enjoy all our new offerings!

Marsha Zinberg

Marsha Zinberg
Executive Editor
The Signature Select Program

COLLECTION

Write It Up!
Elizabeth Bevarly
Tracy Kelleher
Mary Leo

HARLEQUIN®

TORONTO • NEW YORK • LONDON
AMSTERDAM • PARIS • SYDNEY • HAMBURG
STOCKHOLM • ATHENS • TOKYO • MILAN • MADRID
PRAGUE • WARSAW • BUDAPEST • AUCKLAND

ISBN 0-373-83683-X

WRITE IT UP!

Copyright © 2006 by Harlequin Books S.A.

The publisher acknowledges the copyright holders of the individual works as follows:

RAPID TRANSIT
Copyright © 2006 by Elizabeth Bevarly

THE EX FACTOR
Copyright © 2006 by Tracy Kelleher

BREWING UP TROUBLE
Copyright © 2006 by Mary Leo

www.eHarlequin.com

Printed in U.S.A.

CONTENTS

For David,

who made a rapid transit into my life
and thankfully never left it.

Happy Valentine's Day, Sweetie

RAPID TRANSIT
Elizabeth Bevarly

Preface

TESS TRUESDALE, FOUNDER and editor in chief of the ultra-glam, ultra-bad-girl magazine *Tess*, basked in the glow of diffused lighting. She presided from behind her stainless-steel desk while the two other people in her office squirmed in vintage Arne Jacobsen chairs. Danish modern had never been so industrial, so sleek and so uncomfortable.

Tess smiled, content.

No one else did. Or had been. Both states being morphologically impossible for underpaid and overly cynical magazine writers.

"It was one of those karmic things, really." Tess waved the tip of an onyx cigarette holder in a large loop. The mint-green cigarette at its tip burned slowly, a testament to her disregard for the no-smoking regulations in the building and her belief in the mantra she preached monthly to her devoted readers: "Go where no mother has been before, and where no father wants to know about."

"I was enjoying a blissful moment on the deck off the master bedroom of Olympia." Olympia was the "shack" in Southampton owned by Tess and husband number three, oil tanker billionaire Spiros Andreapolis. "Spiros was giving me a foot massage with the new Kiehl's lotion that we wrote about last month, while I was sipping the perfect cosmopolitan. The sun was setting

over the dunes, and there was silence, absolute silence—
except for the occasional beep from the security system,
of course. And that's when the idea came to me."

"That the social season had switched back to the city
one week after Labor Day?" Abby Lewis ventured. One
of the three senior writers on the magazine, Abby had
just returned from a stint at *Tess*'s sister publication in
Milan, Italy. Jet lag, *not* a heavy application of Bobbi
Brown eye shadow, darkened her eyes.

"That salt air can be ruinous for a girl's complexion?"
suggested Samantha Porter, another of the senior
writers. Draped in a chair next to Abby, she wore a
golden Versace ensemble, the tight pants hugging her
pencil-slim hips and the top negligently open to a bejeweled clasp just above her belly button.

Tess flicked the burning end of the cigarette into the
Venetian glass ashtray. "Ooh, I just love it when you girls
talk nasty. It means I've been the proper mentor after all.
Still—" she paused "—I have my moments of inner re-
flection, and not just after having a colonic irrigation.

"You see," she went on, "it occurred to me how
lucky I was with my marvelous good fortune, and that
there must be something I could do—*we* could do as
an organization—to help others achieve some of this
kind of serenity."

"We're going to sponsor a Fresh Air Fund kid to stay
at Casa Olympia next summer?" Abby asked. As if.

"Of course not. I have white rugs. I couldn't possibly have children. No, I realized that what we needed
to do was to help other women obtain my lifestyle."

Tess sat up straight, all business. "What I'm talking
about, darlings, is opportunity. We're going to show
women the quickest, hippest ways to find the right
rich mate."

"You think if we knew the quickest, hippest ways to find the right mate, the right rich mate, *we'd* be sitting here?" Samantha asked.

Tess placed her buffed elbows on the desk and positioned her chin on entwined fingers. "No one ever really leaves *Tess* and all it stands for." She let that pronouncement hang in the air. Then she zeroed in on Abby. "You will delve into the world of ex-dating."

Abby coughed into her hand. "Do you mean extreme dating, as in tandem hang gliding on the first date or making out on the summit of Mount Kilimanjaro?"

"No, Abby darling, that's 'ex' as in former. From what I've gathered, it seems there are women out there who go to great lengths to help hook up their former beaux on this Web site, a kind of online matchmaking service that provides dating recommendations stamped with a type of Good Ex-Housekeeping Seal of Approval. I'm sure you'll find out all about the particulars."

Abby nearly gagged. She clutched her thighs tightly, the imprints of her fingers making deep grooves in the gabardine trousers.

Samantha smirked and didn't bother to hide it.

Tess narrowed her eyes momentarily at Samantha before turning the full power of her LASIK-corrected eyes on Abby. "Now, Abby darling, I don't want to let that little contretemps with your ex-boyfriend interfere with your ability to do this assignment."

"Little contretemps?" Abby practically screeched. "The louse dumped me minutes after I'd won the internship to spend six months in Milan."

"Really, there's no need to be dramatic," Tess replied dismissively. "Besides, the only real tragedy in the whole affair ending as far as I can fathom is that you need to find a new place to live now that you're back in New York."

Abby turned to Samantha. "And who blabbed all the details of my personal life around the office, huh?" It was an open secret that Samantha viewed Abby as a professional rival. When she'd found out Abby had gotten the Milan internship and not she, Samantha had launched her designer-suited-self at Abby's throat. The fashion department had buzzed about it for weeks, totally eclipsing the disappointing London shows.

"Abby, there's no need to point fingers," Tess scolded. "Everyone knows I take a genuine interest in my staff's personal and professional welfare." True, though in Tess's case, everyone also knew she exploited this information for Machiavellian purposes—lavishing an overabundance of care and attention to instill sufficient guilt so that employees wouldn't complain about their measly salary and long hours.

Abby stewed for a moment before accepting the inevitable. "So if I'm ex-dating, what do you have in store for Samantha?" Ah, yes, the other shoe had yet to drop.

"Coffeehouse dating." Tess picked up her cigarette holder and inhaled deeply before taking another breath.

Samantha immediately clutched her nicotine patch. "All those testosterone-impaired, Sartre-spouting losers who are too cheap to spring for their own wi-fi connections?"

"I'm sure some of them read James Patterson," Tess countered. "Anyway, apparently coffeehouse dating works this way. Patrons provide biographical information and photos to the barista, who makes up these matchmaking binders. Then as you sip your skinny double lattes, you can peruse the offerings. Isn't that marvelous?"

Samantha answered by grinding her teeth.

Abby frowned. "You mentioned three writers?"

"Yes." Tess puffed in dramatic Auntie Mame fashion. "I thought Julia would do a wonderful job with speed-dating."

Samantha's jaw stilled. "Julia Miles, the magazine's sweetheart, everybody's sweetheart, doing a piece on speed-dating? The woman who told me she baked a lattice-topped pie for Geraldine in Accounting after her emergency appendectomy. I didn't even know there was a Geraldine in Accounting. Did you?" She looked at Abby, who shook her head.

Tess took no notice. "Unfortunately, she's not in the office right now, otherwise she'd be at the meeting." Tess seemed put out. Her intercom buzzed and she held up her hand. "Yes?"

"Collette can fit you in now," her assistant Ling Ling relayed. Tess went through assistants about as often as a dog marked fresh territory. Ling Ling, the daughter of Hong Kong's leading action-film director, appeared to be able to deflect Tess's jabs better than most.

Tess removed her cigarette from the holder and stubbed it out. "Darlings, I must be off. You *will* bring Julia up to speed for me, won't you? The usual four-week deadline, of course, seeing as this will run in the February issue—in time for Valentine's Day. Remember—first-person point of view. We want our readers to know just how juicy this kind of dating can be, don't we?" She waved them out of her office, a miasma of Creed perfume floating along the length of her well-toned arm.

Abby and Samantha made it partway down the hall before Abby stopped. "So, tell me. What was that all about?"

"You mean the story assignments from hell? To think that the aroma of artificial hazelnut is going to penetrate my pores, not to mention the fact that some black turtle-necked pseudo-intellectual will be drooling over my photo." Samantha shuddered.

Abby shook her head. "No, that's just Tess's usual manipulative behavior to keep the minions on edge. I'm talking about this Collette thing. What was so urgent?"

"Collette?" Samantha waved her hand. "She's the current 'It' girl for giving chemical peels to the stars. Didn't you see the way Tess reacted when I said salt-water wasn't good for the skin?"

"Yoo-hoo, Abby. I've been looking for you." The voice came from the elevators. Julia was racing down the hall toward them. She wore a baby-doll Betsey Johnson dress and ballet flats. Dorothy from *The Wizard of Oz* never looked more wholesome. "Oh, hello, Samantha. Only you can carry off Versace in the middle of the morning." From Julia, that was a compliment.

"So what happened at the story meeting I missed?" Julia asked.

"Trust me—" Samantha imitated Tess lording over everyone with her cigarette holder "—you didn't miss anything, darling." She looked at Abby dismissively. "In fact, I'll leave you to fill in Betty Crocker on the details. I want to catch Ned before he finishes his cover shoot so that he can take my photo. I have to look my most ravishing for the biscotti and café au lait crowd."

"So Ned's still around?" Abby asked Julia after Samantha had sauntered off in her Jimmy Choos.

"According to circulation, there's always a bulge in newsstand sales when his covers appear. Though Tess is complaining that he's too expensive."

"Tess complains that *everyone* is too expensive. What else is new?" She started walking toward her desk in a cubicle around the corner.

"Actually—" Julia took a series of deep breaths.

"Are you all right?" Abby looked concerned.

"It's nothing. Just trying to put in practice some of the stress-busting breathing techniques I just learned about from this tantric sex therapist."

"Yes, well, I can see how Tantric sex and stress might go together." Abby paused. "We're talking about an article for the magazine, right?"

"Of course we're talking about the magazine. What did you think? Oh, never mind. What I really wanted to talk to you about was if you might have some leads on potential apartments? You see, I was planning on having my book group over on Wednesday, and with you camped out in the couch, with all your stuff… Not that you're at all in the way…"

"No, problem. Hey, I've imposed on you long enough. Besides, once I tell you about the latest assignment, you'll probably need to recuperate in a prone position on said couch—just to get over the shock."

"It's that bad?"

"You might want to start those breathing exercises now."

PROLOGUE

JULIA MILES STOOD OUTSIDE the big, ominous door that opened onto her employer's big, ominous office and did her best not to hyperventilate. She told herself that there was no reason to be afraid of Tess Truesdale, that she herself had been a senior writer for *Tess* magazine for a long time now, and Tess had never once made good on her threat to have one of her writers' spleens for dinner. Tess was all bluster and brass and big-shouldered bitching…and Givenchy and Grey Goose and Chanel No. 5. Oh, sure, there was that rumor about the guy from the mail room who'd disappeared and then been discovered months later—in pieces—after misplacing some galleys for the fall fashion issue, but that was different. That had been a guy from the mail room. Julia had never heard of Tess hacking one of her writers to bits.

Yet.

Of course, there was a first time for everything, and the admonitions of Julia's co-workers, Abby and Samantha, still buzzed in her ears. Julia had missed a meeting yesterday about a new assignment for the three of them, and now she would have to suffer Tess's exasperation at having to go over it a second time. Tess hated doing things a second time. If something wasn't done perfectly the first time… Well, that was where the spleen-for-dinner thing usually came in.

Smoothing a hand over her flowered, crinkle chiffon Betsey Johnson dress, Julia lifted a hand to the big, ominous door and knocked.

"Entrez-vous" came her employer's voice from the other side.

Dutifully, Julia entered, closing the door behind her. Tess was dressed in basic black today—in spite of the warm September outside—a mock turtleneck and straight skirt that made her look very much like an older Kim Novak from *Bell, Book and Candle*, one of Julia's favorite movies. Would that Tess would be as sweet as Kim—or would that Julia could perform a little witchcraft like Kim—this meeting might be easier to get through.

"You missed a meeting yesterday," Tess said without preamble before Julia had even completed the dozen steps that brought her to stand before her employer's big, ominous desk.

The comment didn't invite a reply, but Julia did her best to excuse her absence by telling her employer, "I'm sorry, Tess. I was out of the office working on another story." What she didn't add was that it had been a story Tess herself had assigned to her, so if Julia hadn't been around for the meeting, it wasn't exactly her own fault.

Instead of complaining, though, Tess only waved her bejeweled cigarette holder through a haze of smoke in front of her face and said, "I have a new assignment for you and Abby and Samantha. It's for our February issue. Valentine's Day, darling."

Uh-oh, Julia thought. Valentine's Day meant love. Couples stuff. Romantic stuff. It wasn't exactly her area of expertise.

"Valentine's Day?" she echoed with obvious trepidation.

Tess moved the cigarette holder to her mouth and inhaled deeply, holding the smoke inside for several moments while Julia watched fascinated. The woman's lungs must be as black as her attire. Then again, Tess was a stickler for making sure her clothing and accessories matched. She'd doubtless insist on doing the same for her organs.

Finally, Tess exhaled, saying at the same time, "I want you to go out and meet men. Lots of men. And I want you to date them. Then I want you to write about your experiences in great detail for the magazine."

Julia's eyebrows shot up behind her long, medium-brown bangs. "I beg your pardon?" she said.

Tess expelled a sound of impatience. "Darling, you really should have been at the meeting yesterday. It's going to be so tedious having to go through all this again."

Oh, fine, Julia thought. Her editor wanted her to put herself on the block for a virtual gang bang and was calling it tedious? Julia could think of a few other things to call it. Luckily for her boss, she was way too polite to say any of them. And lucky for Julia, too, since saying them would land her on the street without a job like *that*.

"It's called speed-dating," her editor told her. "Have you heard of it?"

"A little," Julia said. What she didn't add was *Enough to know I don't want any part of it.* Because she had a feeling she would have to eat those words if she said them aloud.

"It's the latest thing for meeting people," Tess added.

It was also the lamest thing, Julia thought.

"It's something we're long overdue for covering," her editor said.

It was something that should be covered up completely, Julia thought.

"And I can't think of a better person to write it up than you."

Except maybe someone who actually *wanted* to write it up.

Julia sighed inwardly and mentally cleared her calendar. She was going to need a lot of free time if she was going to be a sacrificial lamb.

Tess tapped the ashes of her cigarette into a millifiore ashtray on her desk and smiled. A predatory, scheming, spleen-eating smile. A smile that told Julia she was about to be coated in a nice mint jelly.

"Darling," Tess said as she lifted the cigarette to her mouth again. "Here's what I want you to do."

CHAPTER ONE

WHEN SHE HEARD THE BELL RING, Julia's first instinct was to come out of her corner swinging. Which was a perfectly appropriate response. Because seated as she was in a bar full of people, wearing her favorite dress fashioned of black lace over pink charmeuse, armed with an appletini (and not afraid to use it), she was here to meet men. And lots of them.

Speed-dating. The words echoed in her head—though it was Tess's voice saying them—as Julia awaited the arrival of her first victim…ah, *date,* she meant, of course. Who had come up with such a concept, anyway? Maybe she should explore the genesis and history of the phenomenon, too, as she researched her article for *Tess* magazine. See if she could find out just where the whole idea of dating en masse for four-minute increments had originated.

Then again, *speed-dating* was a good description for Julia's own alleged love life. In the five years since she'd graduated from college, she hadn't dated anyone for more than a few months. Usually, the guys she went out with disappeared after a few dates. And there had been one or two she wished hadn't lasted more than a few minutes.

Even her college boyfriend, whom she'd dated for more than a year, had been surprisingly easy to get over after he'd dumped her for the captain of the gymnastics team, telling Julia that the whole double-jointed thing was going to be such a boon to his sex life. The joke had been on him, though. It had been sweater-weather at the time, so it had taken a couple of weeks for him to discover that gymnasts have no breasts, and by that point, Julia was *so* over him.

Since then, however, even her breasts hadn't been enough to keep guys around. Or maybe the scarcity of a long-term relationship had been more due to her demand that she be treated with respect and dignity. Hard to tell. Men never seemed able to distinguish between honoring the breasts and honoring the woman.

She shoved a handful of shoulder-length, medium brown hair over one spaghetti-strapped shoulder—thankfully, the September evening had cooperated with her wardrobe by being balmy and dry—fluffed up her overly long bangs, and hoped she hadn't applied her glittery eye shadow and lip gloss too heavily. She wasn't normally one to wear a lot of makeup, but something about tonight's event had made her drop into a Sephora store on the way home from work last night and spend more than she should have on stuff she'd probably never use again.

Or maybe she'd just wanted to adopt a disguise of sorts. The prospect of meeting so many men in one sitting had generated a desire in her to never be recognized on the street. It didn't matter that eight million other people lived in New York, or that one rarely even saw one's next door neighbors in this city. With her luck, every man she met tonight would be standing in line in front of her at Starbucks in the morning. Treating this like a masquerade had seemed like a good idea.

The first man on her list, Julia saw as she glanced

down at her roster of prospective mates for the evening, was Randy 6. Well, now. That sounded promising. It had been a while since Julia had had *any* six…uh, sex. The way she was starting to feel, the randier Randy 6 was, the better.

According to the rules of the game—which the hostess had handed to Julia as she registered for the event, and which Julia had researched even before she arrived—she would have the opportunity to meet twenty-five men tonight. Each "date" would last approximately four minutes, starting and ending at the sound of a bell, with another minute in between for people to move from one table to the next. For the first half of the event—which was being held in the Starlight Roof of the Waldorf-Astoria—the women would be seated at tables and the men would flit from place to place. Then there would be a short intermission for "mingling," followed by another round of "dating," this time with the men seated and the women flitting. It would either be a lot of fun or phenomenally irritating. Julia had yet to decide which.

But she got her first clue—not to mention a jolt of disappointment—when Randy 6 sat down. He looked more like Somethingthecat 8. And then deposited in the litter box. Somehow, Julia managed to curb the urge to strike a line through his name in his presence.

"So. Randy," she began after they'd introduced themselves, already mentally counting the seconds. Just how many were there in four minutes, anyway? She did some quick math. Two hundred and forty? That many? She'd never survive. "Tell me a little bit about yourself."

There. That ought to kill a few dozen seconds at least.

"I don't get out much," Randy 6 said, thereby killing roughly two. Not to mention Julia's appetite. On the up side, her desire for a drink was skyrocketing.

"Well," she tried again, her fingers inching toward her appletini, "you're here now, aren't you?"

"My mother made me come," Randy 6 said. "She's over there."

Then, to Julia's amazement, he turned in his chair and waved at a middle-aged woman on the other side of the room, who, like Julia, was sitting at a table speed-dating. The woman waved back, then made a spinning motion with her hand and mouthed something that even Julia could read as, *Turn back around and talk to her, you big jerk.*

Wow. Speed-dating with one's mother. That gave new meaning to the term "Keeping it in the family." A really icky meaning, too.

"I see," Julia said.

Hard as it was to believe, the conversation only deteriorated after that, and she worried that her session with Randy 6 was going to set a precedent for the entire evening. Sure enough, her next three dates—Ryan 4, Ernesto 18 and Jack 24—were only marginally more scintillating than Randy 6. But the next two, Armand 13 and Michael 19, were relatively interesting. Unfortunately, it was relative to Randy 6. In spite of that, Julia made a quick, surreptitious notation in her notebook about each of the men between rings of the bell, as she awaited the arrival of her next victim...ah, *date,* she meant, of course. For the two allegedly interesting candidates, she wrote, respectively:

If he were the last man on earth, there might at least be hope, if not an actual likelihood, that the human race could continue.

Says Angelina Jolie is too *good-looking, but I'm pretty sure he's lying. Still, could just be being ironic, so might be worth a second look.*

She took a second to flip through her notes. If Armand 13 was as good as it got tonight, the survival of the human race might be a problem. So far, Julia hadn't met anyone she was eager to check off her list as a potential meet-again. Which was what she was supposed to do at night's end—identify any of the men she'd "dated" this evening as someone she might want to see a second time.

The men had a similar list of the participating women and were supposed to do likewise. Their hostess—in this case, a woman who owned a Manhattan dating service—would then compare the lists and see whose names corresponded with whose, and anyone who showed up on both lists would receive notification that there had been a spark of interest on both sides and given the opportunity to make further contact via e-mail.

So if, at the end of the night, Julia put a check mark on her list of men's names by, say, Armand 13—as if—and if Armand 13 put a check mark on his list of women's names by Julia 6—oh, please, God, no—then they'd both be given each other's e-mail addresses so that they might continue with their conversation, and, ideally, a romance. The way things were looking so far, however, Julia was reasonably certain tonight was going to be a bust. Which was okay. Sort of. Because she'd arranged to attend four of these things this month in order to get as full a view as possible for her story.

Gee, had she actually been thinking at first that it might be *fun?* Julia was beginning to wonder. Had she actually attended the story meeting with their editor in chief, Tess Truesdale, discussing the idea—three writers, three styles of alternative dating, no waiting— she could have won one of the other topics. Or maybe changed Tess's mind. Maybe—

Oh, who was she kidding? Had Julia attended the meeting, the outcome would have been no different. She and Abby Lewis and Samantha Porter—all in-house writers for the magazine—would have ended up with the same assignments. Once Tess decided to go with something, there was no stopping her from getting it. Woe betide anyone who thought she could change Tess's mind. No matter what went down in Tess's office that morning, Julia would still be sitting here, nursing her appletini, perusing her notes about unremarkable men, and wishing she was anywhere but—

"Hi. I'm Daniel 9."

She glanced up from her notes with a glib response on her tongue, but it dried up completely when she got a look at her next date. Mostly because there were better things to put on one's tongue than glibness. Like, for instance, Daniel 9.

His sandy hair was thick and tousled, unruly and long enough to let her know he wasn't obsessed with excessive grooming, but clean and combed enough to make clear his desire to look good. And, baby, did he look good, dressed in slightly faded but form-fitting blue jeans, a white oxford shirt open at the collar and a black blazer. His hazel eyes, an intriguing mix of gray and blue and green, reflected intelligence and good humor, as did the scant smile that curled his lips. Even seated as she was, Julia could tell he easily topped six feet, and that every last inch of him was lean and solid.

Oh, yeah. Continuation of the species was looking better and better. As was the species itself.

She extended her hand and hoped her palm wasn't as sweaty as the rest of her suddenly felt. "Julia 6," she said, introducing herself with her first name and her assigned number, as each of the fifty participants had been instructed to do.

Daniel 9 smiled, something that made Julia want to purr and rub against his leg. "Six and nine," he said as he slipped his hand into hers. "Now, why do I think those numbers would go so well together?"

She was so besotted by his dark, velvety voice, and so agitated by the frisson of heat that charged up her arm when her fingers connected with his, that she didn't even care he'd made such an adolescent remark. In fact, she was starting to suffer from a case of overactive hormones herself.

"Have a seat," she told him as she reluctantly released his hand.

He sat immediately, and she made a mental note of how obedient he was. They were off to a *very* good start as far as she was concerned.

"So what brings you to tonight's event?" she asked.

Daniel 9 smiled again, and Julia did her best not to swoon. "It sounded like fun," he told her. And, to his credit, he actually sounded as though he meant it. "I haven't dated anyone seriously for a while, and I've been missing the companionship." He shrugged as if that weren't a big concern of his, but something in his eyes indicated otherwise. "A buddy of mine heard about this thing tonight," he concluded, "and invited me to tag along."

"And how's your evening been so far?" Julia asked.

He pretended to give that some thought. "Actually, I don't think my evening started until I sat down at your table."

Oh, good answer, Julia thought. She was ready to start working on that continuation of the human race right now. She wondered if there was room for both of them under the table.

She smiled, and he smiled back, and suddenly, two hundred and forty seconds wasn't nearly enough. And then she realized she was wasting them by just sitting there ogling him. Oh, wait, no, she wasn't. There was no way a second could be wasted, provided she was within viewing range of Daniel 9.

"So tell me a little bit about yourself," she said.

"Well, I don't like piña coladas," he told her, "*or* getting caught in the rain."

"Excellent," she concurred. "I'm not much for either myself. So what *do* you like? Raindrops on roses? Bright copper kettles?"

"I can handle those," he said, "as long as you don't make me go bicycling through the Alps with a bunch of kids wearing lederhosen made out of curtains."

So he was familiar with *The Sound of Music,* Julia thought, putting another mental gold star by his name.

"What do you like to do in your spare time?" she asked.

He lifted a shoulder and let it drop. "I don't know how to say it without sounding really boring," he said.

"Try me."

And, gosh, smart guy that he was, he totally picked up on her double entendre, because his smile this time was a little suggestive. Oh, goody.

"The usual stuff," he told her. "Movies, music, books, eating out."

"Sports?"

"Some," he said. But he didn't start frothing at the mouth the way some guys did, which was a definite bonus. "I like to watch the Rangers when I get a chance."

Hockey. A manly man sport. Cool.

"And since I grew up in Indiana, I'm really into college basketball."

A small cry of delight escaped Julia before she

could stop it. "I grew up in Indiana, too," she told him. "What part?"

"Indianapolis," he said, obviously as pleased by the discovery as she was. "How about you?"

"Evansville. So do you miss Bobby Knight as much as I do?"

"Hell, yes," he told her. "I don't care what anyone says about him, he was the best damned coach that team ever had."

They launched into an enthusiastic dialogue about college hoops, which was inescapably what Hoosiers talked about when meeting for the first time outside Indiana. Or inside Indiana, for that matter. All too soon, the bell was sounding, announcing the end of their date and Daniel 9's departure.

"Dammit," he muttered, sounding genuinely hacked off.

Oh, they really did have so much in common, Julia thought. She was peeved by the bell, too.

"Intermission's coming soon," he said as he stood. "I'll be looking for you, if you don't mind."

"I'm going to go out on a limb and say you'll find me with little trouble," she assured him.

He grinned at that, lifted a hand in farewell and walked away. But not without looking over his shoulder and meeting her gaze. Six times. Not that Julia counted or anything.

The men who visited her table in the next half hour might as well have had names followed by the number zero, so lacking in *everything* were they when compared to Daniel 9. Nevertheless, Julia made a few perfunctory notes and decided a couple of them might be worth checking off at night's end, if for no other reason than to provide her with some amusing anecdotes for her story.

When the long bell sounded to announce intermission, she couldn't get out of her chair fast enough. She should have been starving for hors d'oeuvres and badly in need of another appletini, but she tucked her notes into her tiny purse and headed for the women's room instead. Not that her bladder was her primary concern. She needed to check herself in the mirror, to make sure she was at her dazzling best. Then she would find Daniel 9 and keep him occupied for the entirety of intermission. With any luck at all, he'd give her an anecdote—or something of an entirely different nature.

CHAPTER TWO

DANIEL TAGGART WAS FIGHTING off a major wiggins at the lusty look he was getting from Edna 12, a woman old enough to be his mother, when the long bell signaling intermission finally rang. With a hasty farewell and without a second thought, he retreated to the men's room, wanting to regroup before he went in search of Julia 6.

What a tasty little morsel she was going to be. In fact, of all the women he was going to, ah, *meet* while researching and writing his article for *Cavalier* magazine, she might end up being the most luscious treat. He quickly scanned the list of dates he'd had so far tonight. Man, the way things were going, she'd be his *only* treat from this batch. Not that he hadn't checked off a number of names. But few of them were women he really, truly wanted to, ah, *meet*. Even for the sake of his article.

He was thankful—and not a little surprised—that the subject of careers hadn't come up while he was talking to Julia 6. So far this evening he'd managed to muddle his way through that mine-filled swamp by lying through his teeth. No way could he tell these women his editor's most recent assignment was a story about the potential for racking up one-night stands through speed-dating events. That was guaranteed to ensure no-night stands with the women Daniel was targeting for his story.

There was something about Julia 6, though, that made him think she'd be difficult to lie to. He couldn't imagine what. He'd gotten extremely good at lying to women, even before he attended his first speed-dating party a week ago.

As if he needed something like speed-dating to fuel-inject his love life. Not that his love life contained anything remotely resembling love.

Sex life, he corrected himself. There. That was more like it. And Julia 6 was going to be a very nice addition to it. Even better, he suspected, than the two women with whom he'd had success at the event last week. And certainly better than the other women he also planned to score with at tonight's.

When Daniel emerged from the men's room, he scanned the crowd until he located Julia 6, at the exact moment she spotted him. They grinned at each other the moment their gazes connected, and, as one, they began to cross the room toward each other. They met precisely in the middle, but not before Daniel noticed what extraordinary legs she had under her short, frilly dress, and how nicely they complemented her incredible breasts.

What was weird, though, was that his gaze kept traveling upward and landed above her neck, and that was where it ultimately stayed. Yeah, her face was as extraordinary as the rest of her, but it was something in her wide green eyes that really captivated him. Not the gaudy, glittery shadow he'd seen turning up on so many women lately, but the fact that the gaudy, glittery shadow seemed so out of place on her. Even weirder was that Daniel usually *liked* to see women wearing a lot of makeup, but now he found himself wanting to know what Julia 6 looked like without it.

The dress, too, as nice as it looked on her, made him

wonder what she looked like out of it. And not naked out, but wearing-something-more-casual out. Which was the weirdest thing of all.

"How many names have you checked off so far?" he asked when they came to a stop in front of each other.

She didn't even look at her list before telling him, "Only one."

"What a coincidence," he said. "I've only checked off one name, too." The lie left an immediate bad taste in his mouth, surprising him. What the hell was up with that? Why did he feel so guilty all of a sudden? He was only doing his job, for chrissakes. "I wish we could leave right now," he added. That, at least, was the truth.

He could tell by her expression she felt the same way. In spite of that, she said, "I can't. I really need to see this through to the end."

"Me, too," he told her. Then, because for some reason he felt that it was necessary to embellish his lie, he added, "For my buddy, I mean. But we should be out of here by eleven," he added. "What are you doing afterward?"

Her eyes widened in surprise at the invitation. "I, um, I really don't have any plans," she said.

"Let's have a drink."

She expelled a soft little sound of surprise that he found strangely erotic. "O-okay," she agreed.

The bell rang to notify everyone that intermission was drawing to a close, and Daniel really needed another drink before facing round two. "Just meet me downstairs in the lobby when it's over," he said. "You need a drink before you head back into the fray?"

Her expression made him think she was a little flustered by the speed at which things between the two of them were progressing. Which was good, he thought. Why should he be the only one here who felt muddle-headed?

She nodded. "Please. An appletini."

"Not a cosmo?" he asked. After all, that was what all the other women he'd met tonight had been drinking.

She shook her head this time. "Too trendy. I don't like to be like everyone else."

He shrugged off the strange irritation that settled on his shoulders at hearing her say that. And it bothered him even more to realize the irritation he felt was for himself. "Consider it done," he said.

With that, Daniel took off for the bar and Julia 6's appletini. Surely that was going to be the *next* trendy beverage of choice for party-girl barflies, he told himself as he went. Because in spite of the naturalness with which they'd connected, and in spite of the ease with which he'd talked to her, and in spite of his singular reaction to her, he reminded himself that Julia 6 *was* like every other woman.

And damned if he wouldn't prove it *tonight*.

BY MIDNIGHT, JULIA AND Daniel were talking again, with a lot more than four minutes allotted them, at Marquee, arguably New York's hottest club. She watched as the bartender placed an appletini and a Scotch and water on the bar before Daniel, who dropped a twenty and a ten beside them to cover the twenty-two-dollar tab, telling the bartender to keep the change. Another gold star, she thought, for the generous tip.

And yet another for the fact that the two of them had been talking naturally and comfortably about everything under the sun since leaving the speed-dating party, without a single awkward moment to muck things up.

Julia couldn't remember the last time she'd been able to talk to a guy with such ease right after meeting him, and she was perfectly content to keep doing it. Talking, she meant. Not, you know, doing it. And looking at Daniel, she could see that he was perfectly content to keep doing it, too. Talking, she meant. Not the other thing. Which earned him yet another gold star beside his name.

At this rate, by night's end, he was going to be his own galaxy.

After collecting their respective drinks, they threaded their way through the throngs of people milling about beneath the boxy yellow-gold lights, until, miraculously, they saw a couple surrendering a table to their right and quickly ducked into it. But instead of sitting opposite each other, they made a silent but unified decision to fold themselves onto the sleek, red-leather banquette by the wall, side by side.

The music wasn't blaring quite as loudly here, and they wouldn't have to shout at each other to talk. Despite that, when they first sat down, they only sipped their drinks and gazed at each other for a moment, as if neither could believe how quickly the night had moved. Julia hated to think about it ending. Then she wondered just how it would end. And if it would still be night— or morning—when it did.

She shook the thought off. No matter how comfortable she felt with Daniel, she barely knew him. Glancing down at her watch, she told herself to find out everything she could ASAP.

"So…what do you do for a living?" she asked, surprised that neither of their occupations had come up yet in conversation.

That was good, though, right? That they'd had so much else to talk about, they hadn't even touched on what was usually the first thing two people getting to know each other discussed.

She wasn't sure, but she thought his smile fell just the tiniest bit as she concluded the question, and he seemed to hesitate for a moment before replying, "I'm sort of self-employed."

For the first time since meeting him, Julia felt a hint of dismay. Had he sounded evasive just then? He'd been answering her other questions straight to the point all evening. Why not now?

"Doing what?" she asked. Surely she'd only imagined his hesitation. It depended on what he was self-employed as. If he said he was a male escort, she could see where it was coming from. And she could see where she was going to. Out of his life. Fast.

Again, he sounded as if he were being deliberately vague when he told her, "I kind of work in the arts community."

Uh-oh, she thought. Maybe he was gay and still in the closet, and that was why he was hesitating. He was by far the most attractive and appealing man she'd met in a long time. He was well groomed and fashionably dressed. And her karma being what it was—namely, *bad*—it would be almost mandatory that any man she was attracted to who wasn't a jerk was either gay or terminally ill, or had a chemical dependency or stalker tendencies.

"What part of the arts community?" she asked.

Seeming resigned now to having to give her a more complete answer, he sighed and admitted, "I'm a writer."

She brightened. A writer? Well, no wonder he hadn't wanted to tell her what he did for a living. "I'm a writer, too," she said. "I'm on the staff of *Tess* magazine."

"Tess," Daniel echoed. "Women's magazine, right?"

She nodded.

"I think I've seen it around."

Well, duh, she thought. *Tess* was only the training manual for every bad girl in the making, telling today's young women not only what to do, say, wear, drink and buy, but also where to go. Uh, for clubbing and shopping and traveling, Julia meant.

"So what kind of stuff do you write?" she asked Daniel.

He seemed to hesitate again before finally telling her, "Right now, I'm working on a…a kind of travel piece that I hope will sell to *Cavalier* magazine."

"Cavalier," she echoed in the same tone of voice he'd used to identify *Tess*. "Men's magazine, right? I think I've seen it around."

"Touché," he replied with a grin.

Oh, she'd love to touché him.

"But it's not exactly a woman-friendly magazine, is it?" she added. "I mean, it's not as bad as *Playboy* or *Penthouse*, but it isn't exactly *The Journal of Sensitive Men*, either."

"I like to think of it as the magazine for men who never quite left their college fraternities behind."

Now Julia was the one to grin. "Apt description."

"And I like to think of *Tess*," he added, "as the magazine for women who think Barbie is the quintessential female consumer."

"No, we think the Bratz dolls are the quintessential consumers," she countered with a chuckle. "Barbie's middle-aged now, after all. Not to mention monogamous. And much too wholesome for the likes of *Tess*. So you're working on a travel piece?" she asked, turning the topic back to him. "I hope you're not just in town for a visit."

He shook his head. "Oh, no. I've lived here since I started as an undergrad at Columbia twelve years ago."

Which would make him about twenty-nine or thirty, she thought, age being another area they had yet to cover. Funny how all their vital statistics seemed of no importance to either of them. They were too busy discussing all the philosophical quandaries of life—and college hoops—which Julia had barely ever touched on with guys before. Now that she thought about it, that went a long way toward explaining why so many of her past boyfriends had had such a short shelf life.

"I went to Columbia, too," she said. "I must have started the year you graduated. School of Journalism, right?"

"Of course."

"We seem to have a lot in common," she pointed out unnecessarily.

"Yes, we do." And, like Julia, he seemed to find that both interesting and agreeable. "So what kind of stuff do you write for *Tess*?"

Julia told herself that was her cue to be evasive and vague, too, that there was no reason to tell him she was writing an article about speed-dating. She'd just started her research and would be attending a lot more parties like tonight's over the next couple of weeks, even going out with some of the guys she met. That was something that could really put a crimp in any potential relationship she might start with Daniel. What guy wanted to date a woman whose objective was to date several men in a short span of time to see who was best?

But Julia discovered, not much to her surprise, that she didn't want to be dishonest with him. Lying could really put a crimp in any potential relationship she might start with Daniel, too. Besides, he was a journalist. He'd understand about getting a story. He'd know the research was just a part of the job.

So, without hesitation or evasion, Julia told him, "Well, as a matter of fact, I'm doing a story on speed-dating. Consider yourself my first primary source."

CHAPTER THREE

SOMETHING ICY AND ROCK HARD slammed into Daniel's midsection at hearing Julia's admission, and it was all he could do not to choke on his drink. "You're writing about speed-dating for *Tess*?" he asked after he finally managed to swallow.

Her laughter was touched by nervousness when she said, "Yeah. Pretty funny, huh?"

He wasn't sure if it was funny, but it certainly answered one question he'd been asking himself all evening. Namely, why would a gorgeous, funny, interesting woman like Julia need something like speed-dating to meet men? And she was covering the event for a story the same way he was. Interesting. He wondered if the objective of her article was also the same as his.

As if he'd spoken the question aloud, she said, "I'm supposed to be looking for Mr. Right. See if speed-dating is a venue where a woman can find a forever-after kind of Prince Charming."

Ah. No. Hers wasn't the same objective at all.

"I and two other writers," she continued, "have been assigned three different types of alternative dating to cover. They are doing coffeehouse dating—you know, where patrons of a coffeehouse fill out forms about themselves and stick them along with their photos in binders that the baristas manage?—and ex-dating.

Which is where a woman sets up her ex-boyfriend with another woman. It's big on the Web. We're all supposed to see if we meet any decent guys for a feature story in the February issue. Valentine's Day."

"And have you?" Daniel asked experimentally. "Met any decent guys, I mean?"

She smiled, and that cold feeling in his belly suddenly went all warm and gooey. "Well, I can't speak for the others—not yet, anyway—but speaking for myself, yeah. As a matter of fact, I have. I met one decent guy in particular at tonight's party."

Oh, that's what you think, sweetheart.

Because Daniel wasn't looking for Ms. Right. No, his editor at *Cavalier* wanted him to look for Ms. Right Now. A never-again kind of Princess Willing. Edward Cabot, editor in chief, had told Daniel that the object of his story was to see how many women he could pick up and have a one-night stand with over the course of a month of speed-dates. And that was exactly what Daniel intended to do.

Julia was right about *Cavalier.* The glossy monthly didn't exactly put women on a pedestal. Unless it was to look up their skirts. The magazine objectified them, poked fun at them and didn't take them seriously for a minute. Daniel had never been bothered by that, because he didn't take women seriously, either. At least, he hadn't before. There was something about Julia, however, that made him want to reconsider.

Bullshit, he told himself. Julia was no different from any other woman he'd met. Hell, she was no different from any other woman period. If he found her sexier or more appealing or sexier or more interesting or sexier or more intelligent or sexier than other women of his acquaintance, it was only because… Because… Because…

Well, just because, that was why. And it was a damned good reason, too.

She *was* just like every other woman he knew, he told himself more adamantly. And just like every other woman he knew, he was going to do or say whatever he had to in order to have sex with her. Then she'd become just one name among many on the final tally for his article. With any luck at all, by morning, Julia would be nothing more than a footnote in his story and a fond memory in his brain.

"Unfortunately, I have to do three more of these speed-dating things over the next few weeks," she said when he didn't reply, sounding a little anxious. Doubtless because of his profound lack of response. "For the story," she quickly added. "I just want to tell you that now, because… I mean, I don't want to be presumptuous or anything, but…" She lifted her shoulders and let them drop in a shrug that was…

Well, hell, Daniel thought. There was no way around it. It was adorable. Dammit.

"Look," she continued, looking and sounding even more nervous now, "I don't want you to think I'm assuming anything, but it seems like you and I are hitting it off pretty well, and I'd be lying if I said I wasn't sitting here trying to get up the nerve to ask you out again. But if I do, and if you say yes, I'm still going to have to go to those speed-dating things and even go out with some of the guys I meet, so I can write about it for my story. I just want to be straight with you about that right off the bat. So if that's going to bother you, or if I'm totally off base about the way things are between us at this point, then be straight with me, too, okay?"

Daniel really wished she hadn't said that. The last thing he could be with her right now was honest. He ap-

preciated her telling him what was what—he hated
when women said one thing while they were thinking
another, which was a malady that seemed to be endemic
to their gender. But he couldn't extend the same
courtesy to her. Not about the subject matter of his
article. Her article, he thought, was really nothing major,
and was actually kind of sweet.

And oh, man, had he really just used the word *sweet?*
Right on the heels of *adorable?* Great. Already she was
turning him into a girly-man. He ejected the thought
from his brain and got himself back on track. With the
speeding locomotive that was his brain, by God.

Her story was a fluff piece, he amended, disregarding,
for now, the fact that he had used the word *fluff,* too. It
was an industry term, dammit. If he told Julia the object
of his story was to sleep with as many women as he
could and then discard them like dirty socks the next day,
there was no way he'd get her into the sack. Not tonight,
not ever. Which would mean he wasn't completing his
assignment as ordered. Ergo, he wasn't doing his job.

That was the *only* reason, Daniel assured himself,
why he didn't want to be straight with Julia. It wasn't
because he was worried she'd think less of him for
pursuing such a story. And it wasn't because he was
afraid he'd never see her again once she knew the truth.
Hell, that was the whole point. To *not* see her again after
the two of them hooked up. And to hook up with her in
the first place.

So donning his most disarming smile—and ignoring
the bad taste in his mouth—Daniel told her, "Okay, I'll
be straight with you. I understand completely. It doesn't
bother me at all."

And he assured himself he was telling the truth when
he said it, even if it felt like a half truth instead. He did

understand why she needed to keep speed-dating in order to write her story. But damned if it didn't bother him.

A lot.

BY THE TIME THEIR CAB arrived at the Chelsea brown-stone that housed Julia's third-floor apartment, it was after 3:00 a.m. Even though tomorrow—or rather *today*—was Saturday, she couldn't believe how late the two of them had stayed out. She was never out this late. The time had just passed so quickly with Daniel. Even now, she didn't want the evening to end. Unfortunately, there was a fine line between good night and good morning, and she wasn't sure she wanted to cross it with him yet.

Strangely, it was because she liked him so much that she didn't want to invite him up to spend the night. Sex was a wonderful thing, and it had been a while since Julia enjoyed it. Sex with a guy like Daniel would be phenomenal. But even before they'd sat down at the club, she'd begun to realize she wanted to share more with him than just sex. If the two of them slept together now, sex would become the defining characteristic of their relationship. And Julia wanted any relationship they might have to be defined by something else. So the sex, she decided, was going to have to wait.

"Thanks for seeing me home," she told him. She opened her purse as she glanced over the front seat of the cab to read the meter. "Since you paid for two rounds to my one tonight, I'll cover the cab."

He curled his fingers gently around her wrist before she could reach her wallet and slowly drew her hand back out of her purse. "I've got it," he said.

Before she could object, he was thrusting a handful of bills over the front seat and thanking their driver. Then, to her surprise, he climbed out of the cab on his side, circled the back of it to hers and opened her door for her.

Julia couldn't remember the last time a guy had done something so, well, gallant. Chivalry really wasn't dead, she thought. Gee, who knew? And it was living in Daniel Taggart now.

They'd shared last names and phone numbers and cell numbers and e-mail addresses before leaving the club—along with middle names, birth dates, political affiliations, childhood injuries and highest spider-solitaire scores. If he wanted to see her again, he knew where to find her. But as the cab pulled away from the curb and he did nothing to stop it, she realized he was thinking he wouldn't have to look far. In fact, he seemed to be thinking the next time he wanted to exchange hellos with Julia, all he'd have to do was roll over in the morning and nudge her.

"You let the cab drive away," she said as she watched the red taillights disappear around the corner half a block down.

"You didn't stop me from letting it go," he pointed out.

"I wasn't thinking," she told him.

He grinned. "Neither was I."

It would be best, she thought, to lay it all out, right up front. Cards-on-the-table time. "You can't come upstairs with me, Daniel," she said as gently as she could. "Not tonight."

His expression changed not at all, so she had no idea what he was thinking. "Why not? I thought we hit it off pretty well."

To punctuate the statement, he lifted a hand to her hair and tucked a few strands behind her ear, then turned his fingers backward and lightly brushed his knuckles over her cheek. The sensation that shot through her in response was nothing short of atomic. Her eyes fluttered closed, and unable to help herself, she tilted her head to the side, so that he might touch her again. He evidently didn't need any more encouragement, because he immediately framed her face in both hands and dipped his head to graze her mouth with his.

It was an extraordinary kiss. He brushed his lips lightly over hers, once, twice, three times…lightly… gingerly…blissfully. Then he took a step closer, bringing his body flush against hers, and covered her mouth more completely. Julia curled her fingers into the lapels of his jacket and tipped her head backward, savoring the sensation of the rough, callused fingers so gentle on her face, the warmth of his body swaying closer to her own, the taste of Scotch that clung to his mouth, the clean masculine scent of him that surrounded her.

As she leaned into him, he dropped one hand from her face to loop it around her waist, pulling her closer still. Julia's fingers crept up over his shoulders, one cupping his nape as the other threaded into his silky hair. It was so soft falling against the back of her hand, and his skin was so warm where she touched him. He curled his fingers under her chin and tilted his head to the other side, and kissed her more deeply still.

Her legs nearly buckled beneath her when he pushed his tongue into her mouth, but she rallied and met him taste for taste, her breathing growing ragged with every new foray. Daniel, too, seemed to scramble for breath as they each grew more insistent. Finally, Julia made herself pull back, end the kiss just as it was about to drag her completely under. The way she felt at the moment, she'd not only consent to Daniel spending the night tonight, she'd be begging him to move in with her.

When she tried to step away from him, he let her go

but caught her hand loosely in his. "Where ya going?" he asked softly, still a little breathless.

She smiled. "I need to go upstairs. Alone," she added before he could challenge her. She truly didn't think she had it in her to say no if he pressed.

But he didn't. And for that, he got a million more gold stars. "Can I see you again?" he asked.

She nodded without hesitation. "Oh, yeah." Although she wasn't sure why she made the suggestion, because it wasn't the sort of thing she did for men, even after knowing them for a while, she said, "Look, why don't you come over tomorrow night—tonight, I mean. If you're free," she hastily added, "and I'll cook dinner for you."

"Oh, I'm definitely free for you," he said. "And I'll for sure come over tonight. But I'll be the one who cooks dinner for you."

She smiled. "How about if we cook together?"

He smiled back. "Cooking together is good."

Funny, but she got the feeling he was talking about something other than dinner when he said that the way he did. And she wasn't quite sure how she felt about that. Good thing they'd be seeing each other again, so she could decide.

"I'll do the shopping and get everything we need," she offered.

He lifted a shoulder and let it drop. With a cryptic smile, he told her, "I might pick up a couple of things myself."

"What, you don't trust me?"

"You shouldn't have to do all the work, that's all."

She honestly didn't know what to say in response to that. So she only asked, "How will you get home? Taxis aren't exactly plentiful this time of night."

"Don't worry about it," he told her. "I'm a very lucky guy."

Before she could say a word in response to that, a bright yellow taxi rounded the corner opposite the one from which the other had disappeared, and it headed right in their direction. Still smiling at Julia, Daniel raised a hand to hail it, and it rolled to a stop at the curb.

"Like I said," he told her, "I always get lucky."

And before she could say a word in response to *that,* he kissed her again, briefly, almost chastely this time, and strode to the waiting car. "I'll see you tonight," he said as he opened the door. "Six o'clock okay?"

Dumbly, she nodded.

"I'll wait till you're inside," he added, jutting his chin up toward her front door. "Then I'll go."

Still not trusting herself to say anything that didn't make her sound like an idiot, Julia fumbled for her keys and made her way up the steps to unlock the front door. When she turned to wave goodbye a final time, managing a soft "Good night," Daniel lifted his fingers to his lips and let them drop again, the masculine version of blowing a kiss. Then he climbed into the cab and closed the door, and the taxi pulled away from the curb. But his face was framed in the back window as the car drove away, watching her.

Leaving Julia to wonder when she would wake up. Because there was no way a man like Daniel Taggart could exist anywhere outside of her dreams.

CHAPTER FOUR

IN SPITE OF JULIA'S HAVING assured Daniel she would shop for everything they'd need to cook dinner, he showed up at her front door with two brown grocery sacks brimming with the makings of a meal that promised to be infinitely more elaborate than the meat loaf and tossed salad she had planned herself.

And he looked even yummier than the food, wearing a pair of snug, lightly faded blue jeans and a light-weight, equally faded forest-green polo that gave the green in his eyes a bit more dominance over the blue. She was glad she'd dressed casually, too, likewise in faded blue jeans, though hers were topped by a colorful, long-sleeved T-shirt decorated with a beaded, spangled art deco French postcard. So accustomed to being in her stocking feet at home was she that she had neglected to put on shoes, which she only now realized as she looked at the heavy hiking boots on Daniel's feet. However, she didn't feel any big urge to go put some on. Already she felt that comfortable with him.

She directed him to her kitchen—which wasn't hard to find since her apartment was roughly the size of an electron—where he deposited the bags on what little counter space was there and began to unpack them. And unpack them. And unpack them. And unpack them.

Whoa. He'd brought more stuff than she would have

thought a man could even *find* in a market, let alone know what to do with. A loaf of French bread, a leafy head of romaine, a bottle of olive oil, free range chiken, she saw with some surprise when she inspected the label—tomatoes, parsley and…a wheel of Brie?

Where were the meat and potatoes? she wondered. Most guys she knew would have brought a half dozen cans of Dinty Moore beef stew and called it dinner.

"And for dessert," Daniel said, reaching deep into the first sack— Good God, what was in the second? she wondered— "Godiva white chocolate torte ice cream. A pint for each of us."

All right. That did it. Julia was ready to propose.

"Wow," she said. "I hope you know what to do with all that. I'm still working on getting the hamburger I'd planned to mix with onion soup mix out of the plastic wrapper. Do you know how that works?"

He grinned smugly. "Not only can I get this chicken out of the plastic," he said, pointing at the product in question, "but I can infuse it with fresh rosemary, poach it in a dry, kicky chardonnay and garnish it with a radish rose."

"My God," Julia whispered reverently. She poked him lightly in the ribs. "Are you sure you're for real?"

He laughed as he turned his attentions to the second bag. "My parents own a restaurant in Indianapolis," he said as he withdrew fresh herbs, red, yellow *and* green peppers, garlic, onions, mushrooms and two bottles of white wine—presumably a dry, kicky chardonnay. "My dad's the chef, my mom's the manager. When I was growing up, while my friends' dads were out in the backyard pitching baseballs to them, my father had me in the kitchen showing me how to broil lamb chops and put the finishing touches on a chocolate soufflé. It goes without saying that I got my ass kicked at school on a regular basis."

Julia smiled. "Yeah, but I bet the girls were crazy about you."

He wiggled his eyebrows playfully. "Good point. And using the blow torch on the crème brûlée was always fun."

"So what can I do to help?" she asked.

"Well, I won't make you take the plastic off the chicken," he told her. "So why don't you open the wine?"

She nodded. "No problem. I'm much better wielding a corkscrew than I am a garlic press. I'm also seriously qualified to choose excellent dinner music."

"That's good to know."

For the hour that followed, and accompanied by the dry, kicky tunes of Michael Bublé, Julia and Daniel worked side by side and shoulder to shoulder—and often hip to hip, so tiny was the kitchen—putting together a meal that was more elaborate, and doubtless more delicious, than anything she'd had since leaving home.

Never before had she realized how intimate—and sensual—creating a meal could be. Along with the sound of jazzy music, the aromas and textures and tastes of the food—to which they frequently helped themselves and then fed to each other—there was the jolt of electricity and the thrill of anticipation that shot through her every time their bodies touched. By the time they sat down to eat, they'd already finished one bottle of wine and opened the second, and they'd sampled enough of the meal to make them leave fully half of their dinners on their plates.

They did, after all, have to save room for ice cream.

But first, Julia wanted to simply bask in the happiness that was dinner with Daniel. He was amazing. Incredible. Too good to be true. Gorgeous, funny, smart, decent. He smelled great—and not just from the garlic, either—was easy to talk to and made her feel as though nothing in the world would ever go wrong again. And he could cook.

There had to be something wrong here, she told herself. No guy could be this perfect and still be available. And she wasn't the sort of woman who experienced this kind of good luck.

So maybe, she thought, finally, her turn had come. Maybe it *was* possible to meet Mr. Right through a venue like speed-dating. Maybe, just maybe, her prince had finally come.

"THAT WAS WONDERFUL," Daniel said at the end of dinner as he twirled his wine idly by the base of the glass.

He hoped Julia would realize he was talking about a lot more than the meal. In fact, he couldn't remember the last time he'd enjoyed himself this much on a date. Probably, he thought, because he'd *never* enjoyed himself this much on a date.

He still wasn't sure what had come over him to make him offer to cook for Julia. That was a side of himself he normally never showed to anyone, male or female. It wasn't that he thought cooking wasn't a masculine pursuit, or that he was ashamed of what his father did for a living. On the contrary, not only was Steven Taggart one of the most celebrated chefs in Indianapolis, whose restaurant commanded four stars from the *Michelin Guide*, he was also the one who had fostered Daniel's love of both basketball and hockey.

But as adept at cooking as Daniel was, it was neither a vocation nor a hobby he had wanted to pursue, and he hadn't done much of it since leaving home. Cooking reminded him too much *of* home. It was something he did with family, in a family environment, something that roused feelings of comfort and affection and happiness and domestic tranquility. Which, now that he thought about it, might be why he'd never wanted to share it with women.

So why had he been so eager to offer to cook for Julia?

She looked great tonight, he thought, pushing the question away without answering it. He liked her better in the jeans and T-shirt and sock feet than he had in the party-girl outfit of the night before. If she was wearing any makeup tonight, he sure couldn't see it. And instead of the curly, flyaway do her hair had been arranged in the night before, tonight it fell in soft waves over her shoulders, enough of it clipped back in a barrette to make Daniel's fingers itch to loosen it.

"It was good, wasn't it?" she agreed, looking at him in a way that told him she was talking about more than just the meal, too. "But now we have to clean up," she added, wrinkling her nose.

"It won't take long with two of us," he said.

And, with two of them, it didn't. In no time at all, they had completed the task and were bringing fresh glasses of wine into the living area—the apartment wasn't large enough for an actual living *room*. But as comfortably as they'd spoken throughout the preparation and consumption of dinner, once they were sitting beside each other with nothing to do, neither seemed to know what to say.

Julia had dropped into one corner of the sofa while Daniel had folded himself onto the other. It was a small couch, and the gap between them probably wasn't more than a couple of feet. Just enough to be annoying, he thought, but still enough that if he scooted himself closer to her, it would be an obvious ploy to get closer to her.

But then, why shouldn't he be obvious about that? he

asked himself. He and Julia weren't in high school, right? Even if, for some reason, he had sort of felt like an adolescent with his first big crush since meeting her. Gee whiz, maybe they could play spin the bottle. Golly willikers, maybe that would give him an excuse for why he had to kiss her and get her girl cooties all over himself.

He blew out an exasperated breath at the thought.

"What?" she asked, obviously hearing it.

He shook his head. "I was just sitting here trying to think up some excuse for why I could move closer to you," he said.

She smiled. "Why do you need an excuse to do that?"

He smiled back. "Good question."

Just as Daniel began to scoot himself down on the sofa toward Julia, she scooted herself closer to him, until they were seated immediately beside each other, *almost* touching, in the middle.

"That's more like it," he said.

"Indeed it is," she agreed.

"So. Come here often?" he asked.

"Occasionally," she replied. "But I don't like to be a regular anywhere. So some nights, I go to the chair over there in the 'burbs, and other nights, I like to go uptown to the table. When I'm feeling really wild and want to party hearty, I head downtown, to the kitchen."

He nodded. "Must cost a fortune in cab fare."

"It's okay. Here in my world, I'm independently wealthy."

He laughed at that. Then, before he could stop himself, he heard himself say, "I really like you, Julia Miles."

She seemed surprised at hearing his admission. Maybe even as surprised as Daniel was to have uttered it. "I like you, too, Daniel Taggart. You're—" But she halted before completing the remark.

"I'm what?" he asked.

She seemed to give that some thought before answering. "Different," she told him.

He wasn't sure if that was a good thing or not. "Different from what? Other guys? Serial killers? Tropical fruit? Waterfowl? What?"

"Just different," she said with a laugh. "From other guys *and* tropical fruit. You're just fun to be with."

"And that makes me different from other guys and tropical fruit."

She nodded. "Yeah. It makes you pretty wonderful."

Daniel thought she was pretty wonderful, too, but he wasn't ready to reveal that to her. Not yet. Bad enough he'd told her he liked her. He honestly didn't say things like that to women. Especially not after having met them barely twenty-four hours before. Hell, how could you even know if you liked someone in that short amount of time?

Strangely, though, he did know it about Julia. He wasn't sure how. And there was something else he knew, too. He knew he wanted to kiss her. Badly. He just wasn't sure how to go about it.

Which was nuts, because Daniel never second-guessed himself with women. If he wanted to kiss one, he kissed her. Something about Julia, though, made him hesitate. He wanted to make sure he did it right the first time. Because he wanted there to be a second time. And a third. And a fourth.

Don't think about it, he told himself. Just do it.

But all he managed was to lift a hand to her face, to cup her cheek in his palm and hold her gaze intently with his. Julia didn't seem surprised by his touch, and in fact lifted her hand, too, toward his face. She skimmed her fingers lightly along the line of his jaw, then down to the back of his neck. His heart hammered harder as her fingers wandered into his hair, fondling the shorter strands at his nape, sparking something hot and frantic deep inside him. Then she hesitated for a moment, her fingers stilling against his skin as if she were trying to decide if she really wanted to do whatever she was thinking about doing.

Daniel held his breath in anticipation, then slowly released it when she moved forward to rest her forehead against his. Her breath stirred the fine hairs at his temple and warmed his face, and her heat and her fragrance surrounded him.

Her mouth was scarcely an inch from his own now, her lips parted slightly in an unmistakable invitation. As if she couldn't quite bring herself to be the one to kiss him, but very much wished he would kiss her. So Daniel closed what little distance still remained between them, slanting his mouth over hers. She gasped softly in surprise and stiffened for a brief moment, as if she honestly hadn't thought he would kiss her. Then, just as quickly, she melted into him, tunneling the fingers of both hands through his hair, kissing him with equal fire, equal need, equal hunger.

Daniel bit back a groan and cupped the crown of her head in his palm, dropping his other hand to curve his fingers over her shoulder. As they warred over possession of the kiss, Julia pushed her body closer to his, and his hand drifted lower, down along her arm, over her rib cage, her waist, her hip, then back up again. As he did, he pulled her closer still, devouring her even more voraciously. When she raked his lower lip softly with her teeth, he drove his tongue into her mouth, then groaned as she sucked him in deeper still.

Something dark and explosive shattered inside him,

and, his mouth never leaving hers, he looped both arms around her waist and tugged her onto his lap. He continued to kiss her as he reached for the barrette at the back of her head and unclipped it, relishing the sensation of soft silk spilling over his hand.

Julia uttered a hushed little whimper in response, then shifted in his lap, roping both arms around his neck. Daniel dropped one hand to her hip, splaying his fingers wide over the denim, opening the other over the small of her back. She felt so good against him, her body fitting so perfectly against his own. She was soft in all the places he was hard, curved where he was angled. She was all the things he wasn't, and somehow that made him want her all the more.

For a long time, they only held each other, kissed each other, enjoyed each other, until Daniel couldn't tolerate not knowing more of her. Slowly, tentatively, he pushed the hand on her hip higher, over her waist, along her rib cage, until he encountered the lower curve of her breast, cradling it in the deep V of his thumb and forefinger. Julia sighed at the contact but didn't pull away. In fact, she leaned in closer, deepening their kiss. So Daniel inched his fingers higher, covering her breast completely with his hand.

The sound she uttered then was wholly erotic, sparking heat deep inside him where he'd never felt it before. She moved in his lap, her bottom rubbing against him, stirring his erection to completion in one swift maneuver. As he gently kneaded her breast, loving how it filled his palm so perfectly, he moved the hand on her back lower. He tugged at her shirt until it was free of her jeans, then dipped his fingers beneath it to open them again, this time over hot, naked skin.

Too much, too soon, he thought the moment their

bare flesh made contact. It was a realization completely out of character for him. To Daniel, there was never enough when it came to sex, and it was never too soon to have it. So it was even more out of character when he, and not Julia, ended the kiss. But, suddenly, he jerked his mouth from hers, pulling back to look her squarely in the eye.

Gasping for breath and groping for coherent thought, he somehow managed to ask her, "What are you doing for breakfast tomorrow?"

She leaned in again, touching her forehead to his the way she had before, a gesture that was sweet and affectionate and should have had him running for his life in the opposite direction. Instead, it made him want to kiss her again.

"Daniel," she said, pulling his name out on a long groan. "I know this is going to make me sound like a tease considering what we're doing. But I don't think I'm ready to—"

He moved his hand to cover her lips, halting her objection before she could utter it. "I'm not asking to spend the night," he said.

And strangely, he realized that was true. Oh, all right, half true. If she had invited him into her bedroom right now, he would, without question, have followed her. But the knowledge that this evening wasn't going to end in sex—and that he was the one who'd put a stop to things—didn't bother him the way it should have. The way it would have, had Julia been anyone else. He was satisfied enough—for now—just to have been able to spend time with her. To have held her. Kissed her. Touched her bare flesh, if only for an instant. For some reason, he didn't want to know any more than that tonight.

"I just meant," he said, "if you're not busy tomorrow, do you want to meet for breakfast somewhere?"

Did he only imagine the look of disappointment that clouded her features for a moment? he wondered. Must have, he quickly decided. Because she was the one who'd said she wasn't ready to go any further. Even if Daniel was beginning to suspect the same was true of himself.

"I'd love to meet for breakfast," she said. "Just tell me where and when to be there. But Daniel," she added with a smile that was almost shy. "You don't have to leave just yet, do you?"

He grinned, withdrew his hand from beneath her shirt and awkwardly tucked it back into her jeans. Then he wrapped his arms around her waist, kissed her once, twice, three times, four, and told her, "No. Of course not. We can still sit here and…chat…for a while." Then he covered her mouth with his again.

And again. And again. And again…

CHAPTER FIVE

"SO. HOW'S THE SPEED-DATING story coming?"

Tess Truesdale asked the question just as Julia was enjoying a forkful of her carryout Waldorf salad, so she had to spend a few minutes chewing before she could reply. After all, dribbled lettuce and grapes would in no way complement her pale blue, pleated, beribboned miniskirt and cropped, ribbon-tied blazer of the same color. Tess had also lightened up today and was dressed in a clingy ivory sheath of pure silk, accessorized by a clunky bronze necklace that could have come from the Egyptian room at the British Museum—and, knowing Tess, it probably had.

Julia had been surprised by her editor's invitation to share lunch in Tess's office, but now realized her employer intended for this to be a working lunch. Which, of course, came as no surprise at all.

"It's going very well," she said evasively, not sure how much she wanted her editor to know about her budding relationship with Daniel. If indeed what she and Daniel had was a relationship, and if indeed it was budding.

It was still too new, too fragile, too personal to talk about—with anyone—having been only a few days since they'd made dinner together. But, Julia had awoken two mornings ago in a much better mood than she normally did on a Monday. That could only be because she'd spent her weekend with Daniel. Breakfast Sunday had led to a movie in the afternoon, then dinner that evening. And then drinks al fresco by the park before Daniel escorted her home, lingering inside her apartment just long enough to kiss her good-night. Twenty-seven times.

They'd spent Monday and Tuesday evening together, too, not to mention lunch yesterday. In fact, since meeting Daniel Friday night, Julia had spent virtually every moment of her nonworking life in his presence. Normally, being with one person that much would drive her nuts. With Daniel, though, the days had seemed to pass too quickly. Already, she was anticipating meeting him again, that night after work.

"And by 'very well,' you would mean…?" Tess asked.

Julia shrugged, hoping the gesture didn't look as awkward as it felt. "I mean it's going very well," she said.

Tess narrowed her eyes suspiciously. "Have you met any men who might be worth mentioning for the article?"

"One or two," Julia told her. The correct answer, naturally, being one. The other men she'd met weren't exactly "worth" mentioning. Except maybe to provide some comic relief.

Tess uttered a sound of exasperation that put Julia on red alert, tossing her fork into her Cobb salad with much flourish. "Tell me you're not wasting the magazine's time," she demanded.

"I'm not wasting the magazine's time," Julia vowed.

"Tell me this article is going to be excellent," Tess insisted.

"The article is going to be excellent," Julia promised.

"Tell me you've met someone special to write about."

"I've met someone special," Julia assured her. And then she smiled. Because she just couldn't help herself.

"Oh, Tess, I've met someone *wonderful*," she added as she leaned back in her chair.

This time when her editor smiled at her, Julia didn't feel at all like the main course. Because this time, Tess seemed genuinely delighted by what she was hearing. "Tell me more," the other woman said.

Julia shook her head slowly, honestly not knowing where to begin. "I didn't think I'd meet anyone even halfway decent doing this speed-dating thing," she confessed, "but this guy…" She sighed eloquently. "He's too good to be true, Tess. Gorgeous, funny, smart, kind, *totally* decent…"

"Nice ass?" Tess asked.

"Great ass," Julia replied with a chuckle. "And he cooks."

"He does not," Tess gasped incredulously.

Julia nodded enthusiastically. "He can poach chicken in a kicky chardonnay."

"Get out."

"And make radish roses."

Tess made a disappointed sound as she moved her fork around in her own salad. "He's gay, darling. He just hasn't accepted it. Find someone else to write about."

"He's *not* gay," Julia said with certainty. "Trust me."

Tess's smile turned satisfied. "Then the two of you have—"

"No," Julia interrupted her. "We haven't. Not all the way. Which is another thing that makes him different from other guys. He's not in a big rush to have sex."

"I hear a 'but' in that sentence," Tess said.

Julia had, too, quite frankly, something that rather surprised her. "But…" she said. "But I think maybe *I'm* starting to be in a rush for it myself. I really like him. A lot. I mean, maybe I even…"

No. She stopped herself before completing the state-ment—verbally *or* mentally. She would not permit herself to say it. She would not permit herself to feel it. Not yet. It hadn't been long enough to know if she even…

No. She halted herself again. Not yet.

Tess nodded with much approval. "Good. I was be-ginning to worry about you, darling. You and Abby and Samantha, all of you. None of you girls has enough epic romance in your life."

And Tess would know, Julia thought, since she was cur-rently working on the third epic romance of her own life.

"It's going to be a great article, Tess," Julia promised again. "Because Daniel is such a great guy. There have even been times this week when I honestly found myself thinking he might just be…"

No. Not yet.

"The one?" Tess finished for her.

For a moment, Julia didn't dare acknowledge anything of the kind, certain she'd jinx it if she did. And also because she wasn't ready to admit it yet, on account of—had she mentioned?—it was too soon for her to know such a thing. Then she realized how silly she was being. Nothing could jinx the way she and Daniel were together. And she was completely crazy about him.

"Yeah," she said softly. "Sometimes, I think he might just be…the one."

Tess sat back in her chair, propping her elbows on the arms and tenting her fingers together. It was her life-is-good pose. "I like seeing you so enthusiastic, darling," she said. "It will serve you well when you write this article."

Naturally, Tess would see it that way, Julia thought, forking up another bite of salad. She herself saw it another way entirely. Forget the article. Having Daniel in her life was serving to make Julia happy. Deliciously so. She didn't know what she'd done to deserve such incredibly good fortune, but she wasn't about to question it.

Daniel Taggart was a dream come true. Perfect beyond words. The answer to every silent plea for Mr. Right she'd ever sent out. Regardless of the manner in which she'd found him, and no matter what Abby and Samantha experienced on their assignments, Daniel *was* Mr. Right.

Tess was right. Life was good. And Julia couldn't imagine a single thing that would change that.

DANIEL HESITATED BEFORE entering the bar his editor had directed him to for yet another round of speed-dating, wondering at the likelihood of running into Julia here. She had said she would be attending three more of these parties herself. Just how many speed-dating events were going on in New York on any given night?

He did some quick mental math. Eight million people, probably half of them adults, then another half of those single, then half of the singles looking, then another half desperate enough to try a half-dozen different types of dating... Half by half by half by half, then a half dozen of that... Drop the zero, carry the two, then divide by pi... Do the hokeypokey and turn yourself around...

Oh, hell. The chances were probably pretty good.

But the bar was packed, he reassured himself as he peeked inside, so he could probably pop in for a quick look around without being noticed. Grab one of the lists of participants for the event to see if Julia's name was on it. Not that anyone was ever fully identified by name at these things, since security was a major consideration, especially for the women. But there were usually first names followed by a number or letter, or people were identified by drink preferences, or celebrity names they chose for themselves, or some character trait like "Loves music" or "Sleeps in the buff" or something. If Julia was on the list, Daniel was confident he knew enough about her by now to recognize her, even under an alias.

And the reason he knew enough about her was because the two of them had seen each other nearly every day in the week that had passed since the night they'd cooked together in her kitchen. And then cooked together on her couch. No, what had happened couldn't be called a one-night stand by any stretch of the imagination. But they had enjoyed quite a nice little makeout party. Then they'd enjoyed some Marx Brothers on DVD. Then they'd enjoyed those two pints of Godiva.

And it went a long way toward telling Daniel how far gone he was on Julia that he'd returned home that night feeling even better than he had after those delirious one-night stands with the two women from that first speed-dating party.

Only a week, he marveled. Damned if it didn't feel as if he'd known Julia for years. He had barely seven days' worth of memories of her, but there were so many good ones, it might as well have been enough for a lifetime.

In addition to the ones from dinner last Saturday, there was spending the day with her all day Sunday. There was lunch at Rockefeller Plaza, where they'd met three days this week because it was located almost exactly midway between their two workplaces. There was the midweek foray to an off-off-Broadway play that was so bad they'd spent two hours afterward improving the writing themselves. There was the trip to the Metropolitan Museum of Art, a place Julia said she visited once a week to keep herself in touch with her humanity, a place Daniel hadn't visited since college. Seeing it again with her, he wondered why he'd stayed away.

He was supposed to have hit on her once to see if he could score, and when it became clear that first night he wouldn't make it past first base, he should have moved on to greener pastures. Greener baseball diamonds. Whatever. Instead, he'd gone home that first night feeling oddly relieved that she *hadn't* invited him up to her place. Odder still was the fact that he hadn't pressed to get her into bed since then. Not even the night they'd cooked together. For the life of him, he didn't know why. He was just having too much fun getting to know Julia. Talking with Julia. Doing other things with Julia. Being with Julia. Yeah, he wanted her. Something fierce. But there was so much else he wanted, too.

The image of her face swam up in his brain then, the way it had a habit of doing lately, her mouth curled into that wry smile, her green eyes laughing at something. She laughed a lot, he'd noticed. She found humor in almost everything, the same way he did. She had a quirky way of looking at things that was unlike anyone else's. In spite of his own protestations to the contrary that first night, he had no choice but to admit she was like no woman he'd ever met before. Daniel liked that. He liked all of it. Hell, he just liked Julia. A lot.

And he had no idea what to do about it.

He glanced down at the list in his hand, reminding himself he wasn't supposed to be thinking about Julia right now. In fact, he should be putting thoughts of her as far away from himself as he could. Because he had a job to do tonight. He had women to meet and charm and cajole into bed. And then abandon. The way he was supposed to have done with Julia.

And dammit, would he never be able to think about anything again without having her slip into his thoughts?

Work, he reminded himself. Work now. Julia later. Then he chuckled derisively at himself. If work turned out the way it was supposed to tonight, Julia had better not find out about "later."

Man, could he do that? he asked himself. Could he really sleep with some woman he picked up tonight for casual sex, just so he'd have a story to write? Well, yeah, since he'd already done it twice. But that was before Julia. Could he do it now? Sleep with some stranger one time and hope that the woman he was beginning to care about never found out? A month ago, he could have answered that question easily, and in the affirmative. Tonight, though…

Damn. He honestly didn't know.

No names, he saw when he looked down at the list in his hand. No identifying elements at all. Damn. The participants for this event were only assigned numbers. There was no way he'd be able to tell if Julia was among them.

He really needed to stay for this party tonight, he told himself. Because the third one he'd attended—the Sunday night after meeting Julia—had been a complete bust. Not a single woman in the bunch had stirred his libido in the slightest, and he'd gone home alone.

And it wasn't as if he had high standards. His main requirement in a woman was that she needed to have produced estrogen at some point in her life. His second was that she have a pulse. His third was that she breathe oxygen. His fourth and final was that she not set off his gag reflex. Yet *still* he'd ended that third party without checking off a single name from his list.

And he'd been so besotted by Julia at the second event that he hadn't even turned in his name list at the end of the night. Thank God for the two women from the first party or he wouldn't have a story at all. Thing was, he could barely remember either one of them now. Good thing he'd taken notes.

All the more reason to focus on work tonight, he told himself. He was in desperate need of material. Which meant he had to go to this party and find a few halfway decent—or rather, wholly *in*decent—women to fill the pages of his story.

As long as, you know, Julia wasn't here.

Still wary of her appearance, Daniel hovered near the front entry, skirting the wall, keeping one eye on the door, in case she was a last-minute show. But by the time the party finally got going, ten minutes late, there was still no sign of her. Obviously she wasn't coming tonight, so he'd be free to pick up women at will. And as he'd scanned the crowd looking for Julia, he'd spied a number of attractive women who might work well for his purposes. At least none of them had set off his gag reflex, all clearly possessed beating hearts, and he couldn't detect gills on any of them. Now, as long as he didn't see any Adam's apples or facial hair...

A tall slender redhead caught his eye as he was pondering her hormonal composition, and she smiled at him. Naturally, Daniel smiled back. He waited for that kick to the gut that usually hit him when a pretty woman smiled at him that way, but it never came. Neither did the heated speculation about what she looked like naked that usually came right after the kick to the gut. Nor did the deep-seated sexual anticipation that had his fingers curling over imaginary breasts.

Which could mean only one thing.

He was so far gone on Julia that it was absolutely, unequivocally, irretrievably *essential* that Daniel get that woman into bed *tonight,* and enjoy every last inch of her. Twice. At least. Because maybe that, finally, would work Julia Miles out of his system, and put him back on the road to eternal hound-dogging perdition, which was where he wanted to be. Right?

Damn right.

Daniel had neither the time, nor the inclination, to be besotted with anyone. Besotment led to even worse things. Things like commitment and monogamy and chick flicks and remembering obscure milestone anniversaries like the day they discovered a gum wrapper on the street together. He had far more important things to do. He had a sensational story to write. A postadolescent dream job to keep. A lifestyle as an arrogant alpha male to maintain. And it was about time he remembered that.

Instead of remembering how good it felt to have his arm around Julia's waist. And how nice she smelled. And how her hair caught the light in a way that made it look like liquid gold. And that soft, husky laugh that was just so damned sexy. And that afternoon they discovered the gum wrapper on the street together…

JULIA CAUTIOUSLY WATCHED the retreating back of her sixth speed-date of the night, whose identifying number looked way too much like what would appear under his mug shot, and wondered again what she was doing here. Oh, yeah. Trying to get a story for *Tess* magazine. She hoped Abby and Samantha were having more luck meeting write-worthy men than she was, and couldn't quite curb the fear that they might have to scrap the whole story. Or at least her portion of it. So far, the only decent guy she'd met speed-dating was Daniel.

Which, okay, might provide her with all the material

she needed for the story, since she'd pretty much decided he was her Mr. Right. But her contribution to the article was going to be pretty short and pretty boring if she didn't have at least a few good guys she could hold up as examples. 40387—yeah, that was definitely a prison jumpsuit number—wasn't anywhere close. She riffled through her notes for the night so far and sighed. Neither was any of the other guys.

And for this she'd dressed in a screaming red, lace-trimmed, curve-hugging slip dress? What a waste of perfectly good designer clothing.

She had flipped to a clean page and was tipping back her glass to suck up the last of her appletini—the way things were going, she needed every last drop of vodka she could absorb—when she saw Daniel sitting at the table of some tarty redhead in the corner of the room. Worse, he was smiling at the tarty redhead in much the same way he had smiled at Julia that first night they met. Worse still, he was holding the tarty redhead's hand. Or maybe the tarty redhead was holding his hand. Hard to tell from this angle. In any event, they were both holding hands and neither seemed to mind very much.

What was he doing here? she wondered as something cool and heavy slithered into her stomach. Why was he still speed-dating when the two of them had been getting along so well? He'd told her that first night he was looking for companionship. So what was Julia? His faithful canine friend?

Okay, so she didn't have any major claim on him, she reminded herself. And they'd only known each other a week. But they'd seen each other nearly every day this week, and they'd had a lot of fun. And, yeah, they'd done a lot of making out. That was part of the fun. Daniel had been totally affectionate with her, and God knew she'd felt affection—and then some—for him. The night they'd cooked dinner at her place had been one of the most enjoyable Julia had ever spent, even before the lip-locking on the couch. And things had only gotten better after that.

Okay, so maybe she hadn't been as ready to do the horizontal boogaloo as he was, despite her claims to Tess at lunch Wednesday. That was actually a good sign. It *was*. It meant Julia cared enough for Daniel to want to make sure she didn't screw things up with him. Sex could make people weird with each other if it came into a relationship too soon. Which—she had to be honest with herself—Julia had finally decided was what she and Daniel had.

Maybe she should have told him that, she thought now. Well, the worrying-about-things-getting-weird thing, if not the actual relationship thing, since guys tended to get *really* weird after that word came up. But she'd been afraid even that small mention of her feelings might spook him. Even when things were going really well between a man and a woman, guys didn't want to cross that emotional bridge as soon as girls did. And if the man and woman weren't progressing at quite the same pace in their relationship…

Something hot and scary splashed through Julia's midsection. She had assumed Daniel was getting as serious about her as she was about him. He'd been as eager to see her from one day to the next as she had been to see him. They'd spent their final moments together every night locking lips in a way that indicated they were both fully sprung on each other.

But what if she was wrong?

Why was he speed-dating? she asked herself again. He knew she was still doing it, too. He had to have realized he might run into her at one of these things. But he'd done it, anyway. Evidently because he didn't care if she saw him here. With a gorgeous, if incredibly tarty, redhead. Smiling at the tart. Holding her tarty hand. Still holding it as both of them stood up to say their goodbyes at the conclusion of their speed-date. Kissing her tarty cheek before leav—

Kissing her cheek? Julia realized in openmouthed amazement. He hadn't kissed Julia's cheek that first night! Just who did he think he was? Why, she ought to march over there right now and tell him—

What? she asked herself, deflating some. He'd never said he wanted to be exclusive with Julia. She'd never said that, either. She'd just figured he felt the same way she did about the way things were progressing between the two of them. She'd assumed he wasn't seeing anyone else because he liked her well enough that he didn't want to see anyone else. The same way she didn't *want* to see anyone else, either. Because she liked him well enough, too.

She was such an idiot.

He was such a jerk.

The tarty redhead said something to him that made him laugh, and Julia's stomach knotted tighter. Before she even realized what she was doing, she was palming her purse and walking slowly across the room. But he left the tart's table before Julia reached them, so she turned to follow him.

She kept her distance as he went to the bar—was he getting the tarty redhead a drink, the way he'd gotten one for Julia that night?—then ducked behind a chatting couple when he turned to look behind himself. But he didn't look back at the redhead, Julia noted. Instead, he seemed to be scanning the crowd, looking for someone else.

Jeez, just how many women was he hoping to meet tonight?

He picked up his order from the bar—one drink, the color of Scotch, she saw with some meager reassurance—and started to make his way back across the room. He was looking over his list of dates as he came toward her, so he didn't see her standing where she was…still cowering behind the same two people who were now looking at her as if she were a complete moron. When someone accidentally bumped him, making him drop his list barely two feet from where she was standing— oh, all right, where she was *cowering*—Julia took her chance. Stepping forward, she scooped up the list just before he would have grabbed it himself, and stood.

He straightened, too, saying as he did, "Oh, thanks for getting that for me. I really appreci—"

And that was when his gaze connected with Julia's and he realized who he was talking to.

"Julia," he said softly.

"Daniel," she replied tersely.

"I…" he began vaguely.

"You," she remarked pointedly.

He smiled, that boyish, self-deprecating smile he'd used so successfully the first night they'd met.

"Oh, no, you don't," she told him, settling her hands on her hips, his date list still clutched in her fingers. "I am not falling for that smile again. I just saw how well you used it on that tarty redhead."

He narrowed his eyes at her, as if he didn't know what she was talking about. "What tarty redhead?"

"Oh, please," she said. Without turning in that direction, she pointed back at the table he'd just left. "That tarty redhead."

He directed his gaze momentarily in the direction she

indicated, then back at Julia's face. "I reiterate—what tarty redhead?"

Now Julia did turn to look where she had pointed and saw that the table was empty. Frantically driving her gaze around the room, she saw no sign of the woman in question. "Well, she was there a minute ago."

"And you're here now," he said.

She looked at him again. "And so are you."

Translation, she thought to herself. *What the hell are you doing here?*

But Daniel was a man, she reminded herself, which meant he probably needed a translator to know what she was talking about. So without awaiting commentary from him, she said aloud, "What the hell are you doing here?"

CHAPTER SIX

DANIEL THOUGHT FAST. Dammit, how had he not seen her before now? Yeah, the bar was crowded, but, good God, look at the way she was dressed. It was a wonder she didn't have every firefighter in five boroughs here trying to put her out. Though maybe that wasn't the best analogy to use. On the other hand, Daniel sure the hell would like to put her out. Or something.

Before he was able to form a cogent reply to her question…demand…summons…shrill exclamation…all of the above—not that he had any idea in hell what to say—she suddenly went limp, crossed her arms over her midsection and lifted one hand to cover her eyes.

"Oh, God, listen to me," she said. "I sound like Bitsy the homecoming queen who just caught her boyfriend Brad under the bleachers with Cherry, the class slut, don't I?"

Although that was exactly what she sounded like, Daniel figured this was one of those times when he should say, "No, honey, of course those pants don't make you look fat."

The lie he actually told was, "I came with my buddy again. He got burned pretty bad that first night by a couple of the women, and he needed moral support."

And damned if Daniel didn't feel genuinely sick when he said it. Never in his life had he felt nauseous telling a lie. Not that he was a pathological liar. But, like many people, male *and* female, he understood the power of the falsified word. He was a writer. He had words, and he wasn't afraid to use them. More to the point, he knew how to use them. To his benefit. To get what he needed. To get what he wanted. And what he wanted right now…

Ah, dammit. He might as well just admit it. What he wanted was Julia Miles. And he didn't want to have to lie to get her. He was tired of lying. To women. To Julia. To himself. This past week with her had been better than a lifetime of weeks before it combined. He wanted to see what more weeks with her would be like. Lots and lots more. No magazine article was worth compromising that.

He set his untouched drink on an empty table and reached for Julia's hand, the one still holding his list of dates for the evening. The list on which he had halfheartedly checked off a handful of names. If she saw that, he'd never be able to talk his way out of this the way he knew he could now. Yeah, okay, he'd lie to her one more time. But that was it. He'd call his editor on Monday and tell him the story was a bust. Then Daniel would hope like hell Julia never, ever found out about it.

She still had one hand over her eyes, as if she didn't want to look at him, so he cupped his fingers gently over the one at her waist—the one that still held the list—and pulled it gingerly away from her body. She dropped her hand to look at him, and he held her gaze steadily as he carefully plucked the list from her loosened grasp. Then he stuffed it heedlessly into his back pocket, opened her hand and pressed his lips softly to her palm. Just as he had planned, she forgot all about what she'd been holding and murmured that quiet little sound that let him know he was touching her exactly the way she

liked to be touched. What he hadn't planned was how
he himself melted inside at hearing it.

The scent of her surrounded him as he moved his lips
to the inside of her wrist, that light floral fragrance she
wore just enough of to make him want to move closer
to inhale more of it. To inhale more of her. To touch
more of her. Taste more of her. Have more of her.

"Julia," he whispered against her soft flesh. "Let's go
someplace where we can talk. Or something."

When he looked at her again, he saw that her pupils
had expanded, that her cheeks had grown flushed, that
her lips had parted fractionally, and that she seemed to
be having trouble breathing. Exactly the reaction he
had known he could generate in her. Exactly the reaction
she generated in him.

She nodded slowly, as if she were having trouble
completely grasping what was going on. "Yeah, we definitely need to talk," she said. "Or something."

Daniel honestly didn't care that he was about to
dump six women at one time, at least three of whom had
made clear their extreme availability this evening—one
had even slipped him a card key to a hotel room she'd
had the foresight to reserve that afternoon, just in case
she got lucky at tonight's event.

If he really wanted to, he could blow off Julia right
now and have just the sort of conquest he needed for his
story. Maybe even two or three conquests if he had the
stamina and organizational skills to manage it. All he
had to do was make up something about why it would
be better for them to talk tomorrow instead of right now,
and then he could enjoy the kind of night most guys only
read about in Letters to Penthouse.

Instead, he wove her fingers with his and said, "Let's
get outta here. Find someplace more private."

For a moment, she only gazed at his face, her eyes never leaving his, and didn't say a word. And in that moment, Daniel knew a heart-stopping fear unlike anything he'd ever felt before. What if she saw through him? What if she didn't believe him? What if she decided he'd been scamming her all along and said she never wanted to see him again? What would he do then?

Never in his life had he feared losing someone. Never had he feared being alone. But in that moment, he knew both. And it was damned scary.

"Julia," he said again, hearing the note of apprehension in his voice, not knowing what to do to cover it. Worried it would only get worse if he said anything more.

After what seemed like hours, she finally nodded. Slowly. Uncertainly. As if she didn't quite believe what was going through her head. Daniel just wished he knew what was going through her head.

"My place," she said softly. "Let's go to my place. It's not far."

He'd been hoping she would say that.

Before she could change her mind, he was weaving his fingers more snugly with hers and guiding her toward the exit. He hailed a cab easily, held the door open while she climbed inside, got in on the other side himself and gave the driver her address. Then he held his breath, waiting to see what she would say next.

"You didn't tell your friend you were leaving," she said.

The remark confused him for a minute, then he remembered what he had told her about going to the speed-dating party with his buddy again. "He'll understand," Daniel assured her. Trying not to think about how that was another lie he'd promised he wouldn't tell her.

"But you're supposed to be providing moral support," she objected.

He forced a smile he was nowhere close to feeling. "I talked to him just before I ran into you." Another one. Dammit.

"You were talking to the tarty redhead just before you ran into me."

"Before that," he quickly amended, wondering how many more times he was going to have to lie to her before he could really promise himself he'd never do it again. "Saw him in the men's room. He said he'd met two great women at that point, so he might not see much more of me tonight. He'll be fine."

Julia nodded, but Daniel could still see caution in her eyes. He never should have lied to her. Not the night they met, not ever. That first one had only led to more, as was the habit with lies. But if he'd been honest with her that first night, she might never have gone out with him a second time. He wanted to be honest with her from now on. But how often would he still be forced to tell her something that wasn't true, to cover up all the things he'd said so far?

She opened her mouth to say something more, and worried about what it might be, that he might have to say something untrue again, Daniel cut her off by leaning forward and covering her mouth with his. He didn't care if they were in the back seat of a cab. All he cared about was not saying something else he'd regret later. So he tangled gentle fingers in her hair, looped an arm around her shoulder, pulled her backward so that they were both leaning against the back seat, and kissed her and kissed her and kissed her....

Until the taxi jolted to a halt, sending them both careening forward.

For a moment, neither of them seemed to remember where they were, then, as one, they smiled at each other. Then they began to laugh. Julia dipped her head shyly and turned away from the driver while Daniel paid him, and didn't wait when he climbed out on his side for him to come around and open her door. She was on the curb waiting when he got there, blushing furiously at their behavior.

But his kiss had inspired the desired reaction in her—she seemed to have forgotten about finding him at the speed-dating party, and her suspiciousness and wariness seemed to have disappeared. This time, when he reached for her hand, she willingly entwined her fingers with his and didn't hesitate when he pulled her close. They said nothing as they climbed the stairs to her apartment, and he waited patiently as she withdrew her key from her purse and unlocked the door. He grew impatient, however, once they were both inside, pushing the door closed behind them, throwing over the dead bolt and hauling Julia into his arms.

He didn't want to think about anything but being with her. And he told himself that everything would be all right. Somehow, some way, it would all work out. He'd scrap the story for *Cavalier*, and Julia would never know the difference. He didn't know what good deed he'd done, what incredible karma he'd earned, to have been awarded a woman like her. But he wasn't going to do anything more to screw it up.

He would just hope like hell nothing he'd done before would screw it up, either.

Julia wasn't sure just when the earth had shifted on its axis, or how she had ended up in such a state of absolute, unmitigated bliss. All she knew was that one minute she and Daniel had been talking in the back seat of a cab—about what, she couldn't even remember now—and the next he was kissing her in a way that made her want a whole lot more than that. And then the next minute, they were in her apartment, fully loaded and ready to go off.

He took a step forward, and she took a step back, an action that left her leaning against the front door with Daniel leaning against her. Then he crowded his body closer still, until he was pressed against her from shoulder to shin, his hands grasping her hips, his mouth slanting over her own. She kissed him back as hungrily as he kissed her, curling one hand over his shoulder and the other around his nape. His skin beneath her fingers was warm and damp, his breathing was ragged, he tasted of expensive whisky and smelled of Ivory soap. And all Julia could think was how much more of him she wanted, and how she wanted it *now.*

She honestly hadn't planned for the two of them to make love yet. She'd been thinking she needed a few more weeks of seeing him before she would be sure it was time. But something about now felt right. She wanted him. Now. Needed him. Now. Couldn't stand the thought any more of not having him. Whatever he'd been doing in the bar tonight, he was here with Julia now. She could tell by his response to her that he wanted and needed her the same way she did him. So why shouldn't they have each other?

Now.

Daniel's thoughts evidently mirrored hers, because he dropped his hand to the hem of her dress and began to push it higher, over her thighs, her hips, her waist. Beneath it, she wore only a pair of pink silk panties and matching bra. In her high heels, she stood nose to chin with him, and, unable to help herself, she tilted her head back and nipped his lower lip with her teeth. His hand at her waist clenched her tighter in response, then moved behind her, dipping into her panties to spread possessively over the lower curve of her ass.

Julia cried out at the intimacy, then pressed her mouth to Daniel's again. His other hand moved higher, covering her breast, kneading it softly, rolling his thumb over the erect nipple through the silky fabric of her dress. Julia dipped her hands beneath the lapels of his jacket and pushed hard, shoving the garment off his shoulders and onto the floor. After that, she went to work on his shirt buttons, unfastening them one by awkward one, tugging his shirttail free of his jeans. Then she opened her hands over his broad chest, loving the feel of the springy dark hair beneath her palms, tracing her fingertips over the elegant musculature of his torso.

And all the while, they continued to kiss, tongues busy now, teeth grazing and nipping. Never in her life had Julia experienced this level of passion, this intensity, this immediacy. Daniel's hand was on the zipper of her dress now, tugging it down, down, down, pulling the gaping fabric wider until the dress fell forward from her shoulders. With a few inelegant wiggles, Julia was out of it, kicking it aside to join his jacket on the floor. Then he was unhooking her bra, too, and tossing it aside.

Half naked now, she surged her body forward, moving sinuously against him, the hair on his chest tickling her sensitive breasts. Daniel maneuvered one hand between their bodies, claiming a naked breast, then lowered his head to open his mouth wide over its dark, tempestuous center. He licked her with the flat of his tongue, then teased her with the tip, tasting her over and over before sucking as much of her into his mouth as he could. Julia panted at the sensations that shot through her, at every jolt of electricity generated by every flick of his eager tongue.

When she didn't think she could stand any more, and wanting him to feel as agitated as she, she dropped her hand to the button of his fly and flicked it open. Then she pushed the zipper slowly down, slipping her fingers inside his blue jeans as she went. Immediately, he sprang against her hand, full and hard and insistent beneath the soft cotton of his briefs. Julia rubbed her fingers over him with much affection, marveling at the extent of his arousal already.

When he jerked his head up from her breast, she knew she had his attention. To make sure she kept it, she tucked her hand inside his briefs and palmed the round head of his shaft, then she wrapped her fingers around him and dragged them back down to its base. He closed his eyes to enjoy the feel of her fingers moving against him, and Julia took advantage of the opportunity to turn their bodies so that he was the one leaning against the door this time. When he tilted his head back in surrender, she dropped to her knees in front of him.

She jerked his jeans and briefs down over his hips and thighs, then took him into her mouth. As she splayed one hand open over his flat belly, she felt his fingers tangling in her hair. And as she drew him in deeper, treating him to more of her tongue, she heard the sharp hiss of his breathing grow more and more erratic. Again and again she tasted him, savored him, devoured him, until his fingers clenched her naked shoulders and he urged her back to standing again.

"I'm really close," he told her as she rose. He smiled a shaky smile. "I mean *really* close. And you haven't had your turn yet."

Oh, Julia did so love a considerate man.

Before she could tell him that, he was kissing her again, taking a few steps forward, guiding her toward the couch. As they went, his hands roved over her bare back, skimming up, then down, then up, then down again. On the final down sweep, he tucked his hands into her panties again and began to pull them down. Over her hips, her thighs, until Julia had to take over and remove them the rest of the way herself. It was Daniel who took them from her hand, however, and threw them over one shoulder. Then, with a gentle push against her shoulder, he sent Julia down onto the couch.

This time he was the one to kneel in front of her, curling his fingers around her ankles, smiling at the high heels she still had on. Gently, he spread her legs wide and draped them over his shoulders. Then he opened his hands over her thighs, urging them apart, before leaning in to cover her damp, heated core with his mouth.

Julia closed her eyes at the exquisiteness of the sensations rippling through her as he darted his tongue against her, then moved it in slow, circular spirals over and through the soft folds of flesh. And when he brought his fingers into the action, locating the sensitive little bud of her clitoris with the middle one, she cried out, her entire body jerking in response.

For a long time, he savored her that way, every now and then slipping a long finger inside her. When he did, she moved her hips forward on the couch to pull him in deeper still, until finally Daniel withdrew his mouth so that he might penetrate her more completely. First with one finger, then crossing it over a second and giving her pleasure that way.

A second orgasm rocked her, and she cried out again. He captured the sound with a kiss as he joined her on the couch, having shed what little of his clothing remained. He'd also rolled on a condom, she noted vaguely—and gratefully—as he pulled her into his lap to straddle him, facing him. He moved his hands to her breasts and captured one in his mouth once more, treating himself to first one, then the other. Julia tangled her fingers in his hair as more ripples of pleasure unwound inside her, urging her body slowly closer to his.

Finally, he moved his hands to her hips and urged her forward even more, so she rose up on her knees and came down again with him sheathed inside her. They both murmured sounds of satisfaction at their joining, and for a moment, neither of them moved, only stilled to enjoy the beginning of their coupling. Little by little, Julia began to move, rising up on her knees, then lowering herself again, drawing him deeper inside with each new descent.

She leaned forward, so that her elbows were braced on the back of the sofa, and Daniel took advantage of her new position to suck one breast into his mouth again. As he did, he moved his hands behind her, cupping one over each buttock, parting them to run a curious finger along the elegant line between them. All Julia could do after that was hold on.

Little by little, slow spirals of heat began to coil inside her, tighter and hotter, until they knotted at her center and shattered. This time, as her orgasm swept through her, Julia could only gasp in response. Then Daniel was coming, too, surging hotly inside her, his hips bucking against her again and again and again.

Then he was turning their bodies so that Julia lay beneath him, and he was collapsing against her, struggling for breath.

"Unbelievable," he said, the word ragged and faint. "My God, Julia, that was incredible."

Somehow, she managed to nod her agreement. "Incredible," she echoed breathlessly.

Because it had indeed been incredible. Phenomenal. Like nothing she had ever experienced before.

Like something she never wanted to experience again—with anyone but Daniel Taggart.

CHAPTER SEVEN

JULIA AWOKE SLOWLY, drifting reluctantly into consciousness from the most exquisite dream state she'd ever been in. Vaguely, she registered the soft whisper of rain hitting her bedroom window and the clean scent of the pillow caressing her face. Daniel's strong arm was draped over her naked waist, and she felt his long, hard body pressing against hers from behind. Warm. He was so warm. She'd forgotten how good it felt to wake up alongside another human being. Especially another human being who made her feel the way Daniel did.

His deep, steady breathing told her he was still very much asleep, so she lay as still as she could, not wanting to wake him. It felt too nice to just lie here marveling at her good fortune, and enjoy the little ribbons of pleasure that wound through her thinking about what had happened the night before. And, better still, about what might lie ahead for the two of them.

Whatever Daniel had been doing at the speed-dating party last night, Julia was confident everything would come clear once the two of them talked about it. No two people could make love the way they had unless they had strong feelings for each other. The way they'd been together last night…

She bit back a sigh of contentment. When she'd been assigned the article for *Tess*, she'd been skeptical about actually meeting anyone speed-dating with whom she might develop a long-term relationship. But the very first night she'd tried it, she'd found Daniel. No, none of the other guys had captured her interest much, she conceded. But that wasn't necessarily because none of them had had potential. It was just that once she'd met Daniel, she hadn't cared about cultivating a relationship with anyone else.

Did Daniel feel the same way, though? That was the question.

Give it time, she told herself. Give him time. Men never came around as quickly as women did. There was no rush. She and Daniel had only just begun to enjoy each other.

A quiet rumble of thunder sounded outside, echoed by the soft rumble of Julia's stomach demanding its morning injection of coffee. Daniel still slept blissfully on, so carefully, very carefully, she extricated herself from his loose embrace and rose from the bed.

Her clothes from the night before, she recalled, were strewn around the apartment, so she plucked a white terry-cloth robe decorated with colorful chenille flowers from the back of her bedroom door and slipped into it, knotting it loosely at her waist to ward off the slight chill of the morning. Padding barefoot into the living area, she saw that hers weren't the only clothes scattered on the floor, and she smiled, recalling how impatient the two of them had been once they'd arrived at her apartment.

Leisurely, she began to gather the garments together, intending to toss hers into the laundry hamper and fold Daniel's as well as she could to place them in the chair. But when she picked up his pants, something fell out of his back pocket—two somethings, in fact—and she stooped to pick them up.

The first looked like a credit card—no, a hotel card key, she saw upon further inspection. That was weird. The second was a folded piece of paper she recognized as Daniel's date list from the bar last night. The memory of him sitting with the tarty redhead, holding her hand and kissing her cheek, replayed in Julia's mind, and all the reassuring she'd given herself since then began to evaporate. She had honestly let herself forget about his behavior once he started kissing her in the cab. All she'd been able to think about after that was how much she wanted him.

Now she remembered. He'd had an excuse for being there, something about being there with his buddy again. But he'd offered no explanation for the woman. And he'd left the bar without even telling his friend goodbye. He'd had an excuse for that, too, she recalled. But it hadn't been a very good one, either.

It was the hotel card key that sent a ragged spur of dread slicing through her belly. Daniel lived in Greenwich Village. So what was he doing with a hotel key?

Telling herself she had no right to do it but needing some answers quick, Julia shoved her hand into the other pockets of his trousers to see what else she might find. His wallet came first, which she shamelessly opened to inspect its contents. Yep, according to his driver's license and credit cards, his name really was Daniel Taggart. And his address was an apartment in the Village, just as he'd said. Nothing out of the ordinary in any of that.

But it was what she found in his jacket pocket when she checked it, too, that was most revealing. A small spiral notebook, much like the one Julia kept in her purse. That wasn't exactly surprising, either. Any writer worth his or her salt would keep a notebook and pen handy. It was what was inside the notebook that made Julia wonder if Daniel was indeed who he said he was. Beyond the name on his driver's license, she meant.

Because his notes, like the ones she kept in her purse, were all about speed-dating. About the women he had met so far. As Julia flipped from one page to the next, she read one name after another, along with brief descriptions of each woman, beginning with a party dated the week before the one where she had met him. Each description was followed by the term "bedability," and then assigned a number.

Assuming the range was one to ten, which it seemed to be, Daniel had found a half-dozen women at that first party who had earned high scores on his "bedability" scale. Two women among those, she saw, had earned a perfect ten, along with a star and the word *Success!*, which was penciled in beside their names. Which, Julia concluded, could only mean Daniel had been successful in bedding them.

Oh, Daniel, she thought as the blade in her belly thrust deeper. *Oh, no…*

No sooner had the realization of what he'd done— of what *she'd* done—unrolled in her head than did he emerge from her room, all bedroom-eyed and sleep-rumpled, looking very, very sexy. He had the blanket from her bed wrapped loosely around his waist, but it dipped low enough to reveal that erotic curve at the base of a man's abdomen that made a woman want to trace it with the tip of her tongue.

"Morning," he said with a lazy smile, scrubbing one hand through his hair. Then he saw what she was holding in her hand and his smile disappeared. "Julia? Why are you going through my pockets?"

For one agonizing moment, she didn't know what to

do or say or feel. She almost couldn't remember who she was. But Daniel... Well. Unfortunately, the confusion didn't last long enough, and she recalled too well who—and what—he was. "I was picking your clothes up off the floor," she said like a good little Suzy Homemaker, surprised at how calm she managed to keep her voice. "And this—" she held up the list "—and this—" she held up the key card "—fell out. I couldn't imagine why you'd be carrying around a hotel key, so I took the liberty of making sure you were who you said you were by looking at your driver's license."

He eyed her levelly, tugging the sheet more tightly around his waist. "That was kind of an invasion of my privacy," he said. "Don't you trust me?"

"No," she said immediately.

His mouth flattened into a thin line, but he said nothing.

"Last night I trusted you," she said readily. "Otherwise I never would have made lo—I never would have had sex with you. But this morning? No. I don't trust you, Daniel. Because this morning I find out that you're not who I thought you were."

When she began to unfold the date list, he bolted forward, saying, "Julia, don't."

She spun out of his way before he could reach her, moving to the other side of the sofa. But he was faster, and maneuvered himself to the other side, as well, snatching the list out of her hand.

Though not before she saw that he'd put check marks by a good half-dozen names.

"You were dating last night," she said, surprised at how level and controlled she managed to make herself sound. "You weren't there with a friend. You planned to hook up with some of those women again, didn't you?" Then she remembered the key card and chuckled once, an anxious, unhappy sound. "If I hadn't been there, you would have gone home with one of them instead, wouldn't you?"

"Julia…" he began. But he said nothing to defend himself, only stood half naked in her living room looking miserable.

No, not miserable, she realized. Caught. He looked like a man who'd been caught doing something he knew he shouldn't, and now he was trying to figure out if he should try to weasel his way out of it, or just throw it all in. And she'd been the one to nail him.

Then again, he wasn't the only one who'd been nailed.

Oh, God, she thought, remembering the last thing that had gone through her head before she'd finally fallen asleep—that she may very well have fallen in love with Daniel Taggart. In love with a man, she realized now, who kept a list of women and a hotel key in his pocket, just in case. A man who had notes in his writer's notebook about the women he'd met—and slept with—while speed-dating. A man who was evidently writing a story about scoring with women in such a venue.

And then another, even worse thought hit her. Had he been planning to include her in his story, too? Was that the only reason he'd come on to her in the first place?

Oh, who was she kidding? Of course it was the only reason he'd come on to her. But was it the only reason he'd stayed around?

No. She didn't want to know. She honestly, truly did not want to know if she had simply been one of a string of one-night stands for him. She couldn't bear it if she had to live with that. She just wanted him gone. Now.

"Julia, we need to talk," he said.

"You don't owe me an explanation," she told him, holding up a hand to stop anything else he might say.

"I've pretty much figured it out. Besides, you never made any promises to me, did you? You didn't even lie to me, not really. No, you didn't tell me the truth about what you were working on, but you did say you were writing a travel piece for *Cavalier*. You just didn't tell me that your destination was my bed." She expelled a single, humorless chuckle. "Your destination was a lot of beds, wasn't it?"

"Julia," he began again. But again, he halted before saying anything more.

"Let's just put this down to…" She remembered how much they both loved old movies, so she called on *Cool Hand Luke*. "A failure to communicate," she said in her best Jackie Gleason, corrupt-Southern-sheriff voice.

Then, somehow, she made herself move forward and tossed him his pants, then extended the key card toward him. "Looks like you've got someone waiting for you," she said as he took that last from her.

"My notebook?" he asked, noting that in her other hand. Until he mentioned it, she'd forgotten she was holding it. Would that she forgot what he'd written inside it, too.

She extended that toward him, as well, but couldn't quite keep herself from saying, "I never got to your notes about me. Too many names ahead of mine. So I didn't see my own 'bedability' score. But considering how everything turned out, I imagine I lived up—or, rather *down*—to your expectations."

He squeezed his eyes shut tight as if she had slapped him, and for a moment, Julia honestly wished she was the kind of woman who would resort to such a thing. Unfortunately, she shared some of the blame for what had happened. She'd made a lot of assumptions about the two of them that she never should have made. She'd slept with a man without having any clear commitment to him, and she really should have known better than that.

But mistakes were only bad if you didn't learn from them. And Julia had definitely learned from this one. From now on, she intended to be a lot more cautious around men. In fact, she intended to avoid them at all costs.

"You'll forgive me if I don't invite you to take a shower before you leave," she said. "And you'll understand, I'm sure, why I want you to leave. Now."

He opened his mouth as if he were going to say something, then, smart guy that he was, evidently changed his mind. He didn't even say her name this time, only collected his things, including his shirt and jacket from where they lay, and returned silently to her room to get dressed. Julia retreated to the kitchen to start a pot of coffee, marveling at how well she was keeping it together, at how polite she was able to be when tossing some bastard out of her apartment on his cold, black heart. Her mother would be so proud of her.

"Julia?"

When he said her name this time, there was only a sad sort of resolution in his voice. She looked up from pouring the water into the coffeemaker to find him standing fully dressed by her front door.

"Would it help if I said I was sorry?"

She almost laughed at that. Almost. "No, Daniel. It wouldn't. It wouldn't change anything. Not the wonderful time I had this week, or the way you and I were together last night, or how I feel about you."

He actually had the nerve to ask, "And just how do you feel about me, Julia?"

She shook her head. Slowly. Adamantly. "No. You're not going to take that from me, too. Go. Please. Now. And don't call me."

"I still think we need to talk," he said.

"No," she repeated. "Talking to you was what got me into trouble in the first place."

He looked as if he wanted to say more, but something in her expression must have warned him off. Instead, he silently opened her front door and started to walk through it. But he hesitated, looking back at her, and in a very soft voice, told her, "You're not in the notebook, Julia. That's why you didn't find your name there. You weren't going to be part of the story."

"So there is going to be a story," she said, even though she'd already guessed at the truth in that.

"There *was* going to be a story," he told her. "Now…"

"What?"

He sighed heavily. "I don't know. I guess it's up to my editor."

It was all the answer she needed. What Daniel was writing about was sensational, tawdry and mean. It would sell a ton of magazines. His editor would make it the feature story.

"Don't call me," she repeated.

He said nothing, only stood there for another moment looking at her. God help her, all Julia could think about was how much she hated it that the last sight he'd have of her was her standing in her kitchen in her bathrobe, looking tired and miserable. He was probably thinking how lucky he was to be making a clean break with her after having gotten what he wanted from her. Was probably glad she was throwing him out so he wouldn't have to do the dirty work himself. Then he took another step through the door, closing it quietly behind himself.

And only then did Julia allow herself to cry.

CHAPTER EIGHT

TWO WEEKS AFTER TOSSING Daniel out on his ear, Julia was still feeling numb. As she slumped behind her desk in her office at *Tess* on a rainy Monday morning much like the rainy Saturday morning when she had last seen him, she realized she honestly couldn't remember how she'd gotten to work. Again. A huge cardboard cup holding a steaming latte sat on the desk before her, so she must have made a Starbucks stop along the way, but she'd done that on automatic pilot, too. Again.

At least her clothes matched, she consoled herself. Sort of. Surely someone somewhere considered a wrap-around turquoise sweater with fluffy marabou trim the perfect complement to a ruffled pink-and-purple flowered skirt. God. Had she been dressing like this for two weeks without even realizing it?

She sighed heavily, jerked open the bottom drawer of her desk and snatched out a black, three-quarter sleeve, lace-trimmed top she kept on hand for emergencies. Though normally, the emergency in question would be a spilled latte or a repeat of the famous Glue Gun Incident, and not having dressed like a preschooler choosing her own clothes for the first time.

Not caring if anyone saw what she was doing, even that smarmy little mailroom swamp rat Eddie, Julia tugged off the blue top and quickly replaced it with the black, stuffing the blue one into the drawer where it could be the spare for a while. Still not the greatest-looking outfit in the world, but at least she wouldn't blind anyone.

God, what had gotten into her? she asked herself. So she'd dated a complete sleazebag. What woman in the world hadn't? So she'd slept with some jerkwad who'd wanted nothing more from her than sex. That made her no different from any member of her gender. So she'd fallen in love with the last man in the world she should have fallen in love with. Yawn. Oldest story in the world. She shouldn't be feeling anything at this point but unsurprised.

Instead, she had been reduced to flashing smarmy little mailroom swamp rats and not even caring.

She had to move on, Julia told herself. She hadn't heard a word from Daniel since she'd told him to leave her apartment. Not that she was surprised. Not that she *wanted* to hear from him. Although she'd made herself go to the last two speed-dating parties she'd arranged to attend, she'd spent the bulk of her time looking for Daniel, hoping, God help her, that she might see him there, hitting on unsuspecting women. And although she'd made herself go out with a couple of guys she met at those parties, she'd spent the entire evenings wondering if Daniel was out with women he'd met, too, and whether or not he was having any success with them.

Stop thinking about him, she told herself. It was over. He was gone from her life. For good. And good riddance, too, she tried to assure herself. She was better off alone than with someone like him.

So why did she feel so miserable?

A quick trio of raps brought her gaze up, and Julia saw her two partners in dating crime standing framed by the door. Samantha looked smashing, as always, in a snug, cropped black jacket and snakeskin mini. D & G, Julia thought. A designer she could never pull off herself. Abby, the more serious and dedicated of the two, looked smart and dapper in her beige Ralph Lauren trousers and tailored white shirt. Julia knew a twinge of relief at their appearance, hoping they might offer some distraction.

Until Samantha asked, "How's your article coming? Tess wants it by Wednesday."

Two days, Julia realized. And she hadn't even started it yet. And, gee, call her crazy, she wasn't very interested in writing it anymore.

"I'm almost done," she lied. Then she closed her eyes, realizing she'd just done to Samantha what Daniel had done to her—lied. Shamelessly and through her teeth.

No, it wasn't the same, she told herself. Her lie didn't hurt anyone but herself. And it wasn't a big lie. She *would* have the article finished by Wednesday. She'd just have to stay up for the next forty-eight hours straight working on it.

"So how did the speed-dating go, anyway?" Abby asked. "We haven't heard much from you for the past few weeks. Tess gave us the impression you were having some decent success."

"*Success* is a relative term," Julia replied.

Samantha narrowed her eyes at that. "No it isn't. Either you're successful with something or you're not. It's like being pregnant."

"Bite your tongue, Samantha," Abby said. "Success is nothing like being pregnant."

"Well you either are or you aren't," Samantha countered.

"You're either drunk or you aren't, too," Abby pointed out. "Why can't we say success is like being drunk?"

"Well, we could," Samantha replied tersely, "but it wouldn't make any sense, would it?"

"Oh, and equating pregnancy with success does make sense?" Abby asked.

Samantha opened her mouth to argue, so Julia hastily cut them both off. "Tell Tess I'll have the article on her desk by Wednesday morning. Are you guys finished with yours?"

Both women exchanged hasty glances.

"Um, not quite," Samantha said.

"Uh, almost," Abby replied at the same time.

"And were either of you successful, pregnant or drunk?"

Samantha sniffed haughtily. "Well, I certainly wasn't pregnant."

"Me, neither," Abby added enthusiastically.

Meaning they'd both been drunk and successful, Julia concluded. And here she'd struck out completely.

"Oh, I almost forgot," Abby said as she pushed herself away from the office entrance. "This came for you by special courier first thing this morning. You weren't in yet, so I signed for it for you."

"Special courier?" Julia asked, puzzled. "What is it?"

"Weird, that's what," Abby told her. "It's something from *Cavalier* magazine. From Mr. Edward Cabot himself."

"The editor in chief?" Samantha said. "Good God, Julia, where do you know him from? Don't let Tess find out. She hates his guts."

Julia scarcely heard the last part of her co-workers' exchange, because her thoughts had become muddled and confused at the mention of Daniel's employer. *"Cavalier?"* she echoed. Then the rest of what Abby said finally sank in. "The editor in chief?" she said incredulously. "I don't know him at all. I don't know why he'd be sending me something."

"Well, he went to an awful lot of expense and trouble to make sure you got this. Whatever it is."

Abby extended a Tyvek envelope, which Julia claimed with nervous fingers. Sure enough, the return address label was decorated with the logo and address of *Cavalier* magazine, along with Edward Cabot's name and title.

She started pulling at the uncooperative flap—what sadist had invented Tyvek envelopes, anyway?—then realized Samantha and Abby were still hanging around her office door, watching with curious eyes. Julia hesitated.

"Was there something else?" she asked.

The two women exchanged another one of those hasty glances, then looked back at Julia and shrugged. Though Samantha did say, "Hey, good to see your clothes matching again. Well, kind of."

Julia ignored the comment. "Don't you guys have articles to finish by Wednesday?" she asked sweetly.

"Yeah, yeah, yeah," Samantha said.

"We're on it," Abby replied at the same time.

Both shuffled off reluctantly, and Julia returned her attention to the delivery from *Cavalier.* Inside the envelope—once she finally wrestled it open—was a slim, paper-clipped manuscript covered by a letter from Edward Cabot addressed to Julia, care of *Tess*.

"Ms. Miles," the letter began without salutation.

Recently, I assigned one of my senior writers, Daniel Taggart, to write a feature article for *Cavalier* which I envisioned running with the title "How Many Women Does It Take to Change a Gigolo?" Beneath it, the chaser, "Trick

Question! You *Can't* Change a Gigolo!" I thought it would be a nice, acerbic piece for our February issue, to counter all the Valentine's Day crap that shows up in women's magazines like *Tess* that time of year. What Taggart delivered instead was the enclosed, with the edict that if I didn't print it, he would walk. Furthermore, he insisted I run it by you first, to ensure your approval of the project, and if I didn't, he would walk.

Quite frankly, Ms. Miles, it sticks in my craw to allow *anyone's* approval over *any* content that goes into *my* magazine. That it's a writer for Tess Truesdale goes beyond the pale. However, Taggart is an amazingly gifted little bastard, one whom I genuinely believe will win a Pulitzer for this magazine someday. That goes a long way toward washing away the bad taste in my mouth that writing this letter has brought with it.

Therefore, it is my great displeasure to submit for your approval a story by Daniel Taggart, which I would very much like to run in my February issue. We're on a deadline here. If you could read the enclosed and get back to me with your yea or nay by Friday, it would be extremely helpful.

By the way, give that harridan you work for my regards, will you?

Yours sincerely,
Edward Cabot
Editor in Chief, *Cavalier* Magazine

When Julia moved the letter aside, she saw Daniel's article beneath it. At the top of the page, above his byline, was the title. "Rapid Transit: My One-Way

Ticket to a Place I Never Wanted to Visit, Then Never Wanted to Leave."

Unable to help herself, Julia immediately began to read.

It was in no way the sort of article *Cavalier* normally ran. She kept up with other monthlies of *Tess*'s caliber, regardless of their audience, and she was familiar enough with *Cavalier* to know that much. Oh, the piece was written in a dry, almost sarcastic tone about the New York dating scene and women in general, and how hard it was for a man of superior intelligence and wit to find an adequate sparring—among other things—partner. And the author spoke frankly about his easy conquests of easy women from the first speed-dating party he attended.

But then the tone of the story changed, right when the author started talking about his second foray into the world of speed-dating. Less sarcasm this time, and more straightforward reporting. And then, little by little, the author began to poke fun at himself, after he met a woman who made him realize what an arrogant ass he was.

Then the tone of the article changed even more, as the author talked about the woman in question. Without naming her by name, Daniel painted Julia as an intelligent, quick-witted, beautiful woman who made him remember that there was more to life than professional ambition, that there was more to male-female relationships than sex, that there was more to sex than physical gratification.

Thanks to this woman, he said, he remembered what it was like to be human. He remembered how to enjoy the most basic pleasures life had to offer. Cooking dinner. Walking in the park. Eating lunch in the sunshine. Kissing in the back seat of a cab. Most of all, though, this woman made him remember that he had the capacity to fall in love.

By the time Julia got to the end of the article, she was very nearly in tears. Then she read the last line, and the tears spilled out. Because that last line said, "And fall in love I did."

She fumbled for a tissue from the container on her desk, but in her teary state, she had trouble locating it. Looking up, she realized that wasn't because she was crying, but because someone had moved the box of tissues out of her reach. And that someone was Daniel Taggart, who was standing on the other side of her desk, holding a tissue for her.

How he had slipped into her office without her noticing, she had no idea. Nor did she know how long he'd been standing there. But since his article had been so eloquent and stirring, and had commanded her complete attention, she supposed that wasn't surprising.

He looked wonderful, damn him, wearing another pair of those lovingly faded blue jeans, a striped oxford shirt this time, sans tie, and a charcoal blazer. His hair was a little longer than it had been the last time she saw him, and there were faint circles under his eyes, as if he'd been having trouble sleeping. He extended the tissue toward her gingerly, as if he wasn't sure what his reception would be. But he didn't say a word.

"So you really were working on a travel article for *Cavalier*," she said by way of a greeting.

He nodded slowly. "In a way."

Somehow, she couldn't quite help herself when she replied, "And here I thought it was just me who was being taken for a ride."

He closed his eyes and his head snapped to the side, as if she had just slapped him. Then his entire body went limp in defeat. "Julia…" he said softly.

"Well, what am I supposed to say?" she asked, hating

herself for sounding so desperate. So hurt. Feeling vulnerable in her seated position, she stood, planting her palms firmly on her desk. "You lied to me, Daniel. And you used me."

He opened his eyes and hooked his hands on his hips, her remark having obviously roused some anger in him, too. "I may have lied to you, Julia, *by omission*," he said, taking care to point out, "but I *never* used you. No more than you used me."

"What?" she cried.

"The night we met, you were looking at me as a potential item for your article, the same way I was looking at you as a potential item for mine. We both went to that speed-dating party for the same reason."

She was shaking her head before he even finished talking. "No, we didn't. *I* was looking for Mr. Right."

"And *I* was looking for a good time. When you get right down to it, it's the same thing, depending on which gender you happen to be."

She opened her mouth to argue with him, then realized to her horror that, on some level, what he said made sense. So all she did was counter lamely, "That is *such* BS."

"Look, Julia, I'm not going to apologize to you for doing my job," he said. "And I'm not going to apologize for being a guy. I write for a men's magazine, and my readership has expectations. Male expectations."

"Then why are you here?" she asked.

He looked at her in silence for a moment, something in his expression tearing at something inside her. He looked so…lost, she thought. So hurt. So scared. He looked the way she had looked every time she saw herself in the mirror for the past two weeks.

"I'm here because I wanted to make sure you read my article," he told her quietly.

"But I'm not your readership."

"Yeah," he said. "You are. It's not the same article I set out to write for the magazine."

"But you told your editor you wanted him to print it."

"I do."

"Why?"

"Because I want everyone to know I'm writing for a different audience now."

Julia wasn't sure what to make of the comment. Or maybe she did but was afraid to hope it meant what it sounded like. So all she said was "I read it."

"And?"

"And what?"

"Judging by your reaction, you either really liked it, or you really hated it."

She moved around to the front of her desk and reached for the tissue he still held in one hand. He looked surprised by her action but surrendered it willingly. Gingerly, Julia dabbed at the corner of each eye.

"Whether I liked or hated it depends," she told him.

"On what?"

"On whether or not you were telling the truth when you wrote it."

"I was telling the truth," he immediately replied. "When February rolls around, and that article shows up in *Cavalier*, everyone will know how I feel about you. Either I'll look like the luckiest man on the planet, because I'll have you with me, or I'll look like the biggest idiot in the universe, because I chased you away."

"You were pretty idiotic, you know," she said.

"Yeah, I know."

"And you still haven't apologized for anything. You've only told me what you're not apologizing for. So I'll ask you again, Daniel. Why are you here?"

He hesitated for a moment, as if he were weighing very carefully what he wanted to say. As if he were still worried about the repercussions. Finally, though, he told her, "I'm here because I want to tell you that I'm sorry I wasn't up front with you that first night, the way you were with me. I can only explain it by saying, hey, I was trying to score with you that night, and at that point, I thought you were like every other woman on the planet, and I didn't care if I was telling a lie—of omission or otherwise. If I'd been honest right off the bat that night, my chances of scoring with you would have dried up. So I didn't say anything."

"Fair enough," Julia conceded. He was a guy, after all. "And what else?" she added.

"And I'm sorry I kept you in the dark about what I was doing, even after it looked like things were going pretty well with us. I can only explain that by saying I was afraid if I told you the truth at that point, you'd think I was a jerk and you wouldn't want to see me again, and I couldn't stand the thought of losing you, even then."

Okay, so that sounded pretty good, she thought. "And what else?"

"And I don't want to lose you now, either."

Something inside her that had been cold for two weeks gradually began to thaw. "And what else?" she asked softly.

"And I promise I will never, ever lie to you again. About anything."

She nodded slowly. He was doing very well, but there was still one thing she wanted—needed—to hear him say. "And what else, Daniel?" she asked.

Without hesitation, he told her, "And I love you."

That was it. That was what she wanted—needed—most to hear him say. The apologies were good. The promise to be honest was better. But the spoken declaration of love… Well. That was stronger than anything in the world. That could never be messed with.

Her eyes were suddenly wet again, so Julia lifted the tissue to them once more, swiping each quickly before indelicately blowing her nose. Daniel smiled but said nothing.

"Why are you smiling?" she asked, dropping her hand back to her side. "You're not in the clear yet."

"Sure, I am."

"How do you figure?"

"You wouldn't have blown your nose in front of me if you were still mad. You would've wanted to be at your best when you told me to piss off, so I'd remember you as your regal bad self."

Although she tried not to, Julia smiled, too. "Yeah, okay, you got me on that one."

"I hope I've got you on a lot more than that," he said softly. "God knows you've got the biggest part of me."

Oh, yeah. Definite melting going on inside her now. "You really told Cabot he had to print this or you'd quit?" she asked.

"I really told him that."

"He's pretty ticked off at you."

"Him I don't care about. It's your opinion I'm sweating."

"Your original story idea was pretty sucky," she said.

"Consider the source, Julia," he reminded her. "When I agreed to write that story, I was just some jerk guy who thought all women were alike. Because I always gravitated toward the same kind of woman. Shallow, clingy and—" he shrugged "—easy to get into the sack. I guess I wanted to be able to justify my prejudice. It wasn't until I met you that I realized women could be so much more. You're right. I was an idiot. But I'm not anymore. Unless I chase you away again."

She narrowed her eyes at him. "You know, this sounds like more BS to me."

He laughed. "I'm telling you the truth." He placed his right hand over his heart. "I promise I will always tell you the truth. From now until forever after. I love you, Julia Miles, and I don't want you making a rapid transit out of my life. I want you to hang around for a while. And instead of speed-dating, I want us to do a little slow-dating. Take our time. Enjoy ourselves. I want us to be together. I hope you want that, too." He took a tentative step forward, then stopped, as if he were just testing the waters and didn't want to go too far. "But I do love you, Julia. More than I thought I was capable of loving anyone."

"I dunno," she said. But her actions belied her words when she took a step toward him, too. "From reading your article, it looks like you're capable of loving someone a lot."

He shook his head. And took another step forward. "Not someone. You. Only you have made me feel this way."

She glanced over her shoulder at the manuscript on her desk, then back at Daniel. And then she took another step toward him, something that brought their bodies to nearly touching.

Really, she thought, when all was said and done, it didn't matter what was written on the page. All that mattered was what was written on the heart. And Daniel's heart seemed to be pretty full. The same way Julia's was.

"Only me, huh?" she echoed as she completed the step that did bring their bodies to touching.

"Only you," he said as he lifted a hand to her face.

Reaching up with both arms, she looped them around his neck, at the same time he dropped his other hand to her hip. Just before she kissed him, she told him, "Wow, what do you know? That's another thing we have in common. 'Cause only you have made me feel this way."

And with that, Julia kicked her office door closed and pushed herself up on tiptoe to cover Daniel's mouth with hers. He'd said all the right things. He'd written all the right words. And he'd used the greatest tool a writer had in his possession.

His heart.

Daniel had finished his story for *Cavalier* magazine, and she'd soon finish hers for *Tess*. And after that, Julia thought as she kissed him and kissed him and kissed him, they could start working on writing their own story together.

To Lex. No question about it.
I always knew you were the one.

THE EX FACTOR
Tracy Kelleher

CHAPTER ONE

So your love affair went flat like yesterday's choco-late soufflé! That doesn't mean some lucky gal won't find your ex to be ab-so-lutely yummy! After all, he had to be special if YOU went out with him, even if it wasn't a case of happily ever after. So register now. Share the delectable details on an old love—the JUICIER the better! And sample the possibilities re-garding a new Mr. Right while you're at it. Just remember. Every scrumptious, lip-smacking ex has been personally vouched for by women IN THE KNOW—women like YOU!

www.exbeaux.com

THE SHEER DENSITY OF exclamation marks and capital letters on the Exbeaux home page was giving Abby Lewis one doozy of a headache, while the food meta-phors were making her amazingly hungry.

She pulled open the top desk drawer, hoping against hope that she'd find a bottle of ibuprofen. The closest she got was a complimentary front-mezzanine ticket to *A Boy From Oz*. Was Hugh Jackman still on Broadway? She looked more closely. The performance was for over a year ago. That was the problem with going away—everybody ransacked your desk and took the good stuff.

"Searching for inspiration, luv?" A lilting baritone sounded above her.

Still holding the theater ticket, Abby looked up. Who needed Hugh Jackman dancing across the footlights when she had Ned Devlin standing next to her? "If it isn't my favorite Irishman! The Gaelic Lady Killer!" she said, very pleased, the first genuine reaction she'd had all day.

"And here I thought you appreciated me for my mind." He sat on the corner of her built-in desk without so much as a by-your-leave.

Not that Abby would have asked him to.

Ned Devlin was a fashion photographer who successfully managed the whole rough-and-tumble, bad-boy image thing—a *Vogue* model on both arms, a pint of Guinness in each hand and, allegedly, a tattoo in a region that rarely saw sunshine. It also didn't hurt that he had bed-head black hair and a grin that reminded Abby of Colin Farrell, only better, because Ned was taller and he would *never* wear a blond wig and let Angelina Jolie play his mother.

"You're like the brother I never had," she'd once confessed after a long day at the office. Ned had dragged her to what he said was one of his favorite pubs—he was one of those guys who seemed to have a favorite pub in any and all cities of the world. They'd celebrated putting a particularly thorny issue of the magazine to bed and clinked their pints of beer together.

"Excuse me, but you already *have* two brothers—one older, one younger," Ned had pointed out.

He had a way of remembering things Abby wouldn't have expected. "Well, a gal can never have too many brothers."

"You sure you couldn't find some other place in your heart for me?"

Abby had laughed. "No, Brad wouldn't like it."

Yeah, that was the era of Good Ol' Brad.

Abby pushed aside memories of her ex. "So have you broken any hearts lately?" She eyed the rough stubble on Ned's cheeks. "Or at least given someone beard burn?"

He touched his jaw. "I ran out of razor blades two days ago, but from the reactions I'm getting, I might keep it." He cocked his head and narrowed his eyes. "Some changes with you, too. I like the new cut."

Abby had always had long, super-curly hair, which she ruthlessly blow-dried straight every morning. On the few days she didn't, she looked like Little Bo Peep with a foot stuck in an electrical outlet.

"I put my head in the hands of Piero della Francesca—I kid you not, supposedly a direct descent of the Florentine painter—and this is what I got." She ruffled the short wispy locks that waved naturally around her face.

Ned crossed his arms. "Very romantic is all I can say."

Which Abby would have interpreted as flirting if it had come from anyone but Ned. "Whatever. The time it saves me in the morning is the main thing."

"Ah, yes. The Abby Lewis that I know and love. She doesn't need to get serious—she *is* serious." He gave her a smart salute.

"Be honest, you aren't making fun of me, now, are you?"

"*Me,* make fun of *you?*" He covered his heart. "You wound me."

"Yeah, right. You want wounding? I'll wound you." She threw the ticket stub at his chest.

He caught it and pocketed it in his black jeans. "So tell me, despite your glorious pragmatic sense, did you take the time to travel to Ravello on the Amalfi coast and watch the sun set over the Mediterranean Sea? And afterward, did you sit in the Piazza Vescovado sipping a martini bianco and gaze into the eyes of your lover?" He paused, reeling in his image. "No, don't tell me about the lover part. You'll never know how much it pains me to picture you and the wonderful Brad doing the dirty."

Abby shook her head. "You are too much. Anyway, Brad couldn't come over." Wouldn't was more like it.

Ned raised one eyebrow. "But did you take my advice and tour around, anyway?"

Should she tell him that, yes, totally out of character, she'd taken a spur-of-the-moment weekend along the coast of southern Italy, to that incredible cliffside village perched halfway between the sky and the sea? That she'd sat in the piazza sipping her drink? And that she *had* pictured herself with a lover, who for some reason, wasn't Brad, but, in fact, was her buddy, Ned Devlin?

Which made no sense at all, since what they shared was a friendship—period. They'd *never* gotten physical, unless you counted the time Abby had a wicked paper cut from the program at the Commes des Garçons spring runway show and Ned had applied Neosporin and bandaged her finger. But then, Abby didn't count that because who, after all, would?

Similarly, she couldn't tell him about the whole Ravello thing, could she?

"Hey, Devlin, some of us are going to meet at this new club in the Meat-Packing District. You want to come?" Ling Ling, Tess's butt-kicking assistant, strode over in hip-high patent-leather boots with six-inch stiletto heels. Her style gave new meaning to the martial arts content of her father's Hong Kong action movies.

Ned rubbed his ear.

"Don't let me stop you," Abby interjected.

Ling Ling glanced at Abby, quickly dismissing her.

No big surprise. The überhipsters took one look at Abby, saw her average height and features that were attractive but certainly not model perfect, and then they looked the other way.

Fine by Abby. She had never thought of herself as a glamourista, and as far as she was concerned, the more people ignored her, the easier it was to listen and observe. And when you combined those two qualities with her funky style of writing and a work ethic that would leave a Puritan begging for a personal day, voilà, you had Abby: überstaff-writer in the competitive world of women's magazines.

"Maybe another day," Ned answered Ling Ling apologetically. "I'm kind of backed up with work, but keep me in mind."

Ling Ling shrugged. "Well, you know where to find me." She puckered up and kissed Ned full on the lips, then strutted away with more leg action than a Jackie Chan fight scene.

"I'm impressed," Abby said. "Let me tell you, they don't make girls like that back in Rapid City, South Dakota." She gave Ned a jaundiced smile. "Listen, don't let me hold you up. I *know* your type, and she is definitely your type." She pointed to Ling Ling's retreating figure.

"Thank you for looking out for my welfare, but I've got a hamstring acting up. I can use a little break from my extracurricular activities." He settled more firmly on the corner of Abby's desk. "So, tell me, what's going on in the red-hot world of publishing?"

Abby frowned. "Well, let's see—and this is not complaining, because I can't stand complaining—merely a recitation of facts."

Ned nodded assuredly. "Just the facts, ma'am."

"Okay, on top of my jet lag, to add insult to injury, I now have the assignment from hell foisted upon me—"

"Another of Tess's inspirations, I presume?"

"What else?" She waved off giving any details. "Then just to provide further spark to that rebaptism by editorial fire—"

"Somehow that's how I've always pictured you." He held up his hands and, closing one eye, framed her face. "A martyr to born-again erudition."

Abby smiled. She'd forgotten just how quick Ned's wit was. "Yes, well, I must remember to put that on my résumé—especially when I come up before co-op boards."

Ned pushed up from her desk. "So you and Brad the Beautiful are buying property?"

The thing of it was, Ned wasn't exaggerating. Brad was beautiful—thick blond hair, lantern jaw and vibrant blue eyes. A schmuck, but beautiful. More or less a golden retriever gone over to the dark side.

"That sounds pretty serious," he went on. "I wouldn't have given him credit for seeing the light, which means I'm forced to take back all the mean things I've ever said about him."

Actually, Ned had *never* said any mean things. The two men had only met once when Abby had suggested that as a way of making nicey-nicey with her colleagues, Brad invite Ned to a pickup game of football in Central Park—one of those super-rough games with macho-competitive lawyers and investment bankers. Ned had proceeded to make any number of shoestring catches and run for several touchdowns.

"I guess not all you fashion types are wimps," Brad had said to him.

Ned had said nothing.

Not Abby, not when she'd been so royally pissed off. "Maybe it has something to do with the fact that Ned played for the Irish National Rugby team, and only gave it up after he had to have shoulder surgery?"

Afterward, Brad had lectured her on the innate differences between rugby and football, and she'd almost upped and left him then and there. But wouldn't you know it, the next day he'd miraculously produced two tickets to a cabaret show, as well as an amazing nosegay of primroses, baby's breath and Old English roses.

How could she leave a man who did things like that?

She hadn't. He'd left her.

Abby cleared her throat. "Brad and I are buying absolutely nothing—because there's nothing between us." She strove for a blasé delivery. It wouldn't have fooled her grandmother, who, bless her soul, didn't register nuance beyond crocheting one afghan to the next.

"Nothing?"

"Nothing." Abby diverted her eyes to the e-mail memo on her computer monitor outlining the production schedule for the upcoming issue. It was so-o-o embarrassing for someone as highly driven as she to be the dumpee in a relationship as opposed to the dumper. It made her seem like…well…like a failure.

Ned waited.

Abby swallowed and raised her gaze. "It seems my decision to spread my professional wings didn't suit the rising legal eagle. He broke things off right before I left for Italy."

"The cad."

"My exact words at the time—well, more or less."

Ned shook his head. "I must not have heard about it because I think I was freezing my butt off in Lapland for a *Travel & Leisure* shoot."

"Could well be. Anyway, the upside was it saved having to write a lot of postcards. The major downside was I lost my apartment. Since coming back from Italy, I've been mooching off Julia, but even she—St. Peach Cobbler of the Upper East Side—has her limits. So, unless I find a place of my own in two days' time, I could be holed up in the back of a burnt-out Chevy Malibu in the seedier section of Staten Island."

Ned frowned, then looked up all smiles—quite a sight, really. "Listen, definitely forget about the Chevy Malibu."

"Delighted."

"I know the perfect solution." He paused. "Don't you see?"

"Aah, no-o."

"Move in with me."

"What? Are you kidding?"

"No, of course not." He plunged his hands in the pockets of his jeans—nondesigner, Abby noted, because, of course, she noted these things, as well as the possibility that this was a new trend.

"I have lots of space," he continued. "Actually, I have hardly any space, but there're two places to bunk, and besides, we've always gotten on well." He waited. "So why not?"

Abby bunched up her mouth in thought. "I don't know. I don't want to get in the way of your extracurricular activities. You know, Ling Ling and the other exotic beauties?"

"If it makes you feel any better, I can put a lock on the door."

She held up her hands. "Trust me, that won't be necessary."

"That's good, because I don't have a door."

Abby blinked. "What kind of place do you have, Ned? Because if it's a loft with a totally open floor plan, I'm not sure that would work."

"Don't worry. It's the farthest thing from a loft. Anyway, I'll pick you up after work?"

Abby still wasn't convinced. "I thought you were swamped."

"I'll be late, but not that late. Why don't you give me your address? You're staying at Julia's place, right? I'll meet you there around nine."

What did she have to lose? In all likelihood, the arrangement would only last a couple of days, and she could use that time to look for a more permanent place of her own. Abby looked at her desk for something to write on. "You'd think as someone who worked at a magazine, I'd have a piece of paper."

"Here." He held out the back of his hand.

She looked dubious. "If you say so." She held his hand as she wrote down Julia's address, trying to ignore the dry heat it put off.

"This is really sweet of you," she said when she finished.

"I know." He turned to leave. "One thing, though."

"Yeah?" Oh, no. Is this where he told her he commuted on the Long Island Railroad from Hicks-ville? That he had pet pythons in the bathtub? That he commuted with the pet pythons?

"You're not prone to seasickness, are you?"

CHAPTER TWO

To: Brad Wahlberg <bradwahlberg@manhattanda.org>
From: Abby Lewis <alewis@tess.com>
Subject: Business to discuss
Brad—
A blast from your not-so-recent past. Hope all is well with you, even if you can't find your Nirvana CDs. Yes, I got your e-mail about losing them when I first arrived in Milan, but things were so hectic I somehow never got around to replying.

Something's come up at work that could use your help. I realize it's an imposition, but I promise it won't take long and won't require any extended contact with me. In fact, you will probably find the whole thing amusing.

It's a little complicated, so could we just get together to talk in person? You can reach me at the office or at Julia's place. You still have her phone number, right? Anyway, thanks, and in case you were wondering, Italy was great.

Ciao,

Abby

P.S. You know your Nirvana CDs you couldn't find? I think I may be able to help you there.

LATER THAT EVENING, Abby stood with her feet braced wide apart, eyeing Ned. Fear and loathing were just two of her emotions. "Please tell me you're not going to make me walk the plank?"

"C'mon. Don't be such a wimp. Where's that hearty pioneer spirit you're so proud of?" Ned hoisted Abby's Kipling knapsack onto his back and headed down the ramp, rolling her two suitcases behind him.

Abby balanced the box containing books and her laptop on her hip and looked at the toes of her sneakers as she gingerly stepped forward. "Where'd you find this thing, anyway? A rummage sale from the set of *The Great Gatsby?*"

"I'll have you know it was the luck of the Irish. I was having a whiskey at my favorite pub in the East Village when this bloke told me he had a houseboat for sale. He was being transferred, you see."

Houseboat was a bit of an understatement. Ned lived on a vintage forty-foot cabin cruiser, all sleek wooden lines and gleaming brass fittings, moored at the Seventy-Ninth Street Boat Basin on the Hudson River.

Abby descended the steps to the boat's deck, and followed Ned as he unlocked a door to the cabin and moved forward. Two captain's chairs and a small round table occupied the deck under the shade of an awning. Inside, the main part of the cabin housed a minuscule galley kitchen, bench-seating area and a rectangular table covered with a checked tablecloth. Narrow shelves along the rich wood walls held CDs, worn paperbacks and leftover Christmas cards. A jumble of sports equipment—skis, a cricket bat, soccer and rugby balls—were stashed to the side.

Abby pulled one of the strings on the butcher's apron hanging from a hook and angled her head to get a better view. It was decorated with a life-size color photo of a frilly French maid's apron, which did little to conceal a well-endowed naked male figure.

"A present from a friend. You had to have been there," Ned explained.

She let the apron drop. "I'm sure."

"My bunk's below deck along with the head. But we'll put you in the bulkhead, with a view of the stars." He ascended a small stairway to the upper level. "You can stow some of your stuff in the built-in cupboards, and what you need to hang up, you can put with my clothes down below."

Abby padded after him and put the box of books down on the narrow bunk. It was made up with a plain navy blanket and white sheets. A reading light was attached above the pillow.

"If you don't like the sheets and stuff, we can easily change them. I can at least promise you they're clean. Nobody's slept here since my Mum came to visit last spring."

Abby stared at Ned. She'd never pictured him having a mother. "No, I'm sure it's fine."

"I'll move the papers and stuff from the desk, and that way you'll have a place to work if you want. There's an outlet and a jack, so you can hook up your computer and go online."

Abby nodded. He actually sounded nervous. *Nah.* She turned and peered out the rectangular windows that ran around the top perimeter and the front triangular section of the roof. "Oh, my God."

Ned stooped down because of the low ceiling and arched his neck upward. "Pretty spectacular, isn't it?"

"'Pretty spectacular' is the understatement of the year." Glittering stars dotted the inky-black sky.

"Just remember that next time the hot water runs out."

"So what other surprises do you have in store?" She turned her gaze away from the nighttime panorama and saw him staring at her.

He hastily glanced away and slipped her knapsack onto the desk chair. "No surprises, but it *is* time for a celebration. If you're up for it?" He turned back, all Ned Devlin smiles.

"Is that a polite way of telling me I look like I'm about to drop dead on my feet?"

"No, it's a not-so-subtle hint that I need a pint, desperately. And as luck would have it, one of my favorite pubs is within spitting distance."

EVEN THOUGH IT WAS a crisp September evening, they decided to sit on the outside terrace of the Basin Café, thereby avoiding the forced bonhomie and desperate urge to get laid among the crowd of singletons inside—the women in their sherbet-colored sweater ensembles and Kate Spade bags, the men in rumpled oxford-cloth shirts and Old Navy trousers.

Abby sipped her beer and gazed at the stars. "This place is great," she said, still keeping her eyes skyward. They were sitting side by side on the bench, their backs to the picnic table.

Ned took a healthy swallow of beer. He had on a decrepit leather bomber jacket, and with his stubble and hair standing on end he looked like he'd just come from an all-night mission deep within enemy lines. "Yeah, it's a real find. I grew up by the sea in Ireland and really miss it. Being here is like re-creating a little bit of home." He drank some more beer. "Having the pub so close by helps, too."

Abby turned and smiled. "I know what you mean.

Not the pub part, but the openness of the sky. It reminds me of nighttime in the Badlands, the uninterrupted expanse, the anticipation that at sunrise I'll see the colors and shapes of the rocks come to life. Not that I'd ever leave Manhattan," she added, taking a quick sip of beer.

"Me, neither."

They sat in comfortable silence until Ned finally spoke. "So what's the story with this latest assignment?"

Abby groaned and gave him the details on the ex-dating story. "So, ever eager to fulfill my professional duties, I e-mailed Brad."

"And have you heard from him?"

"Not yet. I anticipate having to perform major groveling. Somehow I have to convince him that my usual flighty pieces—"

"Let me guess. His turn of phrase?"

"Yeah, how did you know?"

Ned shrugged. "Listen, from what little I saw of him, Brad seemed nice enough—*if* you go for the Ken doll, jungle-predator type. And I mean that as a compliment."

As opposed to all the other remarks he could have made that weren't.

The thing of it was, Ned often wondered why he refrained from bad-mouthing the wanker. True, he'd only met Brad once, when Abby had begged him to participate in some touch-football game with Brad's buddies in the park. He'd gone for the exercise.

No, that wasn't true. He'd done it to please her.

Anyway, Abby and Brad had had some kind of a row afterward, and Brad had come to him for suggestions of how to kiss and make up. "I better get on her good side if I want to get any action tonight" had been his exact words.

"Concert tickets and flowers," Ned had replied, grinding his teeth.

Brad had cuffed him on the shoulder, which Ned really needed to ice down, thank you.

"Long-stemmed roses cost a bundle, but, hey, maybe I can expense them. And Metallica's coming to the Garden, so this will be a great excuse to go."

Attempting to help out this moron, because Abby loved him, Ned had wearily replied, "No, mate, not long-stemmed red roses, something old-fashioned, something Jane Austen-like. And I'd pass on the heavy metal."

Brad had looked wounded, not to mention totally confused.

"Go for more chick music. There's this old-school cabaret singer, Blossom Dearie, who's playing at the Café Carlyle."

"You sure?" Brad asked, who appeared equally per-plexed when Ned gave him the name of a megaexpen-sive florist on the Upper East Side that would under-stand his instructions.

Meanwhile, back in the present, Ned watched Abby press her lips together. And he tried to tell himself that the course of true love never did run smooth.

"You, know—" she slanted her head "—not that I don't think Brad wasn't a complete rat for dumping me the way he did, but—" she looked wistfully at the skyline "—there were times when he could actually be very sweet. I mean, once, he gave me these English garden-y flowers and took me to this funky concert. I practically wanted to cry. Was that the greatest gift to give a girl or what?"

Ned swallowed some more beer and finished his second bottle. "The greatest." He should have known. "So you think Brad'll get back to you about the story?"

He stood and waggled his beer bottle. "Another?" He pointed to hers.

Abby took a large gulp and handed over the empty. "Please." She thrust her hands in her jacket pockets. "And don't worry. He'll get back to me. I hinted that I have something he wants."

Ned arched one brow.

"Trust me, it's not my virtue."

"Trust *me,* a lack of virtue is far more appealing to most men." He clinked the empties together and headed inside.

A few minutes later, he dropped down next to her and passed a beer.

She took the bottle and an appreciative sip. "Thanks. You know, I've finally figured out why people live in those anonymous high-rises in Weehawken." She pointed to the gigantic apartment blocks across the Hudson River in New Jersey.

"Technically, I believe it's Guttenberg not Wee-hawken."

Abby shook her head. "Whatever. No, the reason I believe they prefer living on that side of the river, despite the lousy commute and the constant, and wholly legitimate, slurs about living in New Jersey—" here Ned laughed "—is that they've realized it's too hard to work *and* have a meaningful personal life in the City, that a person can have one but not both."

Ned raised his brows. "That's a pretty pessimistic view of things."

"Oh, yeah? Tell that to the desperate soul-mate-seekers inside. Tell them it really *is* possible to have a long-term relationship."

"I can't because it's something I don't know anything about."

Abby leaned back and eyed Ned critically. "Are you telling me what I think you're telling me? That you've never been in a long-term relationship?"

He rubbed his jaw.

"Medium term?"

He scrunched one eye.

"Did you even make it to a week?"

"There was the one instance I went back and forth across the international date line several times in a row."

Abby leaned back, resting her elbows on the table. "This is amazing! You've never fallen in love, never been so completely enthralled with someone that you forget to eat or sleep. That you go around with this idiotic smile that barely hints at the enormous happiness welling up inside you like some helium-filled balloon, the lightness of which makes your heart soar beyond the clouds to the stars—stars that sparkle with a crystalline purity that reminds you of the tears in your lover's eyes?"

Abby saw Ned hesitate. Then she broke out laughing. "Oh, my God, talk about having too much to drink on top of major jet lag *and* the first full day back on the job. Forget what I just said. No one's ever felt like that—so over-the-top in love. Especially not someone as *serious* as I am—" her voice was laced with self-critical irony "—let alone a serial model dater, such as you."

Ned watched her laugh some more and wondered whether he was brave enough. "Of course not. You're absolutely right," he replied. The answer was he wasn't, not yet, at least.

They looked at each other before turning back to staring out at the water and drinking their beers. The silence and the view soothed Abby as much as the alcohol, and she could almost forget that she was boyfriendless, not to mention discombobulated after her first day back to Life in the City.

"So what do you think?" Ned asked.

"What do I think?" Abby took a thoughtful sip. She rested the bottle on her leg. "I think that if I survive this assignment and settle in some place permanently, life could be pretty fine."

Ned slanted her a smile. "That's what I think, too." He clicked his bottle to hers.

"So can I join you?" a familiar voice asked from behind.

Abby didn't bother to turn around. Because she knew. It was Brad.

CHAPTER THREE

Persephone Wiesbaden and Brad Wahlberg

Richard and Karen Wiesbaden of Boston and St. John, the U.S. Virgin Islands, announce the engagement of their daughter, Persephone Constance Wiesbaden, to Bradford Albert Wahlberg, son of Kenneth and Lois Wahlberg of Crown Point, Indiana.

The bride-to-be is a graduate of the Madeira School, Harvard and Harvard Graduate School of Business. She is currently an investment banker at Morgan Stanley. Her father is the managing partner at Dunlop, Trainer & Wiesbaden LLP. Her mother is associate director of community affairs at the Collegiate School.

The prospective bridegroom is a graduate of Carbondale High School, Northwestern University and University of Virginia Law School. He is an assistant district attorney with the Manhattan District Attorney's Office. His father has retired from the Indiana Harbor Belt Railroad. His mother is a school psychologist.

The couple plans to marry on June 9 in Boston. After the wedding the couple will reside in New York City.

THE PHOTO ABOVE THE STORY showed Brad with his arm around his fiancée's shoulder. The two of them looked blond and healthy and radiant. Brad Pitt and Jennifer Aniston in happier times.

Abby squinted at the picture. "It looks like this was taken on a boat?"

Brad nodded and smiled, as if reliving the moment. "You're right. It was on the sailboat that Persephone's parents keep moored at Peter's Cove in St. John."

She passed the newspaper clipping to Ned. "It's on a boat," she repeated.

Ned skimmed the article and handed it back to Brad. He and Abby had turned around and faced Brad across the picnic table. "Persephone, huh? I'd avoid feeding her pomegranates."

Abby kicked him under the table.

"Really, my congratulations, mate. I'm sure you'll be very happy," Ned said.

Abby noticed he seemed unnecessarily jovial.

Brad nodded. "I know I will. Sometimes you just know when something's right."

Abby couldn't believe his insensitivity. Or maybe she could?

Ned squeezed her forearm. "Can I get you another beer, Abby?" She shook her head. "What about one for you?" he asked Brad.

"That'd be great," he said, further insinuating himself into the scene. Brad stared at the newspaper clipping some more, a dopey smile spreading across his face. "Persephone's very talented and smart."

"Yes, I saw she's a graduate of Harvard, undergraduate and business school." Abby began wondering where her University of Wisconsin diploma was. Maybe back in her parents' home in a scrapbook in the den…

"Which isn't to say she's not a big fan of you."

"Me?" She quickly forgot the den. "She knows about me?"

"Of course. She knows everything about us. Persephone's not one to feel insecure about the past. Besides, she always reads *Tess,* and when I mentioned that I'd gone out with someone on staff, she recognized your name right away. She loved your story on how some women are willing to suffer painful podiatry treatments to look better in their Manolo Blahniks, by the way."

"I'm, ah, happy to hear that," Abby said. That Brad even knew about designer shoes was perhaps more staggering. She took a large sip of beer.

Brad folded the announcement neatly and slipped it into his wallet. "So, you need my input on something at work? A legal matter?"

Ned returned and set Brad's beer on the picnic table. "Here you go. I've got some things to do back at my place, so I trust you'll make it home all right?" He stared at Abby, sending her an am-I-right-that-you'd-prefer-to-handle-this-on-your-own? look.

"Thanks, I'll be fine." Abby sent him a yes-that's-probably-better-and-don't-worry-I'm-a-big-girl-and-can-handle-myself nod. "I'll see you in a little bit."

Brad shifted his head from one to the other, but waited until Ned was out of earshot to lean across the table and whisper, "You and Ned?" He moved his index finger back and forth. "You're an item."

"Brad, you can speak up. He can't hear us," Abby said. "And we're not an item. We're just living together. I mean, we're living together, but, you know, not *living* together. I'm just bunking temporarily at his place. Until I get a place of my own."

Brad tipped his head back and sipped his beer. He

watched Ned's figure grow more distant as he retreated down the dock to the boathouses. Then he turned back to Abby. "So tell me, what did you want?"

Abby stopped peeling the label from her beer bottle. "Well, I *had* been wondering if you'd help me out on this story assignment I have, but now that I know about the engagement, it's probably not going to work out."

"Tell me, anyway. I want to know." Brad inclined forward and cupped her hand in his.

After all that had happened, talk about inappropriate! Abby winced and slipped her hand away. Of course, why his touch still felt solid and comfortable, not to mention achingly familiar, was a different matter all together. One that was decidedly annoying.

Yes, she was weak. And she knew it. But she also needed to get this story.

"Okay, it's like this," she said, and explained to him the details of the ex-dating article.

Brad wet his lips. "It would be kind of difficult. I mean, I'm getting married and all."

"Yeah." Abby stared off into space. Her backup "ex" was her half-crazy college boyfriend. An oboist, he'd spent far too many hours blowing through double reeds.

"Abby? Abby?" Brad repeated, trying to get her attention.

Abby refocused on Brad, who was hunched forward, looking blond and healthy and radiant—just like his engagement picture. "Yeah?" she asked, wondering when she could make her exit.

"I know this probably seems kind of strange to ask, especially in light of my current situation, but do you ever think about what might have been, between the two of us? You know, if you hadn't decided to go off to Italy, and I hadn't acted the way I did, suggesting the breakup?"

"I think you made more than a suggestion."

Brad sniffed. "You're right. I take full responsibility for that happening."

Surprised to hear him say that, Abby sat up straighter.

"So, do you? Do you ever wonder?" he asked again.

She breathed in deeply. "I'd be lying if I said I never did. But as you said, with you and Persephone, sometimes you know when something's right. And I guess it just wasn't right for us."

She started to get up. "Ned's probably wondering where I am. I should get back."

With one hand still clutching his beer, Brad rose, too. He gave her a crinkly smile. "Oh, what the heck. On second thought, why don't I help you out with your story? I mean, it's not like I'd be dating for real, just helping out with your research. And since Persephone is such a fan of *Tess,* I'm sure she'd get a kick out of me participating in something that appears in the magazine."

Abby grabbed the edge of the table to steady herself. "That would be fabulous! I can't tell you how much I'd appreciate it."

"It's the least I can do after how I behaved. Tell you what. Just e-mail me the details—what you need and what I should do to follow up, and I'll go from there."

Abby nodded. "Okay, no problem." She paused. "So I guess we'll be in touch."

"Right, in touch."

She gave him a little wave before turning to leave.

"Abby?" he called out.

She stopped in midstride and turned back. "Yeah?"

Brad pinched his full lips together. "I couldn't let you leave without telling you."

"Telling me what?"

"I don't know exactly. It's just that something about you is different."

Abby shrugged. "It's the haircut."

"You got a haircut?"

Abby rolled her eyes.

"No, it's not that," he said. "Though it does look great."

"You didn't even notice until I pointed it out."

"I noticed, trust me."

Abby cocked her head, surprised.

Brad stepped around the table, coming closer—close enough that only a few inches separated them. "Like I said—it's something else." He glanced to the side, swallowed, then looked back. "I think of you. A lot."

WHEN ABBY GOT BACK to the houseboat, she found Ned in his bedroom, standing in front of a dresser with his back to her. She halted halfway down the open steps. "Hey," she called out.

He looked over his shoulder, startled. "Hey. I've got to get used to having someone else here." He turned completely around and crossed his arms across his chest.

"If it's a problem, I can leave." She made a hitchhiker motion over her shoulder.

"Of course it's not a problem." He gave her a patented Ned Devlin smile, and his eyes glowed with the promise of wicked and fun things.

Whoa, Nellie.

"I'm sorry things didn't work out," Ned said tenderly. She frowned. "Huh?"

"With Brad." He waited. "And your story for *Tess.*"

"Oh, actually, it did work out." Abby pulled on her earlobe. "Brad said he'd do the ex-dating piece for me after all—purely informational, of course. Not that he's looking to two-time Persephone." She looked off into space and replayed the conversation with Brad in her mind.

Ned gazed at her. "That's just dandy." There was a sharp edge to his tone. He swiveled around and pulled out a dresser drawer.

Abby didn't quite know what had set Ned off. She descended the remaining two steps, stopping at the foot of his bed. It had a romantic wrought-iron headboard, she noticed, and a striped Irish wool blanket in rich blues and greens.

She also noticed an ancient-looking duffel bag lying open on top. It resembled a canvas lifeboat tossed amid a sea of jumbled mohair. "You going somewhere?"

He didn't bother to turn around. "I fly out first thing tomorrow for Thailand—a shoot for the swimsuit edition of *Sports Illustrated.* Then it's off to Borneo for French *Vogue.* So, unless you have something more to talk about, I'm kind of busy." He slammed the top drawer shut before opening the next one down.

Abby rubbed a hand up and down her opposite arm. Even though she still had on her camel-hair coat, she felt a chill. She knew she should leave him to get ready, but she also knew she had to ask someone. "You don't think it's wrong of me to impose on Brad this way? With the story, I mean. Seeing as he's getting married and everything?"

Ned sighed and waited a beat before turning around again. He held a pair of black knit boxers in his hand. "I think Brad knows exactly what he's getting into," he said, using carefully measured words.

"Of course he does." Abby nodded her head vigorously. She told herself to look away from his underwear, but she found she couldn't take her eyes off them. "Anyway, it's not as if he would be cheating on Persephone."

Ned sucked in the sides of his cheeks. "If you say so."

"Of course I say so." She walked back to the steps and grabbed the railing. "So, why don't I just leave you to your packing, then? And if I don't see you in the morning, have a great trip."

"Thanks. I'll try to be quiet."

Abby placed her foot on the step. But hesitated. "I really appreciate this, you know. Your letting me stay here and all. I promise to take good care of the place."

Ned stopped and turned to look at her sideways. "About my offer for you staying here?" He swallowed, then rolled his shoulders.

"What? What is it?" If she didn't know better, she would swear he was about to say something important, something soul-searching—something *really* un-Ned-like.

He opened his mouth.

She waited, holding her breath.

Until finally—when her oxygen supply was on the verge of becoming seriously depleted—he shrugged and offered a low chuckle. "Just go easy on my whiskey—that's all I ask."

Then he winked and went back to his drawer.

She nodded, telling herself she was relieved to be spared from male Sturm und Drang. "Okay, I promise. Good night." She pivoted around and gingerly took the narrow steps up to the main cabin.

But she couldn't just leave it at that. "Ned?" She bent down.

He tossed the underwear on the bed and strode to the bottom of the stairs. He stood there, looking up at her, the whole tableau very much the archetypal balcony scene. Abby could almost imagine a swelling crescendo from an oversize string section and a bright beam of light connecting the two of them—kind of a schmaltzy *Star Trek* moment.

He raised his eyebrows and waited.

She let the moment pass. "Why do you think Brad agreed to help me out?"

If he was surprised at her question, he didn't show it. "You must have had what he wanted, after all."

She instantly realized she'd forgotten to mention the Nirvana CDs. "Now that *you* mention it, we never got around to that."

Ned stood there for a moment. Then he picked up the pair of black knit boxers from the bed and stuffed them in the duffel. "Oh, I wouldn't be so sure," he said.

CHAPTER FOUR

A New Ex-Boyfriend for You!

"Court-ly Jester" is the fun-loving, super-achieving guy for you. "*Law & Order* Dude by Day, Grunge Music Worshipper by Night," he knows his way around a habeas corpus, not to mention a mosh pit.

But don't look for Court-ly Jester to tout his accomplishments. Even though this transplanted Midwesterner now pursues a SUCCESSFUL legal career in Manhattan, he'll never brag that he can afford to get you at least two carats at Tiffany's. But he can, girl! So start thinking pear-shaped or square-shaped! And when he's not putting the bad guys behind bars, Court-ly Jester puts away his briefs <g> and dances the night away. His perfect weekend? Snuggling under the comforter with fresh croissants, the Sunday paper and YOU— not necessarily in that order. His perfect partner? Someone who likes meat loaf as much as Vietnamese spicy lobster rolls; who'll take him to the ballet and Alanis Morrisette concerts provided she'll tolerate Schwarzenegger flicks and bad-boy music; but most of all, someone who's true and bright and not averse to sharing the remote. Can you believe it—a man who will give up *Sports Center* for *Friends*?

So how did I lose him? Let's just say my "Leavin' on a Jet Plane" lifestyle put a crimp in those snuggle-up weekends. But if you dance to the New York City beat, let the cross-examination begin!

ABBY PROOFREAD THE COPY she'd just written for Brad's posting on the Exbeaux Web site. The mixture of semi-truths (he'd probably spring for one carat, two was pushing it) and out-and-out lies (definitely the remote control sharing!) seemed about right. Anyway, what girl wouldn't swoon, especially when she saw his photo? As requested, she'd included a JPEG file of him: his engagement photo, to be exact, minus Persephone. Amazing what Photoshop could do.

She hit the send button.

Now her story for *Tess* was in the hands of the gods and single women everywhere.

ONE WEEK LATER, ABBY SAT in Tess's office, the vast expanse of the editor's desk separating their status in life much like the pinch-pleat curtain between first and second class on an airplane. "Tess, like I told you, the ex-dating story is going fine," Abby repeated, trying not to convey her annoyance at being monitored like some junior assistant.

She shifted on her chair, her gray pencil skirt and jacquard sweater clinging to her body. Back in Milan, the Missoni outfit had seemed the epitome of perfect tailoring and masterful knitwear. Here in the office, it just seemed to cling to her boobs and her butt.

"Since I joined Exbeaux and listed Brad, I've been able to view the other ex's on the site. There're a number in New York, mostly Brooklyn, and I'm planning on e-mailing them today. When I finally meet face-to-face with them, I'll let them know the whole context—that I'm working on a first-person story."

"That sounds reasonable. But whatever you do, don't use your real name and *Tess* address initially." Tess tapped her index finger smartly.

"No, of course not. Once you join Exbeaux, you get a free e-mail account, and my user name is Easy Writer."

"Good. It's one thing for residents of the outer boroughs to look desperate. Quite another for a staffer on the magazine." Tess picked up a printout of the Court-ly Jester entry that Abby had posted for Brad and studied it. "I like the part about the spicy lobster rolls." She took a long drag on her cigarette holder.

Today she'd traded in the black onyx for tortoise-shell—*the real thing, darling*. It matched her ensemble, a chestnut-colored ("*The* color this season, darling") turban and fitted suit with a sable collar and cuffs. She was going for the Diana Vreeland effect. *Very* Diana Vreeland.

"Oh, the spicy lobster rolls—that part's phony," Abby admitted. "Brad's never eaten Vietnamese food in his life. I got that from a take-out menu from this great place called Monsoon, on Amsterdam and Eighty-First. Ned left it for me along with a few others."

Tess stopped puffing.

Abby immediately realized her mistake.

To: Ned Devlin <n.devlin@devlinphotos.com>
From: Tess <Tess@tess.com>
Subject: It's All About You
Ned, you naughty boy,

Frolicking in the sun and the sand with all those nubile models. There was a rumor floating around the Hamptons this past summer that SPF 30 has an effect on the durability of latex. Just thought you might like to know.

By the by, I had a certain Oscar-winning actress on the line this morning—no names, darling, in an effort to be hush-hush, though I'm sure you, being you, can put two and two together. Anyway, said actress simply insists that it's you or no one for the cover photo of her for the Feb. issue. What could I say? So don't make me have to call that sweet thing back and tell her I was wrong.

Oh, and by the by—our Abby, the darling, just stopped by my office. Italy has done such wonders for her sense of style. Everyone's commenting on it. To think the girl has been hiding her assets all these years beneath tweed blazers and wool pants. I mean, Ralph Lauren is fine for those occasions when you want to look like a Kate Hepburn redux, but, thank God, I think we can finally call Goodwill to take away all her department store year-end sale items.

Anyhoo—we talked about this and that. Why didn't you ever tell me about the spicy lobster rolls? If I had known, I would have dipped my toes in the water off your boat long ago. Which reminds me, I wonder who Abby's sharing the stir-fried beans with?

Legal has already messengered over the contracts to your office. You know the drill.

Tess

To: Abby Lewis <alewis@tess.com>
From: Ned Devlin <ndevlin@devlinphotos.com>
Subject: So I guess you found the keys
Hey Abby,
So I guess you found the keys I left you on the table before I left. Hope everything is working out OK w/ the boat. And, dare I ask, work?
Got the strangest e-mail from Tess. (When is an e-mail from Tess not strange?) What's this about stir-fried beans?
Yours,
Ned

To: Ned Devlin <ndevlin@devlinphotos.com>
From: Abby Lewis <alewis@tess.com>
Subject: Re: So I guess you found the keys
Ned—
No problem with the keys. Everything's working out great. Why didn't you tell me how friendly your neighbors are? I was wondering who belonged to the large Siamese who likes to curl up on the deck chairs. I found out his name is Izzie—the cat, not your neighbor, Phil, the creative director from J. Walter Thompson? Stir-fried beans? Don't know much about that, but Izzie has developed a great fondness for the short-bread cookies I found in your cupboard.
Hope all is well among the beautiful and exotic. Make sure to use your sun block in all the right places.
Your pale roommate,
Abby

To: Hook 'Em Harry <hharry@mail.exbeaux.com>
From: Easy Writer <ewriter@mail.exbeaux.com>
Subject: Exbeaux listing
Hi, Hook 'Em Harry,
I saw your listing on the Exbeaux site, and I must say, New York's Fire Department has never looked finer. So, according to your profile, you like bass fishing? What a coincidence. I have great memories fishing with my dad in South Dakota (I now live and work in NYC as a magazine writer). We always found that Cheez Whiz made great bait.
I'd love to chat some more. I can understand that you're only looking for friendship right now, having been burned—sorry, you must get that a lot. But I'd love to "hook up" and just talk.
Burning to see you,
Easy Writer

To: Shakespeare in Love <silove@mail.exbeaux.com>
From: Easy Writer <ewriter@mail.exbeaux.com>
Subject: Exbeaux listing
Hi Shakespeare in Love,
You must be the first person I've ever met for whom Titus Andronicus held such sway. It's refreshing to find a man who's read more than the latest John Grisham. Perhaps we have something in common? I am a senior writer for a cutting-edge women's magazine, though admittedly I write more about the latest trendy hot spot than the lot of tortured Hamlet.
Your profile says that you have just received tenure and are seeking a serious relationship. I must confess

that I'm really just looking to talk, but if a relationship clicks, "All's Well That Ends Well."
To be or not to be,
Easy Writer

To: Foot-Long Hero <flhero@mail.exbeaux.com>
From: Easy Writer <ewriter@mail.exbeaux.com>
Subject: Exbeaux listing
Hi, Foot-Long Hero,
Wow! You own a chain of Subway franchises. It must be very gratifying to know that each day you're helping people beat their fried-food habit.
I'm also impressed that you like doing acrostics. That's pretty advanced. My exposure to word games consists of many hours spent playing Yahtzee as a kid. Actually, some people consider my job as a writer for a women's magazine to be a kind of word game.
Anyhow, I'd love to chat some more. I can understand that you're gun-shy about getting involved, having recently been spurned when your girlfriend decided to disassociate herself from all carbohydrates. I can assure you, however, that while I try to watch my calorie intake, I am definitely not a follower of the Atkins Diet. For now, I really am just looking to talk, with or without a roll.
Next in line,
Easy Writer

To: Abby Lewis <alewis@tess.com>
From: Brad Wahlberg <bradwahlberg@manhattanda.org>
Subject: Exbeaux follow-up
Abby—

You wouldn't believe the responses I've gotten to that posting on the Exbeaux site. Persephone said she wanted to be the one to vet the women, but I insisted it was your story, and that you had the say-so, and besides, you're the one who's actually meeting with them, not me.

So can we meet for dinner? Tonight's not good, but how about Thursday? I'll print out the messages and bring them for you to read.

There's this great Vietnamese place, Monsoon, over on your side of town. I should be able to make it there by eight-thirty.

Be there or be square.

Court-ly Jester

To: Tess <Tess@tess.com>
From: Ned Devlin <ndevlin@devlinphotos.com>
Subject: Re: It's All About You
Tess,
You'll get the damned signed contract when you get the damned signed contract. And I'm not putting up with any divalike drama, just so you know.

What have you said to Abby about all the SPF mumbo jumbo? She mentioned sunblock?
ND

To: Easy Writer <ewriter@mail.exbeaux.com>
From: Foot-Long Hero <flhero@mail.exbeaux.com>
Subject: Re: Exbeaux listing
Dear Easy Writer,
What can I say? I never do this sort of thing, online dating, that is. It was my ex-girlfriend's idea. Still, it

was refreshing to hear from someone with a similar love for words. What did you think of last Sunday's New York Times crossword puzzle? I am getting tired of clues themed to the Oscars.

Would your magazine ever consider adding an acrostic column? I would be happy to act as a consultant. Perhaps we can discuss this more fully.

Foot-Long Hero

P.S. If you're interested in watching calories, you might want to try our new turkey wrap.

P.P.S. Do you have a photo?

To: Brad Wahlberg <bradwahlberg@manhattanda.org
From: Abby Lewis <alewis@tess.com>
Subject: Re: Exbeaux follow-up

Court-ly Jester—

Glad to hear you're having success, but Thursday looks bad for me. I promised Julia I'd help her with a Meals on Wheels delivery. What about Friday? Though I don't want to interfere with your weekend plans with Persephone…

Easy Writer (Easy Writer is my Exbeaux moniker. Cute, right?)

To: Easy Writer <ewriter@mail.exbeaux.com>
From: Hook 'Em Harry <hharry@mail.exbeaux.com>
Subject: Re: Exbeaux listing

Yo, Easy Writer,

A fellow angler. Whaddayaknow? So how about we get together? There's an outdoorsmen's equipment show at the Javits Center next week. I understand the new fiberglass poles are something to behold. Afterward we can go for a latte or something, and I'll give you the inside scoop on why firemen wear suspenders.

Hook 'Em Harry

P.S. Can you send a picture of yourself? The guys at the firehouse can't believe a classy chick like you would want to hook up with someone like me.

To: Ned Devlin <ndevlin@devlinphotos.com>
From: Tess <Tess@tess.com>
Subject: Re: Re: It's All About You
ND,
No need for vulgarity. Am I the only one who worries about protecting the poor girl?
Tess

To: Abby Lewis <alewis@tess.com>
From: Brad Wahlberg<bradwahlberg@manhattanda.org>
Subject: Easy Writer?
Abby,
Easy Writer? You may have been cheap, but you were never easy.
Friday's not good at my end. Persephone and I have to meet with florists. What about Sunday?
Court-ly Jester

To: Easy Writer <ewriter@mail.exbeaux.com>
From: Shakespeare in Love
<silove@mail.exbeaux.com>
Subject: Re: Exbeaux listing

Dear Easy Writer,

It was entirely inappropriate for my departmental secretary to post information about me on this Web site. Normally, I would not even reply, but I was intrigued to find someone of your background responding. Perhaps we have something to discuss after all? Have you seen the recent Damien Hirst exhibit at the V & A in London? I find his oeuvre remarkably sophomoric yet strangely compelling in a post-Structuralist manner. It contains the same disturbing dichotomy between the mundane and the metaphysical that is portrayed in Hong Kong action films, another passion of mine. Wouldn't you agree?

Shakespeare in Love

P.S. Please include an image of yourself with your reply.

To: Abby Lewis <alewis@tess.com>
From: Ned Devlin <ndevlin@devlinphotos.com>
Subject: Re: Re: So I guess you found the keys

Abby,

Izzie's cool, but didn't your mother ever tell you to watch out for men in advertising? I have a good mind to call her up now if I could ever get the bloody satellite phone to work, and the resort we're staying at is so eco-friendly, they won't lay any land lines. Who cares if the mosquito netting is by Frette?

Just remember, Phil is the man whose contribution to civilization is the Vistera commercial—you know the one: a man and a woman laughing on a balcony as the fog rolls in, a meaningful smile on him, a camisole barely on her, while we hear, "A week's pleasure in one carnelian capsule."

And if he mentions anything about how I regularly let him drink my Irish whiskey, it's a bloody lie.
I promise I'm staying out of the sun,
Ned

To: Abby Lewis <alewis@tess.com>
From: Ned Devlin <ndevlin@devlinphotos.com>
Subject: Re: Re: Re: So I guess you found the keys
On second thought, just tell Phil to take the whiskey home. Alone.
Did I mention I'm staying out of the sun?

To: Brad Wahlberg <bradwahlberg@manhattanda.org>
From: Abby Lewis <alewis@tess.com>
Subject: Re: Easy Writer?
Brad—
I'm sorry, I can't keep writing Court-ly Jester. It reminds me of this Danny Kaye movie that I know you've never seen where he plays a court jester, and there's this running joke about something to do with wine glasses. If only I could remember it… Aargh! And here I'm supposed to be concentrating on writing a piece on how to get your insurance carrier to cover elective plastic surgery.
Speaking of movies you've never seen, Easy Writer is a pun referring to Easy Rider, this old Peter Fonda, Jack Nicholson film. Never mind…
Sunday is good. Are we still on for Monsoon? Same time?
A
P.S. Eureka! The joke in the film? It has to do with Danny

Kaye trying to explain which wine cup contains poison and which one doesn't—all this darring-do and confusion and even more alliteration. I know, I know, totally silly. But thank God I remembered. Oh, and don't be surprised if I make you taste the wine first at dinner! <g>

To: Abby Lewis <alewis@tess.com>
From: Brad   Wahlberg<bradwahlberg@manhat-tanda.org>
Subject: Re: Re: Easy Writer?
A
Same time: Sunday, 7:00 p.m., but change of venue. Meet on Columbus Circle, the Central Park corner. It's a surprise.
B
P.S. Danny who?

"Abby, Abby? If you're there, pi-ick up…. It's me-e-e, Ned…. Blast, this satellite ph-ph-oh-one is stuffed. For all the money they spend on hair gel, you think they could provide a decent satellite hook u-up…. So wha-at have *you* heard about sun block? *Crackle*. Can y-o-u…hea—m…?"

CHAPTER FIVE

"BRAD, WHEN YOU SAID a surprise, I never expected this." Abby spun around slowly. They'd walked uptown from their rendezvous point, and now that they'd reached their destination, her first thought was, *This is so kitsch.*

Her second was that the outfit she was wearing was grossly deficient—ripped jeans and fisherman's knit sweater, last year's year-end sale at her favorite department store on Herald Square (call her predictable, but how can you not *love* a store that sponsors a Thanksgiving Day parade?).

"Don't you like it?" Brad, looking as if he was ready to bargain a plea, was dressed in a charcoal-gray suit and blue power tie. "I thought it would be kind of fun. Whenever we have visitors from out of town into the D.A.'s office, they always ask to come to Tavern on the Green."

"Brad, do I look like some visiting prosecutor from Peoria? Really, you have to admit the only thing more clichéd would be a suite at the Waldorf-Astoria with champagne on ice and chocolate-covered strawberries in a silver serving bowl."

Abby noticed Brad's pained expression. She immediately realized her mistake. "Aw, don't listen to me. It's just that I'm…um…overwhelmed." She looked around at the thousands of fairy lights adorning the trees and windows. "And it *really* is magical-looking, I admit." She also wondered what the restaurant's monthly electrical bill was. *Never mind.*

"Still, the Vietnamese restaurant would have been fine," she assured him. "You really don't have to spend so much money."

"See, I said you were a cheap date." He held up his hand. "A joke. Anyway, let me spoil you if I want. It's the least I can do."

Brad smiled his Midwestern-boy-made-good-in-the-big-bad-city smile, and held open the door to the restaurant. They walked the curved hallway to the main dining area and waited for the maître d' to seat them at a small table by the windows.

Brad turned to the waiter. "I need as much help as possible, so you better get us some champagne, quickly. A bottle of Veuve Clicquot!" he commanded. Then he laughed in Abby's direction. "And I promise to taste it first—though I can't promise any alliteration."

Abby had always loved his laugh. It was big and guylike and made his eyelids close up into happy crescents.

Brad leaned on his forearms. "Listen, I've got to tell you. I went out and rented those movies you mentioned in your e-mail."

Abby cocked her head. Brad had never *ever* followed up her suggestions on films.

"I didn't quite get the appeal of the Danny Kaye flick."

Abby nodded. "It's an acquired taste. Kind of like stuffed figs."

That had Brad smiling. Abby grinned back. "But I totally got into *Easy Rider.* Early Jack Nicholson, amazing. Plus the bikes." He whistled.

Abby was touched. It wasn't a deep discussion on,

say, the long-lasting merits of *nouvelle vague* cinema, but so what? Besides, a few more sips of champagne and even a plot summary of some teen comedy would sound insightful.

She twirled the stem of her flute. "So tell me about your Exbeaux contacts, and let's figure out how we should proceed."

"I thought you'd never ask." Brad slipped his hand inside his suit jacket and removed some sheets of paper. "My favorite is this Romanian acrobat who's with Cirque de Soleil. They're even in town for an eight-week run."

He unfolded the printouts and smoothed them on the tablecloth. His gray-blues eyes danced with a level of enthusiasm that Abby remembered seeing only once before—right after he'd put away some mafia capo on RICO violations.

But this enthusiasm was different. Because this time Brad's excitement didn't have a competitive, aggressive element. It was something he was sharing—with her.

"You know, I'd never thought I'd say this—" Brad ducked his head and whispered conspiratorially "—but this is fun, working together. In fact, I don't know why we never thought of it before."

For a fleeting, guilt-filled moment Abby thought about Persephone and her Ivy League credentials and her family's Caribbean sailboat. And then the moment passed because, after all, she and Brad were *just* working together.

Or so she told herself as she leaned forward to read the e-mails. "I know. I don't know why, either," she answered, her voice a little wobbly.

Brad shifted those dancing eyes upward and met hers. "You all right there?" he asked, puzzled.

"I'm fine." Conflicted. But fine.

"I REALLY CAN'T TALK now. I'm in the middle of a lunch date," Abby said into her cell phone. She raised her eyes and waved at Hook 'Em Harry, who was getting the two of them hot dogs and water from the Sabrett stand on the corner of Thirty-Fourth Street and Eleventh Avenue outside the Javits Center. She sat on one of the wire chairs clustered on the sidewalk and enjoyed an unseasonably warm fall day.

"It's not Phil, is it?" Ned's disembodied voice had a slight delay as it traveled across the globe all the way from Borneo.

"Phil? Oh, you mean Good Neighbor Phil. No, I haven't seen Phil for days." It was Wednesday. Ned had been gone a week and a half. "I'm here with my fireman—one of the Exbeaux dates?"

"Wait a minute, I thought the whole purpose was to match Brad up with hot chicks, not you with firefighters. Besides, you should know, all they eat is chili."

"How did you guess? He asked if I wanted some on my hot dog. And don't be so critical. Anyway, I've been meeting with a couple of guys whom I've corresponded with for this piece. As soon as we begin talking, I explain the whole article situation."

"So you've been seeing a bunch of them—these Exbeaux wankers?"

"This is my second. Hey, did you know that Subway is the number-one franchise business in America?"

"I'm sure that kind of cutting-edge information will thrill the readers of *Tess*."

"As if."

"So, all this Exbeaux dating must explain why I couldn't get ahold of you on Sunday night. Here I thought it might be because of Phil," Ned threw out oh-so casually.

Abby missed the gnashing of teeth. "Sunday? No, Sunday was dinner with Brad."

There was silence. Also more silent teeth gnashing.

"Ned? Ned? Are you still there?"

"So, how was Persephone?" he asked. The arch in his voice traveled the thousands of miles quite nicely.

Abby cleared her throat. "Oh, she couldn't make it. Tied up with choosing the font for the wedding invitations."

She felt guilty. About dining alone with Brad—even though it was only business—*and* for lying to Ned. "Anyway, Brad told me all about his ex-dating e-mail correspondence, and we worked out how I would follow up and contact the women."

"So he's not going to go out on dates with them?"

"Of course not. Brad isn't like that." She didn't want to debate the subject further because she wasn't sure how rock-solid her convictions were. "So how's Borneo?"

"Tropical. Bloody tropical. I'm lying here naked on the queen-size bed in my hut. There's a paddle fan whirring overhead, but all it does is move the hot air around. And look at that now, will you? A bloody gecko the size of a ruckman is trying to climb up the wall."

"Imagine." Abby gulped. And she could, imagine it, that is—and not the gecko part, either. "Well, it's gorgeous here," she added, once more skirting the issue. "One of those rare New York days when the sky is a cloudless aquamarine, all the taxis are empty and the heady smell of charred soft pretzels and diesel fumes induces thoughts of playing hooky and having sex all afternoon."

Abby blinked. *My God.* Where had that come from? She knew where. And it wasn't imagining the gecko.

Abby waited for Ned to say something. He didn't. "Ned? Ned? Are you still there?"

"Come to Borneo," he said quickly from out there in the digital universe.

For a moment, Abby thought he was being serious. But, hey, this was Ned she was talking to. She laughed. "Good one, Devlin. Get up, put some clothes on and do whatever it is you do with all those skinny models."

She looked up. "Hook 'Em Harry" was cutting a wide swath through the lunchtime crowd. "Sorry, gotta go, Ned," she said. "My firefighter is coming to the rescue. 'Come to Borneo.' You are *too* much."

She clicked off the phone. Hook 'Em Harry—whose real name she'd found out was Chet Schimmerhorn—seemed like a nice guy. When she was arranging their meeting over the phone, Abby had let him know the background on her story, and he had taken the news in stride.

"Somehow I'm not that surprised," he had responded. "The guys at the station had been razzin' me about this whole Exbeaux thing, telling me you were too good to be true, and I guess they were right. But the way I figure it, maybe if you write me up as some hot stud, I'll get a girl, anyway, right? Maybe have 'em touch up my photo, too?"

Abby had also found out that Chet was working toward his bachelor's degree at City College, took the role of godfather to his sister's oldest son very seriously, and enjoyed working out in the gym.

Speaking of working out in the gym, Chet used one of his well-muscled arms to balance two bottles of water and three hot dogs—two for himself, one for her—while he slipped his wallet into the back pocket of his thigh-hugging jeans. One look at his sinewy forearms and Abby had a sudden flash of inspiration.

"You know, Chet, my lack of interest in biceps curls would have doomed whatever possibility we ever had for a relationship," Abby said, accepting the water. "But speaking of too good to be true, I just heard about this woman who's an acrobat, and I bet she'd love to get a look at your fireman's hold."

ON THE FOLLOWING MONDAY, word spread from the guys in the art department: Mary-Kate and Ashley, clutching take-out lattes and Anya Hindmarch leather totes with tassel closures (the guys in the art department knew this type of thing), had just been spotted from the windows on the south side of the building.

Abby rushed out of her cubicle. And *whoomph!* Collision time.

She staggered backward. What had she just hit? Abby looked up. *Oh, my God.* Sometimes knowledge was *not* power.

Tess peered at her bent cigarette.

On the bright side, Tess had chosen to carry a six-inch jade cigarette holder today. If she had gone with one of her usual twelve-inch numbers, Abby's hometown newspaper, the *Rapid City Journal,* would soon be running an obit of her demise due to impaling.

On the not-so-bright side, Abby noticed a round burn mark in her cashmere cardigan, positioned right above her left boob like an ancillary nipple.

Tess removed the smashed cigarette and flicked it unceremoniously into Abby's trash can. "My, my, aren't we in a hurry. I presume you're rushing out to fulfill your groundbreaking reportage on ex-dating?"

Abby thought it best to avoid any and all mention of the super twins. "By all means. And ground-breaking it is."

"As I would expect. Otherwise you wouldn't be working here, would you?" Tess added a little "heh, heh." This might or might not have been an indication of humor.

"By the by," Tess went on, "the mailroom seems to have made an error, and given me something that appears to be for you." She waggled something rectangular back and forth in front of Abby's nose.

Abby followed the motion with her head, narrowing her eyes and trying to focus on what exactly Tess felt was so important to cause her to leave the sanctuary of her office and descend upon the minions.

Only moments before permanent cross-eyedness set in, the object came to rest. Abby squinted. "A postcard? It looks like Hawaii."

"I can tell you're not the travel editor. As anyone with even a passing acquaintance with the Pacific Rim would know, it's Thailand, darling," Tess corrected her.

Abby took the card, flipped it over and noticed the signature. "Oh, isn't that sweet. It's from Ned." She glanced up, smiling, and saw Tess watching her. Abby lowered the card to her side. "He probably sent it to make sure everything's in order at his place. I think I told you I'm temporarily living there. In a separate bunk, I mean, in the forward part of the boat." She pointed upward and out.

"Actually, he seems more concerned that you know he's not mixing his sunblock with anything else."

"You read the message on a card sent to me?"

"*Everyone* reads everyone else's postcards, darling. If someone wanted to write something private, they'd put it in a sealed envelope." Tess pivoted on her Christian Louboutin lizard slides. "Oh, by the way, when you talk to Ned next—about whether or not things are in order at his place—could you also remind him to bring back a sarong? And She-Who-Shall-Not-Be-Named—mum's the word here—requested that his be matching."

"Sorry, you need a sarong? A matching sarong?" Not to mention, who was this She-Who-Shall Not-Be-Named?

"For the cover shoot that Ned's doing, darling. After the *Vanity Fair* session, You-Know-Who insisted she simply wouldn't be photographed by anyone else. You heard what happened then, didn't you?"

Abby shook her head.

"No, of course not. That was right after you'd left for *Milano,* and another of her romantic comedies was about to come out. The story goes that they got into a little energetic role playing and…well…you can imagine what happened from there."

Abby could, and she wasn't sure she wanted to. She stood dumbstruck as Tess withdrew.

"Oh, Abby darling?" Tess called out without bothering to turn around.

"Ye-es?" *What now?*

"If you're going to catch Mary-Kate and Ashley, you'd better hurry."

LATER THAT AFTERNOON, Abby hurried through the heavy, gilt-edged doors of the Waldorf-Astoria hotel and raced up the marble steps to the main lobby. The sides of her coat, which she'd left unbelted, flapped with each brisk stride. She came to a stop, somewhat winded. "This had better be important, Brad. I had to skip out on a meeting with the photo director about the ex-dating story."

Brad bent forward to kiss her lightly on the cheek. Then he frowned. "Have you been smoking?"

Abby saw his eyes fixate on her third "nipple." "Oh, that. Tess burned me with her cigarette, and, no, we're not suddenly getting all kinky at the office. So what couldn't wait?" she asked again.

"Not here." He circled the sleeve of her coat with his large hand—Brad had been quarterback on his high school team—and pulled her toward a bank of elevators. He punched the up button.

"What? Have you got the prosecutors from Robert Blake's murder trial squirreled away in a room upstairs?" She let him guide her into the elevator.

"Something like that." There was a mischievous grin on his face. He splayed his arms out and rested his hands on the brass railing.

"If this is something to do with the story, I've already followed up with various women from Exbeaux. Hey, did I tell you I found the perfect match for the circus performer?"

The elevator glided to a halt. Brad ushered Abby down the hall and drew out a key card. "That's great, but I didn't have them in mind when I extended the invitation today."

He unlocked the door and pushed it open, letting Abby pass through first. It was a humongous suite, with gargantuan flower arrangements of Asiatic lilies and pink hydrangeas cascading over every available hard, flat surface.

Abby circled around, taking in the pastel, overstuffed Grand Hotel decor before resting her eyes on a small table for two set up by the windows. She walked over, spying champagne chilling in a bucket and a large sterling silver bowl of chocolate-covered strawberries. She suddenly had a bad feeling—a really bad feeling. "Tell me you're expecting Persephone?"

He stepped next to her. "No. Right now, Persephone is not in the picture," he said with certitude.

His attitude as much as the words had Abby worrying even more. She opened her mouth to speak, but the pop of a champagne cork silenced her. With bubbly spilling from the top of the bottle, Brad poured two glasses and held one out to Abby.

Abby looked at it askance. "Brad, when I mentioned champagne and chocolate-covered strawberries the last time we were together, I meant it as a joke."

He was smiling, but not in a ha-ha, funny way.

"Tell me I'm completely bonkers in thinking this has something to do with rekindling a relationship between you and me?" she said.

"You aren't completely bonkers."

Abby breathed a sigh of relief. "Thank God. I'll take that champagne, after all." She took the flute.

"But it does have something to do with rekindling a relationship between you and me."

Abby stared dumbfounded as Brad clinked his glass to hers.

She took a large sip and put her glass down on the table. "Brad, I think you need to look at the situation logically—"

"I am," he countered. "You know how much fun we've had these past weeks?"

"Well, yeah, it's been fun, but it's certainly not grounds to resurrect something that's past, let alone jeopardize your engagement to Persephone, who's a smart and successful woman—a woman with a sailboat."

"Unlike you."

Abby picked up her champagne flute and swallowed another mouthful. "I'm not smart and successful?"

Brad squeezed her upper arm through her coat sleeve. "That didn't come out the right way. Of course you're smart and successful. But you also don't take life so seriously. Until these past few weeks, I didn't appreciate your joie de vivre." He peered deeply into her eyes, a vertical line of sincerity bisecting his brow. "Abby, don't let me go through life without experiencing that vitality anymore, without sharing news about

even the silliest things, without expanding my knowledge of old movies."

Then he slanted his head and gave her an achingly
sweet, champagne-flavored kiss.

Oh, my God! She was being pulled in every direction.
On the one hand, she would never be able forgive herself
for hurting Persephone. But, damn it, Brad was hitting
all the right buttons—making her feel needed and
wanted and desired. What woman in her right mind
would purposely throw all that away?

Brad took her hand and parted her fingers with
his. "Stay with me, Abby. I've got the room. It would
mean so much."

Abby wavered. "But what about Persephone? Your
engagement?"

He shook his head. "I haven't told her yet, but it's all
but finished."

He set his glass on the table next to hers and started
to ease off her coat. Then he kissed her behind her ear,
just where she liked it. "I realize now that Persephone
was just a phase I was going through," he murmured.

He trailed little kisses under her chin. "That hooking
up with her right when you were deciding whether or
not to take the job in Italy was a mistake, a big mistake."

Abby pulled her head back. "Hold on." She placed
one hand on his chest. His suit jacket was unbuttoned
and his dress shirt felt stiff with starch. "I need some
clarification here. You hooked up with Persephone
before I left for Italy?"

Brad cleared his throat. "You have to understand, it
was a particularly confusing time for me. I was feeling
abandoned, and then when I met Persephone at this
party at City Hall, you know…the Easter Egg Hunt they
have for the kids of municipal workers…"

Abby narrowed her eyes and dredged up distant recollections. "Why is it that I distinctly remember you telling me you were too busy to go even though you knew I loved it from the year before?" She rotated her head and stared at the sweating champagne bucket. She might be from South Dakota, but that didn't make her naive.

She glared at Brad. "You knew ahead of time that Persephone would be there, didn't you? You went babe trawling with her in mind."

"I think one of the other assistant D.A.'s may have mentioned something about bringing a friend, who just happened to have invited Persephone along, too." Brad attempted some verbal back-pedaling.

"Just happened. I bet." Abby was disgusted.

"I swear. I was just so conflicted, what can I say?"

"Please, don't start swilling the same psycho-babble that *Tess* throws at its readers. Remember—I'm the one who writes that stuff. I know what a load of hooey it is."

She reached across the table and lifted the champagne bottle out of the bucket. Chilled water from the bath of melting ice ran down the sides and dripped on the carpet.

"Whoa there." Brad held up his hands defensively. "You're not going to hit me with that, are you? Because I have to warn you, if you injure me, it could be construed as manslaughter two."

Abby shifted her focus from the bottle to Brad's horrified face. The one-time high school quarterback no longer looked in charge of the game. "Hit you? I wouldn't waste a two-by-four on you. No, I intend to drink this." And with that, she stormed out of the room.

CHAPTER SIX

ABBY BANGED THE HOUSEBOAT door shut and shifted the champagne bottle from one hand to the other as she ruthlessly disentangled herself from her coat. Somewhere in the walk across town, it seemed to have sprung several extra sleeves, which made the process particularly difficult.

Successful at last, she let it drop to the floor and stepped over it. "Forget the lights," she cursed, and foraged in the dark for the table. Locating it with her hipbone, she plunked the bottle on top. Then she took an unsteady step backward and began stripping her sweater over her head. After sending that flying, she turned her attentions to her trousers, undoing the waistband button and letting them hit the deck as she kicked off her shoes.

The whole episode with Brad had left her feeling filthy. She itched to rid herself of anything connected with the encounter, cleanse herself of her disgust.

"Don't let me stop you from taking off the rest." A disembodied voice floated up from deep within the boat.

Abby grabbed the empty champagne bottle and held it over her head in a menacing fashion. "Whoever you are, I'm armed and dangerous."

The lights flicked on.

There stood Ned—at the bottom of the stairs to his

bedroom. He wore an old T-shirt and a pair of gray sweatpants that bulged at the knees.

Abby blinked. "Oh, my God, it's you. When did you get back?"

"About an hour ago." He ascended the stairs and rubbed the stubble on his tanned cheeks. "I was so messed up from the time difference I sacked out as soon as I arrived. Your banging woke me up."

He reached out and liberated the champagne bottle from Abby's grip. He regarded the label. "It's not a vintage year, so I don't think it would have been too dangerous."

Abby peered closely and noticed Ned displayed a truly sexy case of bed head. "I wasn't banging," she protested.

"If you say so." He turned and trotted back down the stairs.

Abby took a step after him and swayed, bumping into the corner of the table, a different corner but just as painful. "Ow." She rubbed her hip—the same hip. "Where are you going?"

Ned bounded up the stairs and stood next to her. "To get you a dressing gown." He held up the short black bathrobe. "You might not realize this, but you don't have any clothes on."

Abby looked down her front. "What? Not used to the sight of a woman in underwear?" She stared at her nude demi-cup bra and boy shorts—the latter, all the rage in Italy while she was there. *"La thong e molto passata,"* the fashion editor had informed her.

Abby snapped her head up. "I'm sure your swimsuit models wore far less."

"They weren't *my* swimsuit models and just humor me." He slipped the silky robe over her and tied the belt securely around her waist.

"There we go." He stepped back, but when he saw

Abby was sniffling he gently grabbed her shoulders. "What's wrong? It's not that fireman, is it?"

Abby wiped her nose with the back of her hand. "No, it's not the fireman. It's Brad."

Ned rolled his eyes. "How could I not have guessed?" He eased Abby over to the bench along the side of the cabin and lowered her onto the cushions. "So what happened?" he asked, his head bent close, his arm circling her shoulders.

Abby stiffened. "I don't want to talk about it. I just want a drink."

Ned eyed her dubiously. "You look like you've had quite enough already." He cocked his head toward the empty champagne bottle.

"Don't be a prude, you of all people." She grabbed a large tumbler from the shelf above the bench and held it out. "How about some of that famous Irish whiskey you don't like sharing with your neighbor?"

"Okay, if that's what you want? From bitter experience, I warn you that I don't recommend it."

Abby nodded squarely. "I want."

Ned slipped his arm from out behind, pressing Abby against the pillows. Then he got up and opened the cabinet under the sink to retrieve the whiskey, before reaching up to get a tumbler for himself. It seemed necessary under the circumstances.

He uncapped the bottle and poured two stiff drinks. As he brought his own glass to his lips, Ned watched her take a sip, then close her eyes and swallow. Her pale skin stood out against the low V of the robe's neckline.

Ned wet his lips and took a large swallow, feeling the hot liquid coat his dry throat. "You know, I think you're right. I think it's better if I don't know what happened."

Abby opened her eyes, drank another generous

mouthful and proceeded to tell Ned everything—*every-thing*. By the time she was done, she had wheedled another double shot out of him and had tears dripping down her cheeks and off her chin. A true gentleman, he offered the bottom of his T-shirt for her to wipe her nose on.

Ever practical—not to mention wasted—Abby accepted. Then she raised her wobbly head. "I can't believe what a rat Brad is. Wanting to sleep with me while he's still engaged to someone else, and before that, taking up with someone else while he was with me." She pounded her chest with her empty glass.

Ned took the glass and rested it on the cushion. "Easy, tiger. You don't want to do yourself any more damage."

Abby bunched up her mouth in a look of dismay. "Maybe it's me? Maybe I'm just so focused on my career that I can't manage this whole personal relationships thing?" She rested her forehead on Ned's shoulder and closed her eyes. "Was I right to go to Milan in the first place, Ned? Could all of this have been avoided if I'd just realized it was better for me to stay here?"

Ned stroked her hair. "Any man who truly loved you would have encouraged you to take that internship. Would have realized how important it was to you and would have waited." He cupped her chin and pulled her head back, gazing into her teary eyes.

Abby eked out a smile. "How come you're so nice?"

Ned hesitated before dropping his hand. She was too vulnerable, too tipsy. This was not the time to make a move, as much as he wanted to. "Trust me, I'm not."

"That's not what all the models say."

"You believe anything models tell you? These are women who haven't eaten a decent meal since hitting puberty. All that starvation has made them more delusional than most of the contestants on *American Idol*."

She laughed at his joke. Then she burst into tears, even harder this time. "Oh, I am so screwed up," she moaned.

"Let's have none of that," he soothed her. "Listen." He grasped her hands and waggled them in his. "I know just the trick for exorcizing an ex."

Abby closed one eye and peered at him sideways. "More whiskey?" She leaned around him to find her empty glass.

Ned pulled her upright. "No, I think we've had enough of that."

"Not even a wee bit?" she pleaded.

"That is the worst Irish brogue known to man, and, no, not even a wee bit." He turned her hands over so that her palms were facing up. "What I'm proposing instead is a game of X Marks the Spot."

Abby made a yeah-right-I-cannot-believe-you-just-said-that face.

"Don't be so quick to dismiss it. I personally guarantee that after enough rounds of this you will be incapable of remembering the identity of your ex or even why you ever thought he was worth kissing."

"Can we not talk about kissing?" Abby pouted her lips.

Ned averted his eyes. "Yes, that's probably a good idea." He cleared his throat. "Okay, it works like this." He slid the loose material of one of the robe's sleeves up to her elbow and rested her forearm on his lap.

"X marks the spot." He made a small crisscross on her arm. "Dot, dot, dot." His fingers mimicked his words. "Once around. Up and down." He slid his index finger gently from her wrist to the inside of her elbow, and back again. "This will give you the chills." He danced two fingers up and down her skin.

Abby tried to pull her arm back, but Ned held her hand firmly. "That tickles," she complained.

"That's the whole point. Now, are you ready for the advanced version?"

"The advanced version?"

"That's when you close your eyes."

Abby looked at him from beneath her eyelids, something that was decidedly difficult after consuming as much alcohol as she had.

"Trust me." His voice was low.

And she did. She closed her eyes and tried not to flinch while he slowly repeated the process once, and yet again. He did it slowly—very slowly—and she bit down hard.

He did it a third time—very slowly—and there was practically nothing left to her lower lip. "Stop, stop," she shouted between uncontrollable bursts of laughter. She rested her free hand atop his. "You're killing me."

"Death by giggling. I like that." Ned smiled back. "This is payback for all those snarky remarks you made about my social life."

"As if you never criticized *my* social life?" Abby answered back. "Actually, you never did, but never mind. Give it here."

"Give what where?" He looked as if he didn't comprehend.

Abby was buying none of it. She wiggled her index finger. "Now it's your turn to feel the power of *my* hands."

"Whoa." Ned pulled back. "I don't know about that."

"C'mon. It's only fair play." And she grabbed his hand and rested his arm upside down on her thighs. It was solid and warm. Abby told herself to ignore those two intriguing sensations and concentrate on the game.

"Close your eyes," she ordered. "No peeking." And she began to play, with her patented Abby Lewis intensity, seriously applying just the right amount of constant pressure with her fingertips, over and over, in geometric patterns, all with achingly slow precision, up and down his arm.

Her face was the picture of concentration.

And Ned's? It looked more like a losing battle with the darker forces of Comedy Central. Talk about a complete and utter meltdown.

"Oh, how the mighty have fallen!" Abby exclaimed triumphantly. "Ned Devlin—playboy of the western world, playboy extraordinaire of the western world—turns out to be totally, and I mean totally, ticklish."

"Enough!" he shouted, wiping the tears from his cheeks, and yanked his arm away.

Abby grabbed his hand back and swung it in a circle...well...not quite a circle, more like an ellipse with a giant pimple, her large motor skills being sufficiently impaired to prevent her from performing symmetrical gestures. "Who i-is ti-icklish? Who i-is ti-icklish?" she sang along in a particularly childish way. It felt so-o much fun.

Ned wrestled with her to stop. "Would you desist with this ridiculous blarney?"

Abby attempted to sit up straight. "I'm drunk. I'm allowed to go on and on."

"Well, that you are, but quit it."

"Why should I? I let you torture me."

"That was therapy. And it worked. Look—you're laughing. Whereas what *you're* doing is cruel and unusual punishment. And as you so clearly remarked earlier, *I* am a nice guy."

"That you are. Very nice." She jutted her chin forward and studied him through half-mast eyelids. "And a handsome devil, as well."

The two of them looked at each other. In silence. For

what seemed like an eternity. A silent eternity more tor-
turous than any tickling game, advanced or otherwise.

Abby didn't blink, but slowly, ever so slowly, she
slanted her head and leaned toward Ned's. "I've decided
that I'm going to kiss you."

Ned stiffened. "You think that's wise?"

Abby continued her slow advance. "I'm a healthy,
thirty-year-old woman, who by most standards other
than the high fashion world is good-looking, and who
on this very night in question—"

"I didn't question anything," Ned interrupted.

"Don't interrupt," she scolded, and bent forward even
more. "And who, on this very night in question, turned
down—yes, turned down, I say—her ex-boyfriend's
offer to get laid, *even though* she hasn't had sex in more
than six months and may never have sex again if her life
continues on in the same fashion, and you want me to
be wise?" Her voice went up an octave as her lips
stopped within millimeters of his.

Ned swallowed. "I guess not."

So she kissed him.

And he kissed her back, a light whisper that blended
warm breaths with the sweetness and tartness of various
alcohols. Then it gradually changed into a long, slow
drink of something far more intoxicating—longing,
sadness, surprise. Promise.

And when they finished, Abby rested her forehead
against his. And sighed.

Then she started snoring.

Startled, Ned pulled back, barely catching her from
doing a face-plant in his lap. He shook her gently. Hell,
he shook his own head.

To say he was disappointed was the understatement
of the year. But as much as he was disappointed—no,

more—he was also relieved. He didn't take advantage of drunken women. Even if…

"Yeah, even if," he said softly, and cradled her in his arms. "Abby Lewis, I hope you remember tomorrow morning what a noble guy I was." He staggered to his feet, lifting her in his arms. She was cuddly against his chest. Also a bloody deadweight.

One thing was for sure; it would be next to impossible to carry her up to the small bunk, given the low ceiling and cramped quarters on the upper deck. There was only one solution.

Ned gingerly descended the small flight of stairs to his bedroom and laid her in the middle of his bed.

He sat down on the edge and rubbed his bum shoulder. Then, because he told himself that she would be more comfortable and not because he wanted to see more of her creamy skin and curvy body, he loosened the belt of the robe.

And even though he hadn't intended to see more of her creamy skin and curvy body, he couldn't help noticing how her breasts, while of modest size, had a round, soft fullness that was clearly real, quite an anomaly in the world of fashion.

Swearing under his breath as he reminded himself that he was ever the gentleman, Ned pulled the wool blanket up around Abby's chin. He bent forward, brushed a lock of her curly hair aside, and placed a light kiss on her forehead.

Her eyes fluttered but remained shut.

So he whispered, "I love you, Abby, that I do."

OH, GOD. WHEN ABBY WOKE the next morning, her mouth tasted as if she'd had a prolonged and particularly unsuccessful encounter with charred seaweed. And her head? It felt like a thousand buffalo wearing rain boots had decided to trample her skull while looking for grazing land.

She stumbled up the steps from Ned's bedroom. "Please tell me the end of the world is nigh." She grabbed a corner of the table, balanced herself—kind of—and covered her face. "And could you make the boat stop rocking so violently."

Ned smiled at her cheerfully. "That's merely your knees buckling. Here, eat this. You'll feel right as rain." He placed a bowl in front of her. "There's a spoon, milk and brown sugar on the table."

She rubbed her forehead before daring to open her eyes. "What's that?" she asked when she had managed to curve several cracking vertebrae in her neck downward.

"The Irishman's cure for a hangover. Oatmeal. And not the revolting instant stuff you Americans are so fond of."

Abby groaned and lowered her body onto one of the benches. "What happened? Last night, I mean." She would have tried to finger-comb her curls, but she wasn't sure if the action would destroy whatever gray matter she had left in an un-pickled state.

"You came home upset after an encounter with Brad, and having already sampled French bubbly, decided to cross the English Channel and taste and retaste what Ireland has to offer in the way of adult beverages."

"That much I remember. And after that?"

"After that we played a perfectly innocent game of X Marks the Spot, during which time you may remember thoroughly humiliating me, but I can assure you, that's purely a false illusion brought on by alcoholic overconsumption."

"And I was in your bed because…?" She attempted to twist around and indicate his room but realized the gesture required greater coordination than she currently possessed.

"You passed out, and rather than test my manly strength and your bunk's limited headroom, I thought the easiest way out was to let you sleep it off in my bed."

"And I just…I mean…we just, slept?"

"Yes, you in my bed, and me in your berth. Frankly, you were so out of it, I was afraid if you rolled over on top of me in the middle of the night, I might never be able to disentangle you from my delicate and highly sensitive body."

"If you say so." She went to shake her head. Big mistake. She pressed a hand to her forehead. "I must have really been out of it because somehow I have this vague memory of you whispering to me—what, I'm not quite sure."

Ned cleared his throat and slid the china creamer closer to her bowl. "Milk?" he asked, a little too casually.

Abby, whose ability to measure degrees of casualness was sorely lacking this morning, didn't register Ned's tenseness. "I know, I know. It's best just to ignore me when I get delusional, right?"

He didn't say anything but instead looked at his hands.

She sucked her tongue to the roof of her mouth and negotiated lifting her spoon. She held it above the hot mixture in the bowl.

"The idea is to eat the stuff, not merely have the steam do a number on your pores," Ned coaxed. He sat at the end of the table next to her.

"I'm not sure I'm quite ready for the Irish cure." Abby pushed the bowl away and looked up. "You're not dressed in your usual unrelenting and overly sexy black."

Ned glanced at his outfit, a loose-fitting top that

somehow crossed in front of him but exposed quite a lot of chest. "You don't approve?"

She couldn't help noticing the scattering of dark curly hairs on said chest. "What's not to approve?" She cleared her throat and searched for a quick recovery. "But you should know—if you're going for the pirate look? You should really be wearing a billowing shirt that's snowy white and not—" she peered between narrowed eyes "—deep crimson."

"Didn't you get the invitation from Tess? Sorry, *command* is more like it. She's throwing the annual company outing at her place in the Hamptons. Today as it so happens. And I am merely dressed in costume according to this year's theme—Gypsy Magic."

Abby groaned. "That was the e-mail I purposely didn't open. Oh, well, I have a perfectly legitimate excuse for not going."

"Sorry, a slow recovery from a night of inebriation is no excuse. If it were, half the art department wouldn't make it into work each day."

"No, smarty-pants, I can't go because I don't have anything to wear." Speaking of smarty-pants, Ned chose that moment to get up from the chair and walk across the room to the counter by the sink, and Abby noticed that he was wearing black satiny trousers that he'd tucked into a pair of low black boots. Despite the billowing around his legs, they managed to cup his tight, rounded butt.

He turned and walked back to the table with a wrapped parcel. "Here. I picked this up. It's a silky sarong-kind-of-thing. That should do you nicely. I can wait for you out on the deck while you shower and dress. Though I warn you, I already used up most of the hot water."

Abby fingered the string around the package, then looked up. "I thought the sarong was for She-Who-Shall-Not-Be-Named—you know, *that* actress?"

He poured a mug of coffee. "Screw her."

Abby watched him leave. "I thought that was the idea."

CHAPTER SEVEN

THE ONLY SAVING GRACE of the three-hour drive out to the party was that Abby slept the whole way. If only Ned hadn't shaken her brusquely after he'd parked the rental car.

"Let me go back to sleep," she protested even as she stumbled out of the car. Her high-heeled silver sandals took on a chalky powder as she crunched along the crushed shell driveway.

"Hold up," Ned called out, pocketing the car keys and coming over to her side. "I think you're losing some of your gypsy flair." He tried straightening out her outfit.

After dashing through a frigid shower, Abby had attempted to wrap the deep purple-and-gold sarong around her in some off-the-shoulder peasant-y way, cinching the whole thing together with one of Ned's Zegna ties around her waist. "Maybe if you'd had a few more safety pins, I wouldn't be in danger of losing more than my flair," she complained.

"I don't know why you didn't let me use the staple gun." He adjusted the folds of the skirt portion of her outfit.

"Enough." She batted his hands away. "It will just have to do. With any luck, no one will even notice I'm here." She wobbled toward the sound of the festivities.

The party was outside on the back lawn of the beach house. Acres of grass gently rolled toward the water's edge—the triumphant result of drastically altering the natural contour of the coastline, adding a mountain of high-grade topsoil, and the regular attention of a six-man lawn crew. Gaily colored paper lanterns hung from strands of fairy lights that looped among tent poles. Brightly painted Sicilian wooden carts and wandering jugglers wearing weird headscarf things, which looked like babushkas with street cred, conjured up an atmosphere of gypsy caravan madness. Or at least a Madison Avenue version.

"My God, it's like the backlot of RKO, with the added advantage of Lycra, of course," Abby said in amazement, her words nearly drowned out by a band of gypsy musicians who had descended to serenade her and Ned.

All eyes turned toward them.

Ned crossed his arms over his chest and bit back a smirk. "So much for making an anonymous entrance."

Abby fiddled self-consciously with one of her large gold hoop earrings and wondered why she had only taken three Extra-Strength Tylenol. "Maybe you could take our new friends here and make them wander off somewhere else, preferably far out of my hearing range?"

"My pleasure." Ned made a large bow. "This way, fellows. Time to play for the babes by the pool." Ned crooked his finger and sauntered off, his strolling minstrels trailing—and playing—behind him.

Abby looked both ways and tried as stealthfully as possible to make her way to the open bar and order a Bloody Mary.

"How very Bollywood—your outfit, that is," Samantha purred behind her.

Her comment didn't deter Abby from removing the stalk of celery from her Bloody Mary and crunching it loudly.

"Something new from Armani this upcoming season, I presume?" Samantha went on.

Abby breathed in deeply, attempting to achieve an inner serenity, despite the safety pin digging into the underside of her breast. She turned and offered Samantha a weary smile. "Not everything in the world emanates from the fashion houses in Milan."

"Oh, really? Which doesn't at all explain why you were so eager to accept that internship when there were others more talented than you."

"Give it up, Samantha. I've got a whopping hangover, so I'm physically incapable of exposing my claws, let alone enjoying a good catfight." Abby munched on the celery.

Samantha cast a knowing glance in Ned's direction, which had Abby looking as well. There he was—it was hard to miss his shirt, not to mention his chest. Next to him was Tess's assistant Ling Ling, doing a commendable imitation of shrink-wrap in the way she applied her scantily clad body all over his.

Samantha brought her gaze back to Abby. "I saw the two of you arrive together. That and your little drinking problem clearly indicates a story." She clucked.

Abby momentarily closed her eyes. "There's nothing to tell. I'm just staying at Ned's until I get a place of my own. The drinking was something I managed all on my own after seeing Brad."

"You saw Brad?" Julia came up next to her. "I'm sorry. I couldn't help overhearing." Concern was written all over her subtly made-up face. The natural look never looked so wholesome. "I've been so worried about how that would go, and I even mentioned it to my book group. This is, after all, a delicate time for you, Abby, being back in New York after so long, with things the same but not the same." She pressed her open palm over the smocking of her embroidered peasant blouse.

"Really, I'm fine," Abby assured her. "The only way I'd be better would be if this outfit would stay somewhere in the vicinity of my shoulders." She pushed up the material.

Samantha snorted. "I think I'll let you girls have your little touchy-feely moment alone." She turned to Abby. "You should really wear a strapless bra, you know." Then she sashayed off in her bare-midriff costume that was something out of *I Dream of Jeannie*, if *I Dream of Jeannie* had been transplanted to the Caucasus Mountains.

Abby looked at her boobs. "Is it that obvious I'm not wearing a bra? I don't see any nipple action, do you?"

"None at all. It's more that Samantha is worried that she's starting to sag," Julia assured her.

That little snide comment had Abby turning in surprise.

"Anyway, a wardrobe malfunction is the least of your worries." Julia emphasized her point by holding up her glass.

Abby looked at the clear bubbly liquid and knew, given that Julia *was* Julia after all, that it was probably Diet Sprite. "Okay, you're right," Abby admitted. "Dealing with Brad all over again has been a little trying."

"Little?"

"All right, more than a little." She gazed toward the water and watched the gentle waves of ocean lap the sand. "And truthfully, it's made me think a lot about the difficulties of having a successful relationship *and* a successful career."

"Of course you've been thinking about that, but you're at a very vulnerable time in your life. Don't give up hope." Julia placed a hand on Abby's upper arm, scooping up the slipping material of Abby's costume at the same time.

As if on cue, the gypsy musicians reappeared—with an energetic rendition of what sounded suspiciously like Roberta Flack's "Will You Still Love Me Tomorrow."

"Argh! They refuse to leave me alone." Abby grabbed Julia's arm. "C'mon, let's get out of here." She pulled Julia into the thick of the party, but the gypsy musicians scrambled after them, playing at an accelerated tempo. Abby peered back over her shoulder. "I don't believe this. Quick. We need to move faster to lose them." She picked up speed—only to find the musicians responding by kicking up their heels and cranking the music up to presto.

Julia pointed off to the left. "I know, why don't you nip in there, the fortune-teller's booth?" She was breathing hard.

Abby pulled up. The lead violinist lowered his violin and mopped his brow with a large handkerchief. "You think?" she asked.

"Well, it's completely private, so they can't follow you in. And who knows, your fortune might provide insight as to your future."

Abby laughed. "Oh, please."

Julia opened the flap of the striped tent and thrust Abby inside. "Do it. For me if not for yourself. I don't want you landing back at my place one night in tears—especially when the book group is there."

The gypsy violinist settled his instrument under his chin and signaled the others with his bow. What choice did she have?

Abby plunged inside the tent.

Into total darkness. The only source of light came from a glowing crystal ball. It creakily rotated around and projected inaccurate representations of the constellations on the ceiling and walls of the tent.

As Abby's eyes adjusted to the dimness, she saw that

the globe stood in the center of a small round table, which was draped with a dark felt cloth covered with sparkly stars and crescent moons. A small boudoir chair stood empty on one side. On the other, facing her, was the fortune-teller.

Bad hair day did not begin to describe what was happening on the woman's head. A raccoon with mange was perhaps the best description. As for the rest of her, she was smothered in enough robes to clothe a whole clan of bedouins. She beckoned Abby toward her with a set of sequin-adorned ruby-red nails. "Come, my pretty. Have zee fortune told." Her accent combined shades of Zsa Zsa Gabor with the Wicked Witch of the West.

Abby tiptoed forward and grabbed the back of the empty chair.

"Do not be afraid. Zee cards, they do not lie," the fortune-teller intoned.

Abby slowly lowered herself into the flimsy chair. "That's what I'm afraid of."

From beneath her robes the fortune-teller pulled out a deck of tarot cards and, after shuffling them with the dexterity of a Vegas croupier, laid them out in neat rows. She bent forward and tapped one enormous fingernail to her lips.

Abby craned her neck over the crystal ball. "So, what do you see?"

The fortune-teller started rocking in her chair, her eyes closed, her enormous false eyelashes casting long shadows across her face. She hummed loudly. "A ch-great lo-ve a-vaits you," she murmured.

Abby turned her head to the side. "Are you sure you don't have a cookie stuck in your throat?" She narrowed her eyes and tried to figure out who was responsible for this amazingly bad performance, but it was too dark and the woman's makeup too heavy.

The fortune-teller stopped rocking. "Please, no one on an Atkins diet would consider having zee cookie, let alone have eet get stuck in her th-ch-roat." Then she cleared her throat and resumed her trancelike state.

Chastised, Abby sat back. "So tell me more about this great love."

The fortune-teller's index finger swooped down on one card. "This card here—zee lo-ve card—indicates that it is someone you already know. Someone from your past, someone you already have a relationship with but who is terribly misunderstood—by you."

Abby peered at the card in question. It showed a man, dressed in foppish clothes, standing atop what looked to be a shoe-shine box. "All that from one card, huh?"

The fortune-teller tapped her finger imperiously. "Look carefully. Zee cards, zey do not lie." She raised the card and let the light from the crystal ball illuminate it more brightly.

Abby gasped. Could it really be what she thought it was?

She pushed back her chair and rose suddenly. "Thanks but I have to go. Now." She pressed open the heavy flap and rushed out of the tent. She blinked repeatedly to adjust to the sunlight. Then she took off.

Her slim heels dug into the grass, causing her to lose her balance. She stopped to rip them from her feet, then resumed running through the crowd, moving so fast that she hardly noticed that the gypsy musicians were playing Rimsky-Korsakov's "Flight of the Bumble-bee"—in a rendition that owed much to the light of a campfire and the shuffle of tarot cards.

CHAPTER EIGHT

NED AMBLED THROUGH the throng of people. He carried two "gypsy cocktails." He tried one and nearly gagged on the mix of slivovitz and sweet vermouth. He was looking for Abby and curious as to whether her costume was still covering the essentials.

Sidestepping the pegs in the back of a striped tent, he barely escaped getting smacked senseless when a portion of its canvas wall came thrusting out in his direction. He juggled the drinks. Then he heard the distinct click of a lighter and looked up…

To see a fortune-teller, a fortune-teller smoking. In fact, a fortune-teller smoking with a long cigarette holder.

"Tess?" Ned inquired, not quite sure. The formidable figure in front of him looked more like Dame Edith after her senior—very senior—prom.

Tess enjoyed a long puff. "None other, darling," she finally said, acknowledging Ned.

Ned wondered how best to get away. "If you're still concerned about the cover shoot with that actress, I can assure you that I've already signed the contracts."

Tess viewed Ned with a jaundiced eye, not an easy thing to do with so many layers of foundation. "Actress smactress," she said and tut-tutted. "Sometimes I think the world is too celebrity obsessed."

"You do?" This was a side of Tess that Ned had never

seen before. Maybe it was brought on by the weight of her humongous wig and the fact that it looked as if it was made of synthetic fibers?

Tess took another thoughtful puff. "Yes, I do. Sometimes it's more important to look deeply into your heart—or other people's hearts." She scanned the crowd.

Ned followed her gaze and saw that she was watching Abby, running away from them.

"I just told Abby her fortune," Tess said, still watching Abby's flight. Tess related the details.

Ned swallowed. "Someone she's already had a relationship with, you say?"

"That's right. So, who would you say she's off to see?" Tess turned to Ned.

He worked his jaw. "I wouldn't know." *Brad*, he sneered to himself.

He took a large gulp of gypsy cocktail—strictly for medicinal purposes—and smacked his lips. "But one thing I do know—" he viewed the throbbing crowd "—*I* see someone particularly delectable." He bid Tess adieu and sidled his way up to Ling Ling, offering her the second cocktail. She was clad in ropes of gold coins and very little else.

The gypsies switched to a minor key.

ABBY RACED BACK UP the beach and smiled distractedly at various people from the magazine. Someone bumped into her shoulder, causing her sarong to dip precipitously into the sunset, but she was more concerned about not losing any of the clear liquid in the small jar she held in her hand.

Where the hell was he when she wanted him? She pushed aside a few more partygoers and searched frantically.

"Looking for someone, darling?"

Abby glanced in the direction of the inquiry. "You? I mean, Tess?" In the clear light of day, Abby recognized her editor in chief. "You were the fortune-teller?"

Tess patted her hair. "Rather remarkable, isn't it? It's part of an original costume from *Cats*."

Yes, the wig did have that certain longest-running quality about it, Abby thought. And it should have kept running—far, far away.

Tess nodded dubiously at the jar in Abby's hand. "Are you looking to give that to someone? If so, I hope it's not some kind of specimen."

Abby went back to scanning the crowd. "It is," she answered distractedly, "but not the kind you think. I was actually trying to find Ned." She looked back at Tess. "You wouldn't happen to know where he is, would you?"

"Last I saw, he was heading off in the direction of the cars with that lovely little assistant of mine, Ling Ling, in tow. The firmness of her thighs is just amazing, don't you think?"

Abby shook her head. "I try not to."

"Abby, darling, my little fortune-telling act didn't upset you, did it?"

Abby rubbed her forehead and tried to focus at least part of her attention on Tess. "On the contrary, I never thought I'd say this, but you actually brought clarity to my life."

Tess batted her false eyelashes. "So what have you decided to do about it?"

Abby scrunched up her mouth and took a moment to think. She refocused on Tess. "Ned drove me here, and if he's already left, I need a lift into the city."

"Why not use Spiros's Bentley?" she offered, referring to one of her husband's cars. "The chauffeur is always on call."

Abby was flabbergasted. "Gee, Tess, it's one surprise after another."

"Surprise is the very essence of *Tess's* philosophy." Tess swept her cigarette holder in a wide arc. "Suddenly, I feel another story idea coming on."

"Great, let's talk about it—only later. Right now…" Abby waggled her hand in the direction of the driveway.

"Yes, right now, be off." Tess gave her the queen's wave, all limp wrist and majestic shoulder rotation. "And just remember, I predicted I would show women everywhere the quickest, hippest ways to find a mate."

ABBY HELD UP THE HEM of her sarong and rushed down the gangplank to the houseboat. She hopped down to the deck and headed for the door. Then stopped.

There sat Ned. On a deck chair.

Alone.

She glanced around. "Hold on, would you?" she said as she opened the door and peered inside. She held herself still and listened. Satisfied, she let the door go and turned to face him. "You're alone. I thought for sure you had company. Ling Ling or someone like Ling Ling, not that anyone is quite like Ling Ling."

Ned rested his arms on the chair. In one hand, he clenched a small piece of paper. "I decided I wasn't in the mood for kung fu fighting." He raised his head. "How come you're here? I thought you'd be riding off into the sunset with the man of your dreams—Brad." He saw Abby frown. "Tess told me, about the fortune? About you getting together with someone you already had a relationship with?"

"Well, duh!" She dropped into the chair next to him and cradled the jar on her lap. "Let me explain to you in words of one syllable—not that I'm claiming to have figured this out that long ago myself. I mean, it's amazing what one ridiculous fortune-telling session and a three-hour limousine ride can do for putting things into perspective."

She took a deep breath. "For your information, I am not getting together with Brad, nor do I have any intention of getting together with Brad. The supposed re-awakening of his love for me is just a smokescreen to avoid commitment. Don't you see? It's the same behavior he pulled on me before I went away to Italy, only now he's doing it to his fiancée."

Abby looked Ned squarely in the eye, those incredible baby-blue eyes. It was time to face the truth head on. "I don't love Brad."

Ned lifted a brow. "Those are definitely words of one syllable."

"Well, here are a few more. This mysterious man out of my past? The one who is meant to be the love of my life?"

He tipped his head and waited.

"He's you. It was written in the cards—in fact, Tess pointed to this tarot card of a dark-haired man standing atop a houseboat, and it wasn't Noah and the ark, I swear. But that's beside the point. Even if the picture had been of Scooby-Doo, I'd know you were the one, because, you see, I know that I love you, that I've always loved you. I was just distracted by other things."

Ned stared at the water. "Do you remember when you asked me if I'd ever been involved for longer than a day?"

"Yeah."

"The answer is yes. I've been in love with someone for years, only until recently, she was taken by another."

He shifted his gaze back to Abby and saw right away how downcast he'd made her. "Oh, no, Abby. There's no reason to be upset. That someone?"

She nodded.

"She's you."

Abby went to press her hand to her heart, only the small glass jar got in the way of her rib cage. She passed it over. "Here. This is for you. I brought it from Tess's."

"Thanks." He started to take it, but saw he still had the piece of paper in his hand. "Let me just put this down." He placed it on his lap.

Abby recognized it. "The ticket to the Hugh Jackman play that I found in my desk? That's what you were holding?"

"I thought it was the only thing of yours I'd be left with."

Abby swallowed, starting to believe that maybe, just maybe, true happiness was possible. "Well, forget the ticket and take this instead." She pushed the jar into his hand with renewed conviction.

Ned held up the jar to inspect it more closely. "If this is one of the gypsy cocktails from the party, I've got news for you. They aren't particularly good."

"Trust me, this is." She nodded as he peered through the glass. "After Tess read me my fortune, I knew what I had to do. I ran to the beach and got you some of this. It's seawater. You see, I remembered how you said how much you missed Ireland and the ocean. Well, this is ocean water from the other side of the Atlantic, but maybe, just maybe, it might have touched the coast of Ireland in its travels."

She waited expectantly as he rotated the jar this way and that. "So?" Abby asked.

Ned leaned over and lovingly rested it on the deck between their chairs. Then he reached across and helped the sarong slip further down her shoulders. "I think it will do nicely. Very nicely, thank you."

Then they went inside, and the houseboat started to rock. And it had nothing to do with the tides.

EPILOGUE

To: Easy Writer <ewriter@mail.exbeaux.com>
From: Hook 'Em Harry <hharry@mail.exbeaux.com>
Subject: She flew thru the air with the greatest of ease
Yo, Abby,
What can I say? The woman from the Cirque de Soleil? SHE'S THE ONE. We've already planned a fishing trip for the Delaware River. Can wedding bells be far behind?
Call me if you ever need a free fire inspection,
Chet

To: Foot-Long Hero <flhero@mail.exbeaux.com>
From: Easy Writer <ewriter@mail.exbeaux.com>
Subject: Coupons
Hi Manesh—you will always be my Foot-Long Hero. I can't tell you how delighted I was to hear that since the publication of the article, you've gotten back together with your ex-girlfriend. It's nice to think that my story had an impact. I think her decision to ignore the restrictions of her Atkins Diet in favor of her deeper feelings toward you shows how strong her love really is.

As to getting a subscription to Tess, I'm afraid you will have to deal directly with the Circulation Department.
Abby (Easy Writer)
P.S. I will pass on your offer to do a regular acrostic at the next editorial meeting.
P.P.S. Many thanks for the Subway coupons. My fiancé Ned and I have really enjoyed using them.

To: Shakespeare in Love
<silove@mail.exbeaux.com>
From: Easy Writer <ewriter@mail.exbeaux.com>
Subject: Have I got a girl for you
Hi Shakespeare in Love,
Thank you for your congratulations regarding my engagement announcement that appeared in the New York Times. And here I thought I was the only one who read those.
Speaking of good news, I remember you mentioning something about a passion for Hong Kong action films. Well, have I got the gal for you...

To Aaron Watkins and everyone who loved him.

And to Cait Marcoux-Watkins for her courage and remarkable dedication.

I love you both.

BREWING UP TROUBLE
Mary Leo

CHAPTER ONE

I HAD SENT ANDY HOME right after our last round of orgasmic bliss. We'd had three, which wasn't unusual considering he was leaving for Atlanta in the morning and I wouldn't see him again for months.

I liked to store up orgasms like squirrels stored up acorns and dig one up from my memory during those harsh winter months when the land is barren and comfort can only be had from something mechanical.

Andy had wanted to spend the night and take me out to breakfast in the morning, but I'd insisted he return to his hotel and order room service. I argued that he'd be far too busy in the morning with cab rides, valets and airport schedules to think about what kind of eggs to order.

I didn't have to argue long; he was practically asleep during the debate. Three times can really take a toll on a guy. I put the spent-libido soldier in a cab around midnight and cheerfully sent him on his way.

Actually, I wasn't a morning-after kind of girl. Breakfast scared me. All that sunlight and bacon was enough to give me heart palpitations and sweaty palms, not to mention the added calories. Breakfast meant starting the day together. Planning an event for that afternoon. It was a symbol of a new beginning. A new start. An actual relationship. A from-this-moment-on type of thing. The whole scenario smacked of romance and commitment, both of which I wasn't up for, especially not with someone who lived in another state.

Not that it wouldn't be great to someday share a side of hash browns, or a fruit cup, with a guy I was all gaga over, but Andy just wasn't the gaga type. At least not for me. So, I sent him packing and told him to consider finding someone closer to home. I wasn't ready for the breakfast commitment.

After that, I couldn't sleep. Not really. I tried, but it just wouldn't happen, and according to my digital clock on my nightstand it was now 3:38…3:39 and I was completely wide awake.

Three-forty.

Again.

But what was the big deal about sleep, anyway? Who said a person needed eight hours of the stuff? Where did that magic number come from? Was there something wrong with six hours, or in my case, none? Why was it absolutely necessary to actually sleep?

My boss, Tess, a chronically observant woman, claimed that lately I'd been looking like the walking dead. I'd made the case that I simply wasn't wearing my usual amount of makeup, but she didn't go for it. In reality, lately, that was exactly what I'd been feeling like. A flatliner, walking.

Perhaps it was the age thing that had finally taken hold. Like some midlifer in a crisis. Never mind that I was only twenty-seven. Other girls my age had already written and produced their own plays, made an important documentary, run a couple of marathons, a couple companies, and discovered a cure for some exotic disease. And most of them had done it all before they took their first legal drink. I was losing and hadn't even made it to the right game.

I tossed off my blanket, thinking I should get up and do something, write something or learn something to keep my edge. Keep my advantage. Keep my job before Tess gave it to the next eighteen-year-old who walked through the door with an idea.

But wait. I had ideas. Great ideas! I just couldn't think of any at that exact moment.

Coffee. I needed coffee to spin my mind back into greatness. I was stimulant-deprived and my body was rebelling. Perhaps my new walking-dead look was simply the result of my caffeine intake, which I'd substantially cut down due to shaking hands and those pesky heart flutters.

Not that I had any medical reason to back off. It wasn't as if I was on the verge of some major heart crisis. At least I didn't think I was. I'd actually been trying to clean up my act. I mean, thirty was just around the proverbial corner and I already had grown a couple wrinkles that my latest peel wouldn't remove. My facial therapist blamed it on my obsession with coffee and cigarettes, so I stuck a patch to my ass and cut down the caffeine to eight hits a day.

Big mistake.

I needed coffee, a whole pot of coffee and about a thousand cigarettes. Perhaps the combination would lull me back to sleep.

Could happen.

Better still, I remembered the coffee in my orange mug behind my clock. It couldn't be that old. I'd just poured it that morning…or was that yesterday morning?

It didn't matter. Coffee's coffee and these were desperate times.

After gulping down the remainder of the French roast with slightly sour milk, and lighting up a vanilla-flavored cigarette, I decided to jump on the Web and learn Chinese or, at the very least, do some research on sleep deprivation, while still in bed, of course. I was hoping that simply by remaining in bed for at least another four hours, it would somehow count toward my eight, and with the coffee and cigarettes I'd feel and look like my old self again.

I was thinking that part of my sleep-deprivation research should include an in-depth interview with my friend Nico, a brilliant cosmetic chemist. The man probably knew everything there was to know on the subject of sleep problems and facial deterioration.

The vision of my deteriorating face was enough to make me go screaming into the night. However, I wasn't adequately dressed for the occasion, so instead I pulled my laptop up from the foot of my bed to begin my research.

I was never too far from my laptop just in case I needed to look something up, or write something down. More important, I had a deadline looming on "Alternative Dating in the Twenty-First Century" for *Tess* magazine where I worked, but for some reason I couldn't get an angle on it. My story centered around finding love at your local coffeehouse, an idea that Tess herself had whipped up. "We're going to show women the quickest, hippest way to find a mate, a rich mate," she'd said.

The piece was divided up between three of us—Abby, Julia and myself. Abby's assignment centered around women who found lovers for their ex-boyfriends, Julia had to cover speed-dating and I was assigned coffeehouse dating. Patrons provide their personal stats and a photo for a matchmaking binder that the barista managed. Personally, I thought Tess used these assignments as her own matchmaking service. She wanted each of us to find true love, or at least someone who could pay part of our bills.

Actually, it wasn't as if I was totally opposed to finding love, I just didn't want it now. And certainly not with Atlanta Andy. Not when I was working on my career and had to keep up with the eighteen-year-olds. No, I believed the best thing that could happen from all of this was I wouldn't have to dig up those orgasmic memories. Instead, I might make some new ones.

The thought of all that sex gave me an idea.

"Sex, Coffee and a Dating Service."

I leaned back and stared at the title. I liked the way it read, at least for the moment.

The glare from my bedroom light bounced off the screen, causing my eyes to sting. An odd sensation considering I slept with the lights on every night, the lights and the TV. Always. Constant. Twenty-four/seven.

I had this thing about quiet and darkness. Didn't like either one. It was my mom's fault. She had insisted we live over our bakery in Hoboken. My two sisters and I shared the front bedroom, the bedroom with the bakery's neon sign hanging directly underneath our windows that illuminated our room all night long. Where the street noise was nonstop. The continuous chatter of the TV somehow reminded me of that time and also of my older sisters, who both moved to Maryland, married doctors and had two kids each. I didn't really know what kind of sex lives they had with their husbands because they didn't like to talk about it, especially Natalie, the oldest.

Although, it was curious about the doctors' connection...

My laptop chimed and a message popped up.

nico: samantha, you should be sleeping

I swear the man had a sixth sense. Every time I wanted to talk to him, he was right there.

samantha: i am

I hit the enter key and my answer zoomed across the ocean to Milan, Italy. Ah, Italy. Home to Michelangelo's David and Nico Bertuzzi. Somehow, I pictured Nico with the same attributes.

nico: how can that be? you are on your computer

He simply didn't understand.

samantha: i know, but I'm in bed

nico: what does this mean?

samantha: i have a new theory about sleep. as long as i'm in bed it counts toward my eight hours. what do you think of my new theory?

nico: fascinating! can i join you?

I immediately conjured up a vision of myself and Nico lying in bed together. Naked. Sweaty. In the afterglow. My head resting on his David-like chest…but we were just friends. Distant friends, so I threw the vision aside and dreamed up something much more soothing: window-shopping at Bloomingdale's. I'd had enough sex for one night, thank you very much.

samantha: not tonight, honey. i want to sleep. BTW, i broke up with Andy

nico: i thought you liked him?

samantha: he wanted to go out for breakfast

nico: some men never learn

samantha: but now i can't sleep. you think you can help?

He didn't answer. My clock clicked off a minute. A whole entire minute and nothing. Another minute passed. Then another and still nothing.

The whole thing with Nico had started several months ago when I was researching an article on perfume and needed to consult a chemist. I couldn't exactly remember how I'd gotten his name, probably from Tess. The woman had an endless contact list. She seemed to know everybody on the entire planet. No six degrees of separation with Tess, only one degree and she was the one.

Anyway, I phoned Nico for a brief interview and we

ended up becoming friends and setting up instant messaging.

nico: are you lying down?

I crushed out my tasty little cigarette and lay down, eager to start our late-night tryst.

samantha: yes

nico: mmm...bella! are you comfortable? a woman should be comfortable when she wants to sleep

Oh, God was I ever. I scooted up on the bed.

samantha: yes

nico: but you must turn off the lights

A reasonable request, but I didn't think I could honor it. The question was, should I lie to the man or should I tell him the truth? I pondered this for a moment, reluctant to give up the security of Thomas Edison. I had to opt for truth or my nose would grow and I'd end up like Pinocchio...I tended to base most of my ethics on kids' stories. It just made my life easier.

samantha: you know i can't when i'm alone...at night

nico: but you are not alone. i am there with you. you can feel safe with me. safe enough to turn off the lights

I clapped my hands and my light went off, but the TV remained on in a low murmur. I couldn't have it totally dark or I'd freak. As soon as I got comfortable again, I let out a great big yawn, grabbed my down pillow and hung on.

At one point, I had genuinely thought our friendship might have turned into something more. That was my reasoning behind wanting that internship Tess had offered. It was in Milan at our sister magazine. I should have gotten it, but Tess gave it to Abby, my sometimes friend. She hadn't exactly known how much I'd wanted to go, so I couldn't legitimately blame her, but still, she should have asked me.

Okay, so it was my own fault and I shouldn't take it out on Abby. I had opened my big mouth and made a pact with Tess to help her quit smoking. So how could she possibly have sent me all the way to Milan during our pact? Of course, neither one of us has actually quit smoking, so the whole thing was a complete bust!

But wait. Perhaps it wasn't the pact. Perhaps it was Abby's age. Tess sent Abby because she was younger than me, and I'm an old hag.

Argh!

I made a mental note never to use the word *old* when referring to myself. Better still, I needed to strike that barbarous word from my vocabulary.

I pulled up the blanket and tucked it in all around me, leaving one hand out to do the typing.

samantha: okay. it's dark and i'm imagining that you're here with me

I hit Send and closed my eyes for a moment, trying to throw out all the negative thoughts in my head. I focused on my vision of Nico…and Bloomingdale's… Nico in a window at Bloomingdale's. After that little vision, I had to open my eyes.

nico: i want you to relax and dream of a full moon in a sky filled with stars as we lie under it

samantha: not good enough

nico: then, you are watching a fashion show by your favorite designer…who is it?

He knew me too well.

samantha: Dolce & Gabbana

nico: you have superb fashion taste. I…well, we will save my story for another time. first we will concentrate on your sleeping. you are watching the models on the runway, one after another wearing fabulous creations

I closed my eyes and saw a flash of color, an endless parade of models wearing crazy blends of textures, styles and flair. They were all around me. Catwalks stacked up to the heavens. It was glorious.

samantha: now you're talking

nico: try not to think of anything else but this moment. relax. float on my words. breathe slowly, deeply

I turned over onto my side, taking in slow, deep breaths, concentrating on his words, the moment. I suddenly felt light, lazy, and ready to think of what it might be like to …

CHAPTER TWO

WHEN I FINALLY AWOKE at 9:19 there was a message on my screen:

nico: abbia un giorno bello, samantha

Nico was telling me to have a beautiful day. How could it not be? I'd actually slept almost six straight hours. An all-time record. I'd have to use that boy again. He was better than sex. Well, maybe not better than, but somewhere close.

I yawned and stretched, feeling about as good as I did when I was a kid waking up to the smell of freshly baked bread and Mom's pot of coffee, which was exactly what I needed…a pot of coffee.

I wanted to write Nico and tell him about my luscious night of sleeping pleasure, but my digital told me that I was already late for the office. No doubt, Tess would be looking for me.

Still I felt positively fabulous, and couldn't wait to get into work….

Wait. That was way too scary.

I had to slow down here, or I'd be e-mailing Nico every night just to get some sleep. Of course, I had to consider that some of my euphoria could possibly be due to the fact that it was Fashion Week in New York City, and I loved to dress the part.

I jumped out of bed, something equally disturbing, went to the kitchen, considered making myself breakfast, but then realized I may be taking this happiness thing a bit too far, and put on a pot of coffee instead... Italian coffee in honor of Nico.

After fifty sit-ups, thirty push-ups, a few weight-lifting exercises and my morning hygiene routine, I slapped a new nicotine patch on my left butt cheek—hoping that it might actually work this time—and donned the latest in Victoria's Secret. Then I weighed myself, something I did every morning, and came in at one-twenty-one, which meant I had to restrict myself and get rid of a pound today. I tried to keep my weight at an even one hundred and twenty pounds. That was plenty for my five-foot-seven frame.

I took the time to style my hightlighted hair around my oh-so-fabulous face and shoulders, dabbed on plenty of makeup, especially around my steel-blue eyes...I loved dark, sultry shadows. Today I wore a dark smoke color to go with my new Dolce & Gabbana black shirt and a gold black-and-silver psychedelic skirt, which made my legs look incredible. I slipped on black, ultra-decadent fishnet stockings and gold stilettos with a small sparkly brooch on each shoe.

Or was the brooch thing last year's craze? It didn't matter, they looked gorgeous and I loved them.

Actually, I loved everything about me today.

I drank down two quick cups of coffee, checked myself in the mirror one last time, and out the door I went, so totally ready for the day that if I were my own friend I'd have to gag myself.

TWENTY MINUTES LATER, I arrived at my favorite coffeehouse, Uptown Perk, for my second bout of morning brew and my first actual interview for my story. Rio Jackson, the barista and owner, just happens to run a matchmaking service along with serving up some of the finest coffee in the entire city.

"Samantha, I've found you the absolute perfect man," Rio yelled while she steamed up a batch of milk in a silver pitcher. "And if my Mr. Perfection doesn't work out—which is doubtful considering I know my stuff—at least you'll get some firsthand research for your story."

The coffeehouse smelled luscious as I took in its eclectic ambience. It was relatively slow this time of the morning, with a few late-morning customers standing in line who looked as if they'd all had terrible nights and needed Rio's coffee just to open their eyes. Three young-looking women, all somewhere between puberty and the next Broadway star, worked behind the coffee bar with Rio. One of them had a large dragon tattooed on her forearm. I had to admire her courage. I'd always wanted a tiny dragon tattooed on my stomach, but could never bring myself to do it.

"Rio, I hate to be the one to tell you this, but I am not dating one of your lovelorns," I declared while sitting myself down on a stool at a long purple bar. Rio handed me a blue mug filled with frothy java delight. I didn't even have to tell her what I wanted to drink, she simply knew. Rio was the best barista in the entire city. Hard liquor or caffeine, there was none finer.

Rio Jackson opened Uptown Perk when she was twenty-three-years-old in 1997, right after she broke up with her boyfriend, Harold-the-house-painter, and moved to New York City from Upper Sandusky—the town Doris Day made famous in *That Touch of Mink*. Rio was about as opposite to Doris as a person could be. For one thing, Rio was an African American with attitude, and positively no fear of sex, and would definitely never get caught up in a love game to make a Cary Grant-type jealous. Not her style.

Rio was a prime example of a woman who could do it all and run a successful business as a bonus feature. She'd worked hard in Upper Sandusky as a waitress, bartender, a short-order cook and a part-time model while she studied for her business degree. The woman had been saving all her money for the big out-of-control wedding to Harold, also a business major. But when Harold took a right turn and she took a left, she decided to invest all her hard-earned cash in an espresso machine. The rest, as they say, was coffeehouse history.

"Of all the people in all the world who need my dating service, you're certainly top of the list. You need a guy who lives within a thirty-mile radius, honey, not three hundred." She leaned in closer to get a better look at me. I wanted to run. The woman could get anything out of me, and I didn't feel much like spilling this morning. "So come clean. You look too good today. Too happy, which we all know, *happy* is not an adjective to describe Samantha Porter. Was there some *hot and heavy* going on last night? Was one-night-stand

Andy in town or did you find some other out-of-towner to take his place?"

"Andy and I broke up."

"You were never really together so how could you break up?"

"I'm having a good day, don't mess with it."

Her forehead furrowed and those whiskey-colored eyes of hers darkened. "I'm not messin'. I'm just askin'. And you're wearing perfume, too." She took a deep, loud sniff through her shiny nose. "Chanel. Ooh, Mama. Who's the new man?"

I didn't answer. Instead, I took the first sip of my Mocha-Choca-Double-Espresso, a house specialty, and licked my lips with pleasure. "Just got a good night's sleep. Nico helped."

"Nico! You're doing it again, honey. Isn't he the guy who lives in Italy?"

I nodded, taking another delicious sip.

"This guy's even worse than the others. He won't even show up for a weekend. It's like having sex with a dildo. You can come, but you can't do, and the doing is half the fun."

"It's nothing like that. We're just friends and he helped me sleep. You know how much trouble I have sleeping."

"What you need is a permanent man in your bed, honey. Not an elusive one in your head."

At this point in the conversation, if it was anyone other than Rio, whom I considered a friend, I'd tell her to take her unwanted advice and shove it. But I liked her. Plus I needed her story.

I changed the subject. "So, tell me how this whole dating service works. How did you get it started? And what are some of the results? Like how many marriages came out of it? Stuff like that. We can talk about my lack of a local boyfriend some other time. Right now, I'm here to gather information."

"Always the reporter."

"Always the adviser."

We stared at each other for a moment.

"Let's sit at a table. It might be easier," she offered.

The place was beginning to get crowded, and by noon finding an actual table would be impossible. I spotted one in the corner, sat down and took out a notepad and a pen and waited for Rio.

Uptown Perk looked like a funky liquor bar with sofas and scuffed chairs and tables scattered in no particular order. The walls were three shades of gold, with a little burnt orange thrown in for excitement. The furniture, comfortable contemporary, came in various shades of red, yellow, green and purple. A long bar complemented one end of the room with brushed-metal stools lined up in front of it, with seats that matched the colors of the furniture. The place was once an actual bar that served up cocktails, but now served up coffee-based drinks. Rio ran a different kind of coffeehouse. She could mix just about any kind of liquor with your coffee, or serve it up straight. She didn't serve wine or beer or martinis. If you couldn't drink it out of a cup or a mug, you wouldn't find it at Uptown Perk.

Rio also served up matchmaking. A little something to nibble on while you enjoyed your cup of jazzed-up java.

She came over and made herself comfortable across from me. Rio had an exotic face with sparkling eyes, creamy skin and a tiny silver nose piercing. She wore her hair short, but filled with big droopy curls. Rio loved bright designer clothes and copied them whenever she could. The floral dress she wore was probably a knockoff that she'd put together on a weekend. The woman was amazing with a sewing machine.

"Here's a picture of Jason Rocket, the guy I want you to meet." She opened a three-inch black binder and shoved it in front of me. A smiling head shot of a Banana Republic kind of guy with a flashy smile and loose-fitting hair stared up at me. "Jason comes in here about three times a week. He owns his own real estate company. The man does exceptionally well for himself. He's twenty-nine and, get this, he lives right here in New York City. I know that scares you, but you should give it a try sometime. You might like it."

"I don't have a problem with dating local guys. I've just never met one that I've been interested in." Which was absolutely true. I couldn't understand why the woman insisted otherwise.

"Yeah. Uh-huh. You're talking to Rio now, honey. You can't lie to me. I know you too well."

"I've dated plenty of local men."

She sat back and folded her arms across her chest. "Name one."

I thought for a moment. True, most of the guys I had dated recently didn't actually live here. But wait! There was that one guy with the Southern drawl. "Garret," I blurted out. "Garret... Something. He owned a condo on the Upper East Side. A lavish condo, I might add."

"Owning a timeshare doesn't count. The man lived in Dallas."

She had a point, but still...

"My man Jason, on the other hand, actually lives in the Village. I think this guy is just edgy enough to handle you. He's your perfect match. Want me to set it up? Besides, it's good research."

"No," I said, using my most definitive voice. "I don't want to be set up with anybody, thank you very much."

"Why not? Are you afraid you might actually like the guy?"

"I came in here to find out how this whole thing works, not be your latest victim. Besides, if I was going to do this research right, I'd stick my own mug in this book and wait until some lucky guy gave me a call."

"That might take a while."

I didn't like her answer. Like, what? I didn't fit the profile to be included in her Loser Yearbook? "What are you trying to say?"

"Nothing against you, honey. What I mean is, not too many people use this binder anymore. I only keep it around to remind me of how it all started. Plus there's a few people in here who don't want to be up on the Web. They prefer my personal attention. When's your story due?"

"A couple weeks."

"The fastest way to get a date is to go on my Web site. Answer a few questions, add some hobbies, some likes, dislikes…you get the general idea…type it into a database. You'll get more exposure that way. Then you and some lucky guy can meet right here, or any number of coffeehouses. I'm connected to a bunch of places both here in the city and across the country. But for your personal purposes you need to concentrate on the locals."

"And how much does this whole thing cost?"

"Pocket change. You can afford it. Or tell your mag

to pick up the tab. Do you want to try it?" she asked, all sugary sweet.

I could tell she was setting me up. As if she heard church bells in my future and saw white dresses and lace. She always was a sucker for a wedding. My instinct told me to run, but I had a story to do. And besides, maybe she was right.

Before I could come to my senses, I said, "Okay. I'm going to try this. From now on I'm only dating local guys. No more out-of-towners. Where do I sign up?"

Actually, it would make for a more accurate article if I went through the process, at least that was my on-the-spot reasoning for this lunacy. It made me a better reporter if I got down in the trenches, walked the beat and intermingled. And perhaps it *was* time I made an effort to date somebody local.

Hell, why not!

"That's my girl." She slipped me her business card. "Just go to my Web site and click on Dating and fill in the blanks. The price info is right there in black and white. It's a monthly thing. Keep it going for as long as you like. Simple. Nothing to it."

I took her card and shoved it under my coffee mug for later. "Can I ask you one more question?"

"Sure, anything."

"If this dating service works so well, why aren't you dating the perfect man?"

"I am, honey. Didn't I tell you? He's coming by tonight and we're planning our trip to Miami. I think there're wedding bells in my future."

"That's great news! Why didn't you tell me you were serious about somebody?"

She grinned, and I instantly knew she was kidding. For some reason, Rio could always get me to believe her stories.

"You're making this up, aren't you?"

"It's good publicity."

"You're such a bitch."

"I know, but it's so much fun."

I threw her a look.

She laughed and went back behind the safety of her coffee bar while I moved to a table with an Internet jack, brought up her Web page and dutifully filled in the blanks.

Not ten minutes later, I received five e-mails from potential dates.

All locals.

CHAPTER THREE

I ARRIVED AT WORK sometime after lunch, and Tess was having a stroke over something the art department did or didn't do. I made a dash for my cubicle so I could stay out of her line of fire. I was still riding on my morning high and didn't want Tess to bring me down. She'd developed the habit of bumming a cigarette right after one of her episodes, and lately I'd rather she did her de-stressing in the next guy's cubicle. But I knew Tess well enough to know that I should get mentally prepared for the onslaught.

The argument ended and I could hear her heels clacking across the wooden floor. I thought about hiding under my desk, but knowing her, she'd just dive right under there with me.

She stepped into my tiny air space and sat in the blue chair across from my desk like a demanding queen wanting her subjects to respond to her thoughts. She looked fabulous in what had to be Stella McCartney's latest: black slacks tucked into shiny black knee-high boots, a tweed fitted cropped jacket with a large gray paisley silk scarf taking up room on her shoulders. Tess had attended the festivities when Stella opened her New York shop during Fashion Week in 2002, and there was no doubt Tess would be spending most of this week over at Bryant Park with Stella and the other hot designers.

I allowed Tess to sit in silence for a moment. The storm needed to settle. I'd found that a moment's silence was the best way to handle her in these situations.

Finally, after several minutes, she opened her royal mouth and spoke. "I should fire everyone involved. They're simply too old to do their job. They don't think young enough anymore." She liked to use her hands when she spoke, and when she got angry, look out. Those arms were flying.

"Who?" I asked, and rolled my chair out of her line of attack.

"The art department, of course. I bet they're all way past thirty."

"You're past—" I stopped myself before I said something stupid, like reminding her of her forty-something age. She'd stopped counting sometime around puberty.

"I can hire a couple of nineteen-year-olds who could do a better job for less money. Kids who would appreciate the opportunity to work for me," she said, all pissy. I hated when she got like this.

The woman was lucky to have this art department. They were some of the best men and women in the business.

I went for some logic. "Your newly promoted assistant art director *is* nineteen, and the rest of them would be hard to replace. They're ridiculously talented and instinctively know the look you want. Besides, most of them have been with you since you launched this magazine. You love these people. They're like family."

She took in a quick, loud breath and let it out again.

I cautiously rolled my chair in closer. The wind had lost its force. We had calm once again.

"You're looking well today," she offered, standing for a moment, then planting her butt on the corner of my desk. "One of your lovers fly in?"

"Actually, I'm done with that. I broke up with the last one last night. From now on I'm dating only local men."

A tiny dismissive grin spread across her face. "Whatever you say, darling." I wanted to defend my decision, but I knew better. Arguing with Tess never got you anything but a migraine.

She leaned in closer. "Let's sneak out for a quick one," she whispered as if anyone other than me might actually hear her. As if anyone other than me would care. This was *so* like her. The woman only complimented you when she wanted something. As if that was going to make the difference. It was her magazine. She could say I looked like dirt and I'd still do what she wanted.

"Tess, we don't have to sneak. Everybody knows we smoke."

"I'm wearing my patch today. They think I'm seriously trying to quit." She spun around to show me her exposed nicotine patch riding just above her ultra-low-rise slacks.

Tess liked to live with denial. It kept her safe in her own little A-list world.

"You're right. The entire staff looks up to you as an example of willpower," I lied, but it was necessary under the circumstances. The one thing I'd learned about working for Tess Truesdale Andreapolis, if you wanted to keep your job and your sanity, you told her exactly what she wanted to hear.

She grinned and flicked her blond styled hair over her shoulder. "Do you have any of those cranberry-flavored ones in the cute little pink papers? I've been craving one all morning."

She pulled out her diamond-studded cigarette holder, ready to install her nicotine fix.

"You know, if you wore that patch every day, you wouldn't have these cravings."

"But then I'd have to actually quit smoking."

"Isn't that the idea?"

"You're causing me stress, darling, and you know how I hate stress."

A bald-faced lie. Tess thrived on stress. She sucked it up like air. It was part of her genetics. Part of her soul. She liked to think she was this easygoing woman who only stressed when outside forces got in her way, but Tess woke up stressed and just increased her tension as the day went on.

However, this might not be the correct tactic. "You're right." I opened a drawer and fortunately I had a fresh pack of the requested cigarettes. I pulled them out and tossed them to her. At once her whole body seemed to relax.

"I knew there was a reason why I keep you around even though you're late for almost every meeting, and your attitude is sometimes less than gracious."

The best thing to do here was to offer her another entire pack of cigarettes and suck up. Tess didn't know about my sleep problems, and I certainly didn't want to tell her now.

"Sorry. I was in the middle of an interview with a barista. Have you tried the vanilla-flavored cigs? Fantastic." I pulled the pack out of my bag and eased them across my desk, like bait, hoping she'd bite.

She glared down at them but didn't move. I slid the pack back and forth. Still, she didn't react. In public, Tess preferred the more refined blends of tobacco, like a Nat Sherman product. But in private, she was a Camel slut all the way. I picked up the pack and took a long sniff. "They smell so good. You should at least smell these." I felt like a drug pimp. A pusher. A demon from *Buffy*. This was just wrong. But I held the pack out in front of her nose, anyway. Tempting her with its sweet fragrance.

I should have been shot.

"I *love* vanilla," she cooed.

"Take the pack. I've got more."

She grabbed it out of my hand and headed out. After taking a few steps, she turned to face me. Always in charge. "Don't think this makes up for that crack about my age."

"Never," I told her, but we both knew the truth.

"Good. As long as we're clear." She walked out, grinning while hiding her cheap nicotine fix in her pockets.

"Crystal," I said out loud, and sat down behind my desk, thankful that I'd gotten through another bout with Tess and still had my job.

I brought up my laptop and the familiar tune filled my cubicle. I should have started on my story or completed a few other projects I had going, but avoidance took over and I wrote to Nico instead.

samantha: i had a fabulous sleep…thank you, but my good mood was almost ruined by tess. however, i refused to let her get to me and managed to quiet the storm with a pack of flavored cigs

No answer. My Buddy List showed that he was logged on, but perhaps he wasn't sitting at his computer and I'd have to…

nico: if only my boss could be as easily tamed. perhaps you should come to italia and teach me how this is done

I could feel the knot forming in my stomach. The Abby wound was still very fresh.

samantha: love to, but tess won't let me. she thinks she can't quit smoking without me

nico: but didn't you just provide her with cigarettes?

samantha: yes, but in her mind, if everybody thinks she's trying to quit, it must be true

nico: then, i'll fly there

The thought of Nico flying into JFK was almost surreal. Like that would ever happen. The man worked twenty-four hours a day. He had no life and no time to travel, but if he did, it would be kind of fun. I'd show him New York, store up more sex and wave bye-bye at the airport. What could be better?

samantha: how you tease

nico: and you are not?

samantha: never

nico: me neither

samantha: you're doing it again

nico: what?

samantha: teasing/flirting

nico: why do you not believe me?

samantha: because i know the real you

nico: apparently, you do not know me at all

It was great to watch an ego at work. I decided to play along.

samantha: fine. i'll leave the key under the mat

nico: you can do this in new york city?

samantha: no, but it sounds good

nico: is this not teasing?

samantha: you bet it is

nico: then, not only do you tease but you lie

samantha: it's what makes me so endearing

nico: and alluring

samantha: i'm at work. you shouldn't talk to me like this

nico: but i am at home, sipping wine, listening to music. there is a fragrant breeze blowing in through the open windows from the rose garden below. i know how much you like roses, white roses, and these are magnificent. i wish you could see them, smell them, bathe in a tub filled with...i can hear the people in the piazza talking. laughing. it is a beautiful night for love

The man was way over the top on the romance scale. I might have to rethink our weekend in the city.

samantha: sounds like you need to get out there and find it

nico: what?

samantha: love...

nico: love is not something you can go looking for. when it is ready, love will find you

samantha: oh...pul-eeze!

nico: oops

samantha: what?

nico: this teasing is fun but i must go now or I will miss my date. ciao, samantha. abbia un giorno bello.

samantha: ciao, nico

Date? The man had a date? For some reason I found that a little disturbing. Not that I didn't think he dated, but he'd never mentioned it before and it took me by surprise. Perhaps I needed a dose of reality. No guy who sounded like him would be single. He had to have a girlfriend. It was only natural. I wondered if she actually lived in Milan or was she from Rome or Naples?

I shook it off and clicked on Rio's Web site to check on my date requests. There were twelve and each of them worked in and around Manhattan. I could have an actual in-town boyfriend in a matter of weeks, or days, or even hours.

The thought gave me a shiver, so I ran after Tess. I was in desperate need of a cigarette.

CHAPTER FOUR

THE NEXT NIGHT, I braved my first coffee date. Actually, I'd scheduled three dates right in a row at a couple different coffeehouses. I would give this whole matchmaking business a try, and be as fair about it as I could. My story depended on fair and balanced reporting.

Yeah, right.

At one point of absolute weakness, while I sat in the back of a cab stopped in traffic, my heart beating in my throat, I phoned Andy but then hung up when I heard his voice. He instantly returned the call, but I didn't answer. I was determined to go through with this project with an open mind, as if I was really looking for a boyfriend. A rich boyfriend, like Tess had suggested. I would just be my fabulous self and let the dating games begin.

Of course, the problem of when to tell the prospective dates I was actually working on a story loomed over my head. I decided I wanted to capture the real person. That first-impression kind of stuff everyone used on a first date. Then I'd drop the story bomb sometime right after our third or fourth latte…and then only if I wanted out of there. Otherwise, I'd simply let the night unfold, like everyone else who signed up for a dating service. At least that would be the plan.

I ARRIVED AT MY FIRST coffeehouse on West Forty-Ninth Street, in the theater district, around seven-thirty. I wore my favorite DKNY jeans, a Diesel loose-fitting brown blazer, a cropped striped sweater, a couple silver necklaces, a thin fuzzy scarf, and a pair of tri-colored Chanel heels with round toes. My clutch was vintage Louis Vuitton. I was a fashion designer's fourth of July, and prime bait for any man…or woman, for that matter.

This first guy, Brando Formosa, just happened to be a graduate of Parsons School of Design, and according to his own description of himself, he was an up-and-coming fashion designer with an active role in Fashion Week, whatever that meant. If nothing else, maybe he could get me an invitation for an up-close-and-personal with Marc Jacobs, one of my favorite designers.

I ordered a mocha latte, and told the red-haired girl behind the counter my name and that I was there to meet Brando. She smiled and told me to please wait for a moment while she finished an order. All way too formal for my liking.

The place had a homey-enough atmosphere, with overstuffed rolled-arm sofas and cushy chairs. There were a few tables and hard-backed chairs scattered around the large room. The walls were a deep shade of plum, but no pictures, and no real ambience to the place. I wasn't terribly impressed.

However, the coffee I had ordered was good and strong the way I liked it. A definite point in their favor.

The redhead, who couldn't have been more than sixteen years old, escorted me over to Brando. On our way she smiled and asked, "Is this your first time?"

We walked toward a back room. I felt as though I was a budding virgin getting ready to be deflowered and somehow this smiling young thing knew more about it than I did.

"Yes," I answered in a wispy voice, à la Marilyn Monroe.

"Well, don't be nervous. Everybody here is so nice. We'll try to do everything in our power to make your first time memorable."

"Thanks," I said, all surgery sweet, not wanting to spoil her fun.

Brando, a dark-haired Cuban who liked candlelight dinners and midnight walks up Broadway, sat alone at a table staring at the other customers. I knew his hobby, intense video games; his dream, to be the next Ralph Lauren; his favorite music, jazz; and how many kids he wanted, two. I even knew what size shoe he wore, eleven and a half. I knew more about Brando than most of his friends did and I hadn't even met the guy. Yet. Something didn't seem right about me knowing all that stuff about a complete stranger. I, on the other hand, with the exception of my vitals, had exaggerated or lied about almost everything I'd put down on the form and, looking over at Brando, dressed in his off-the-rack outfit, I'd bet my perfect little Chanel heels that he did the same.

As soon as Brando spotted my escort, he jumped up a little too fast and bumped the table. His coffee spilled, but he extended his hand to me as if this was a business meeting and the spilled coffee was some other guy's problem.

Right away I wanted to call it a night, but then he smiled and his face lit up, so I took his hand, gave it a shake, then sat down across from him while my escort went for a towel.

Not exactly what I had envisioned, but he had potential.

"Wow! You came," he announced, staring at me as if he was amazed by my very presence.

"Not yet," I mumbled, just to see what I was dealing with.

"Pardon me?"

Obviously, not much.

"Nothing. It was a joke."

He stopped and pondered what I just said, then let out one of those great big hee-haw laughs that echoed throughout the entire room.

I gulped down my coffee, told him who I was and about the piece I was writing, got him to answer a few questions in between more horsey laughs. And before his spilled coffee was cleaned up and replaced, I was outta there.

I HAD MY NEXT DATE lined up with thirty-one-year-old Jake Falkener. He was in marketing at some shoe company he didn't list, was the third son in a family of five children, liked extreme sports, exotic vacations and didn't want any kids until he was in his forties. I figured he *must* be at the very least, savvy and hip to the current fads and fashions. And hopefully, he had a sane laugh.

Plush Café was located at Twenty-Second and Third Avenue. Dim lighting, jazz music and an eclectic clientele made up its ambience. Plush had the customary sofas mixed in with tables and chairs. The place also served up wine and beer. I ordered a glass of pinot noir, thinking I could use the buzz. Once again I was escorted to meet my date. Only this time, my date was lounging on a sofa, glancing through the *Times*. He had a nice rugged look to his face, and an infectious smile that he threw my way as I walked up to meet him.

So far, I was liking what I saw.

"Jake Falkener, I'd like you to meet Samantha Porter," my male escort said.

Jake's hand stayed at his side, and he didn't budge from the sofa. "Nice to meet you," he said, but there was a slight edge to his voice that I wasn't too sure about. As if there was a dark undercurrent going on that maybe I didn't want to know about.

"You, too," I answered, and forced out a slight smile. I took a couple of sips of my wine, thinking I was probably way too critical or overreacting to his laid-back demeanor.

My escort walked away and I wanted to run after him.

"Take a load off," Jake said, patting the sofa next to him. Already, I was thinking this was never going to work.

"Sure," I answered, and sat on the edge of the sofa, a safe distance from where he was sitting. Somehow spider and bug came to mind, but I let it pass.

"Well," he said while sliding down on the sofa and resting his head on the back cushion. "Man, what a day I've had. You wouldn't believe what kind of crap I had to wade through. It was so deep I had to take a shower when I got home just to get rid of the stench. It's not that I don't like my job, I do, but…"

He dumped for the next twenty minutes, until I couldn't stand listening to him anymore. I told him I was going to puke if I didn't get home soon. I blamed it on the wine, but the wine only helped me get through the twenty minutes. I gave him my card and briefly told him I worked for *Tess*. He then went on for another twenty minutes about women and dating, and what he thought of the whole scene. His ideas were classic Neanderthal, and he insisted I quote him. I told him I wouldn't have it any other way and then ran out of there as if the place were on fire and hailed the first cab I could see. Jake actually followed me out the front door, so I gave him some advice. "Honey, do the world a favor. Get a vasectomy."

Somehow, in Jake's twisted mind, he took that as a compliment. He leaned over to talk to me through the open back window of my cab, holding my card in his hand. "You are so right. Kids'll just get in my way. Let's get together after I get it done. I'll call you. You can write about my love-making techniques in your magazine. Maybe take some pictures. I look good in bed."

I reached out, smiled, ripped my card out of his grubby little hands and said, "Tell you what, I'll call you."

MY FINAL DATE WAS BACK at Rio's, Uptown Perk. It was now close to ten o'clock and all I wanted to do was go home and throw the covers over my head.

I smoked about three cigarettes in the cab on the way over. The driver, an articulate older man with a sense of humor, was a smoker as well. We commiserated on the woes of trying to quit. He showed me his patch on his forearm and wanted to see mine.

What the hell. When I got out of his cab I gave the guy a thrill and flashed him my butt patch. He whistled and I was flattered. He was a sweet guy, with a real personality, unlike the two guys I'd just left.

I arrived at Rio's realizing I'd had a better time with

the cab driver than I did with both my dates. So far, this prearranged dating experience wasn't offering much by way of finding the right guy. Of course, I'd chosen these guys from a long list of hopefuls, which, in the scheme of things, didn't say much for my choosing abilities.

Somehow, I wasn't holding out much hope for the final date. He was a publicist who liked to work out six days a week, and run ten miles on the seventh. Maybe he was too much of a jock for me, or maybe he was just too much.

Rio had wanted me to contact that Jason guy she thought was so perfect, but he was off somewhere on business. Just as well. He was probably a loser like the last two dates, and Rio would never be able to accept it. After all, if there wasn't something wrong with a person in the first place, why on earth would they need a dating service?

Okay, so maybe they worked too many hours and didn't have time, or maybe they were new to the city, or…okay, so there were a lot of reasons, but so far, I hadn't run across a legitimate one.

As I approached the front door, I decided that I wasn't going to stay to make small talk with another desperate coffeehouse boy. I'd simply make my excuses to Rio and go home before I could meet the guy. I was scheduled for three more dates tomorrow night, one more on Saturday, with a final date on Sunday morning. That should be quite enough research for my story, and quite enough in-town dating for the entire year.

"Let me get that for you," a male voice said from behind me. I turned around as some guy standing next to me reached for the door. He had the most intense green eyes I'd ever seen.

"Thanks," I told him, waiting as the door swung

open. He brushed his arm along mine and I caught his scent, Chanel for Men, one of my favorites.

The place was jammed with late-night coffee drinkers. I couldn't see Rio anywhere and I was tempted to just leave, but I couldn't be that rude. It wasn't something Buzz Lightyear would do.

Suddenly, I was squeezed up against the guy with the intense green eyes.

"Excuse me," he inquired, "but have we met?"

What a line. I thought that went out with disco, but I decided to play along.

"If we did, I'd *remember* you." I even fluttered my eyes.

He backed up a little. "I can't tell if that's a compliment or sarcasm."

He smiled, and I had to admit, he had that Matthew McConaughey thing going on that I was a total sucker for. He actually did look a little familiar, but I didn't want to take the time to think about it. Plus, I was a little put off by his sincerity.

"I'm sorry. I thought that was just a bad come-on."

"No. I mean, you really *do* look familiar. Sorry if that sounds strange, but I think I know you from somewhere."

Okay, now I had to know if this guy was on the level. "I'm supposed to meet someone here, but I really don't want to. Any suggestions?"

"You could call this person and make it for another time."

"No good. I don't have his number."

"You could blow him off, but…that wouldn't be right."

A guy with morals…this was getting better all the time. "Right. I can't do that."

"You could find him and tell him—"

"I don't really know what he looks like. It's one of those dating-service things."

He stared at me for a moment and I stared right back at him: lips made for kissing, eyes to swoon over, high cheekbones, a chiseled nose and honey-blond hair that he kept short and messy. Now, why couldn't Rio have fixed me up with this guy?

This guy, I could like.

He asked, "Can I buy you a coffee while you try to find your date?"

"Sure," I replied, actually looking forward to sitting down over steaming coffee with somebody I was attracted to. "By the way, I'm Samantha Porter."

"Hi, Samantha," he said while looking down at me. He was at least six-three. I loved a tall guy. "Jason Rocket." He flashed a smile.

There was an awkward moment of silence when I tried to understand the situation. I mean, Rio's Jason was supposed to be on a business trip. Or at the very least, I was supposed to dislike him the moment I saw him.

Instead Rio was right.

Jason Rocket was perfectly perfect.

CHAPTER FIVE

As it turned out, my coffee date never showed up. It seemed that Patrick O'Reagan had a good thing going with Nancy Witkowski, another girl he'd met through Rio's dating service, and didn't want to mess it up. I would have been suspicious, but the girl with the dragon tattoo on her forearm convinced me otherwise. "He called about fifteen minutes ago. Said he was really sorry and wanted to make it up to you, so he paid for two large coffee drinks."

I considered this for a moment. "With liquor?"

"Uh-huh. Anything you want."

"Then bring me a Café Royal." I looked over at my new coffee date, whom I knew very little about other than Rio's recommendation, but after my last two dates, I was happy about the possibility of getting to know him.

"I'll take a Mexican coffee, but I'll pay for it."

Already I liked this guy.

We were sitting at a small round table against a back wall. The place was crowded and noisy, just the way I liked it, but Jason couldn't seem to take his eyes off me. He was much better-looking in person than his photo had suggested. Sexy. Very sexy. I liked a man who could give me his undivided attention. Perhaps he was thinking about what I would be like in bed. I stared back at him, thinking, I'm better than you can even imagine. I'm fabulous. I'm the answer to...

"You're a regular here, aren't you? That's why you look so familiar to me."

"Well, I—"

"In the morning. You're usually here in the morning."

Okay, he wasn't thinking about sex. Just face-recognition.

"Well, yes, I—"

"I never forget a face. Just something I picked up when I was a kid. I like to be aware of my surroundings."

I didn't know if I should be offended or flattered. After all, he was comparing me to furniture.

"So, I'm part of the ambience?"

He leaned forward, tilted his gorgeous head, blinked and said, "You are the ambience."

Right answer. The man was not only pretty to look at, he also knew how to charm a girl.

Our drinks arrived and he sat back in his chair. A good move on his part because I was starting to pant.

"I'm in real estate. What do you do, Samantha?"

I was a little leery about telling him so early in the game. Usually, I liked to wait until the timing was right before I sprung it on a guy. Sometimes they were intimidated by it, and other times they would drill me about specifics. Neither of which I was in the mood for.

"I write for a magazine. What about you? What kind of real estate are you into?"

He smiled. "Let's try a different subject. Seems that neither one of us wants to talk about our daytime lives. How about animals. Do you have a pet?"

A rather odd topic, but nonthreatening in that what-movies-have-you-seen-lately kind of way. "No, but I always thought I'd like a cat. A loving little bundle of fluff. And you?"

The words had come out, but I wasn't saying them. At least that was what it felt like. A bundle of fluff? If anything, I'd want a cat with attitude who could open its own can of tuna and change its own litter box. I had barely enough time for myself let alone a bundle of needy fluff.

"Huh, I never would have guessed it about you, and usually I'm a pretty good judge of character. Me? Actually, I love cats. I have two. Fraidy and Isabella. Both Persians."

"Fraidy?"

"As in fraidy-cat. She's afraid of her own shadow."

We chuckled a little. "Cute," I teased, and gulped down half of my drink.

The rest of the evening went on just about the same way; him being truthful and me playing some kind of role. I couldn't figure it out, so sometime after my third Café Royal, and right before we started down the road of favorite reality shows, I told him I needed to go home.

"Oh, is it that late already?" he asked, checking his obviously expensive watch.

I stood and grabbed my bag, thinking it had been an odd but fascinating evening. "Yes. I like to get up early in the morning." I almost cringed on that one. Me? If I could sleep, which I couldn't, I wouldn't get out of bed until noon, and even then I would hit the snooze button one more time.

"So do I. How about that. I know it sounds corny, but I look at each day as a new beginning."

I wasn't going to touch that one, so I simply smiled and nodded.

He stood and followed me outside. "Can I drop you somewhere?"

"You drove here?" I didn't understand people who drove in the city. It was like asking for stress.

"I have a driver."

Why didn't that surprise me?

"No, thanks. I'm not far."

"Then let me walk you home."

We both knew what he was fishing for, but I just wasn't ready for a one-night stand with Rio's perfect man.

"I, um."

"Hey. It's just a walk home. Nothing more. I promise."

How could I refuse such an offer? "Sure. It's only a few blocks from here."

We walked and just like in the movies, his driver, in a black Mercedes, followed.

"What is it you do again?" I asked, wondering about the price of drivers and cars.

"I buy and sell real estate. And you?"

"I write for a magazine."

We both smiled and let it go at that. If he wasn't ready to spill the details, then neither was I. Besides, I could use some of this for my article, and if I told him the truth, he might get a little uncomfortable. I decided to wait.

When we got to my apartment building, we stopped out front.

"You want to do this again?" he asked.

"What? The walk?" I knew what he meant, but I was searching for a delay.

He smiled. "Yeah. The walk and coffee. Or how about dinner next time?"

"I could do dinner."

"Tomorrow night?"

I was booked with coffee dates. I really couldn't. He ran his hand up my arm. "Sure," I told him, thinking I'd somehow work around them.

"Is seven all right?"

My first coffee date was at six. "How about eight? I like to stay up late."

"I thought you liked mornings?"

A guy who remembered the details. I'd have to be more careful. "I'm not much of a sleeper." At least that was the truth.

He stepped in closer. "Not enough sex."

Where did that come from? "Are you offering?"

He smiled, and leaned in as if he was going to kiss me, but stopped short. "Not tonight. I like to keep my promises."

I could feel his warm breath on my face. I was dying to taste him. "So, you're a man of your word, then."

"You can bank on it." He gently slid a strand of hair off my face, and I wanted to bring him right up to my apartment and rip his Armani clothes off his athletic little body. His lips were a heartbeat away from mine.

"Some other time, then," I whispered. He took a step back. I nearly fell into him, but I caught myself.

"I'll pick you up at eight tomorrow night." He took another step backward and grabbed my arms to steady me. I stood up straight and searched around inside myself for some composure. I wasn't finding it.

"Sure. Yes. Tomorrow. Eight o'clock."

He handed me his business card, which consisted of his name and a phone number centered in black letters on a white background. I wondered if he'd had them made up specially for picking up chicks at bars. "This is my private number. You can reach me anytime, night or day."

Then he turned and walked to his awaiting car. When he got there he turned back and yelled, "How does Masa sound?"

Masa, on the Upper West Side, was one of the top restaurants in New York City, with a price tag to prove it. You had to make your reservation a month in advance. Tess and her husband had a standing reservation every other Friday. She would have a minor stroke if she heard I was in there with a guy who could afford the place. It would be like a dream come true for her. I thought about saying no just so I wouldn't have to hear about it from Tess, but "Sounds perfect" came out of my mouth and that was that. Now all I had to do was think up something fabulous to wear.

Jason got in his car and drove off into the night. I stood on my stoop and watched as his taillights mixed with the other traffic on my street. The whole evening had been amazing and I couldn't wait to tell Nico all about it.

nico: he is not the man for you

samantha: he's perfect

nico: he likes cats

samantha: so do i

nico: you are lying. your nose will grow

samantha: leave pinocchio out of this

I was sitting up on my bed. The Animal Planet channel had a pet-star program coming on about a spunky black kitten that I didn't want to miss.

nico: i can't. he's part of who you are

samantha: okay, so maybe i don't like cats and jason does. it's a minor drawback in an otherwise perfect man

nico: there is no such thing as a perfect man. we are all imperfect creatures trying to fit into a woman's world. we do and say things to please the woman

samantha: so, it's a woman's world, then?

nico: it cannot be otherwise.

I liked his reasoning.

samantha: anyway, i had a good time. and did you have a good time on your date?

I hit Enter and then regretted having asked that. It seemed that what my fingers typed was no better than what had come out of my mouth that night. I was simply out of control.

nico: how could i not? she is the perfect woman

My fingers rested on the keyboard, unable to write. Frozen. Suspended in cyber-talk. I found it all rather ironic, in a weird sort of long-distance way. It was fine for me to tell him that I'd found the perfect man, but suddenly it was totally different when he said he'd found the perfect woman. My head began to ache. I needed coffee.

samantha: does she like cats?

nico: we didn't speak of such things

I wanted to ask him why not, but then thought better of it. I really didn't want to know any more details of his "perfect woman." Not tonight. Not after I'd met my own perfect date.

samantha: i'm tired. i'm going to bed

nico: do you need any help getting to sleep?

samantha: no, thanks. i think i'm fine tonight

nico: then this jason is good for you

samantha: yes, jason is good for me

The cursor flickered, but there were no more messages. The little buddy guy flashed up on my screen, telling me that Nico was unavailable.

I lay back on my bed, closed my eyes and was instantly surrounded by dozens of fluffy white felines all crying for my attention. Their little mouths agape, showing pink nubby tongues and sharp pointy teeth. They wanted food, or water, or worse, my attention.

I heard myself moan, and instantly opened my eyes.

The balls of demanding fluff were gone. It was just me, alone in my bed, with a dozen or so cats swarming some guy on TV. The vision gave me a shiver, so I turned it off and pulled the covers over my head.

As I lay there in my silent, dark cocoon, I could think of only one thing: Jason…Nico…Jason.

CHAPTER SIX

"I KNEW YOU TWO WOULD hit it off," Rio announced so that half the coffeehouse could hear her. "It's just another one of my success stories."

"We just met, Rio. Don't ring those church bells yet," I protested.

"Excuse me," a tall blond-haired woman said. She was standing at the counter directly in front of me. "I couldn't help overhearing and just want to say that I met my fiancé through Rio's dating service. Rio actually handpicked my very first date and we fell in love the moment we met. The woman is amazing!"

"Me, too," a guy with bed-head standing behind me interjected. "I was into that whole dating scene and I could never pair up with anybody I really liked, until Rio convinced me to try her dating service. After only three dates, I met Mia. We're getting married this summer."

I felt like I was caught in a reality infomercial.

"You're going to be next," Rio teased. She handed me a large black coffee. "So where's he taking you on your date?"

The two people who'd joined the conversation waited for my answer along with another middle-aged woman who threw me that you'll-come-around smile.

"I have to go to work. I'm late," I explained as I grabbed my coffee to leave.

"You're always late. Is it Masa? Jason loves that place. Or maybe it's Jean George. That might actually be better. But there's always Atelier inside the Ritz-Carlton. That place is dynamite for a first date." Rio kept talking, while I tried to slip a heat shield on my cup and get the heck out of there.

"Oh, I think Daniel is more romantic, if that's what he's going for. It's right out of an Italian movie, red velvet and gold silk." The blonde sighed one of those weak-knees kind of sighs. An obvious out-of-control romantic. "Of course, he may not be that kind of a guy, and it's rather pricy."

"It's Jason Rocket," Rio explained, beaming.

In complete unison, as if they'd rehearsed it, the group said, "Wow! Jason Rocket."

I stared at Rio. "Why are you doing this? Do you enjoy seeing me squirm?"

She smiled. "So spill it. Where are you two going?"

I took a few steps away from the group of strangers who suddenly seemed to know far too much about my life. The bed-head nudged me as I tried to get past him. "Make him take you to Alain Ducasse. The guy's probably richer than Trump. He can afford it."

I had to get out of there, so I turned around and made a beeline for the door. As I left, I could hear everyone still fussing over where the date would be. I decided that perhaps I needed to do some research on Jason Rocket; if he was richer than Trump, what would a man like that want with a dating service?

"YOU HAVE A DATE WITH Jason Rocket?" Tess asked as smoke encircled her face. We were in her office discussing my story when Jason casually came up in conversation. I really didn't know why I'd brought him up, only that I wished I hadn't.

"Yes. Tonight," I mumbled. "I also have five more coffee dates in the next couple days. All with highly successful men, and one woman."

"You made a coffee date with a woman? I never would have guessed…"

"I'm not," I insisted. I had to cut her off before she started spinning stories about me. Not that I was entirely opposed to a lesbian affair, I just didn't want to date anyone who could borrow my clothes. I was very territorial when it came to my clothing or my shoes or my bags, especially my clutch bags. They were far too beautiful for my lover to leave in a cab. I would never be able to forgive her and our affair would end and she'd cry and I'd cry and… "No. I just wanted her perspective."

"It's not that I care what you do, darling. I had a short affair with a sweet little…"

"Hold it, Tess. I don't think I need to know this. It's way too personal."

"But my life acts as an inspiration to other women. I have no problem sharing it, especially if you're having difficulty deciding. I'm here for you."

The thing about Tess was, deep down inside, she really did care about her employees and her friends… from time to time.

"Let's get back to my story."

Tess leaned forward from behind her desk and pulled her diamond cigarette holder away from her face. Smoke tracked in a long spiral up to the ceiling. I had to admit, I loved the smell and was oh-so-tempted to light one up, but instead, I pressed my patch tighter on my forearm. "I can tell you're a little nervous about it," Tess whispered. "Don't worry. We all go through that initial phase of self-doubt, but after that first kiss…"

There was a knock at the door and Tess's assistant, Ling Ling entered. "You have a hair appointment with Collette in twenty minutes."

"I'm off." Tess stood up, put out her cigarette and grabbed her two-thousand-dollar Bottega Veneta bag from inside a locked drawer. "I'm glad we had our little chat. Sounds as if you're right on schedule." I stood up and she glided past me, her Creed perfume surrounding me as a reminder of her dominance. "I can't be late, or she'll cancel my appointment. Collette can be so difficult."

"Hmm, I can't imagine."

THAT NIGHT, BEFORE I got ready for my coffee dates, I went online to do a little research on Jason Rocket. Unfortunately, he wasn't listed on Rio's dating Web site, but he was listed everywhere on the Web. Seemed the man owned several buildings both in the city and all over the world. He was the fourth generation of Jason Rocket's. Power and money had permeated his family since his great-grandfather bought his first hotel on the Upper East Side in 1902. He couldn't be a better date. It was as if Tess herself, and not Rio, had picked him out for me.

Of course, if she had, she would have probably dropped her present husband, Spiros, and kept Jason for herself. According to Tess, you could never have too many ex-husbands or too much money.

But the burning question still remained: why would a man of Jason's stature still be unattached?

My laptop chimed.

nico: it has been a long day and your sleeplessness has rubbed off on me. i have been thrashing around on the bed like a fish on the shore. how do you live like this?

In all the months I'd been writing to Nico he'd never had a sleep problem. I found it a little disturbing.

samantha: gallons of coffee...it's the only way

nico: but that is good for staying awake. what do you do if you want to sleep?

samantha: i talk to you

nico: then, i will talk to you

samantha: i can't. i have to leave here in about ten minutes

nico: oh, yes. your date with mr. perfect. call and cancel. stay home and talk to me

samantha: i have three coffee dates before him

nico: sounds like work. i am much more fun

samantha: it is work. it's for my story. i have to go

nico: that should only take an hour. come home afterwards and we can talk

I'd never known Nico to be so demanding. It was a side of him that I wasn't quite sure I liked.

samantha: what about my date with mr. perfect?

nico: am i not more important?

samantha: you're teasing, right? you don't really want me to blow off a date with a guy who might be my soul mate just so i can help you sleep? he's the first guy in years that i've dated who actually lives in the same zip code, and you want me to dump him?

I waited, but there wasn't an answer. I waited some more, but still nothing. I couldn't linger any longer. I had to go, but I hated leaving it like this. I wanted him to understand the situation.

samantha: are you there?

nico: yes, but i can not talk anymore. someone has come with a pillow

For a brief moment a pang of jealously swept through me, but then I realized that I was being silly. What was there to be jealous about? We each had our own lives, and it could never be any different.

But still…

I was thinking of what else to say to him, when the "Nico is unavailable" message popped up…which was just fine with me. I was meeting Mr. Perfect in just under three hours, and if things went my way, I wouldn't be available, either.

MY FIRST COFFEE DATE turned out to be a sweetheart of a man with a fabulous smile, thick black hair and blue eyes. His name was George Taylor, and if it wasn't for the fact that he was old enough to be my father, I might have actually considered the next step. Not that I had anything against an older man, but an older man who was purposely looking for a younger woman, a really younger woman was just freaky.

I told him up front that I worked for *Tess* magazine and was merely doing a story on the whole prearranged dating scene and George opened right up. I asked him what he was expecting out of all of this. "Fun, sex with a beautiful young woman and no commitment. I had twenty-six years of commitment and all it brought me was heartache. Now I think with my penis, not with my heart. It's easier."

I was busy taking notes on that one, when he said, "It's not that I have no feelings. I do. But they're overrated and I can get along much better in life without them."

"But what about the women you're dating? Aren't most of them looking for love?"

"I tell them right up front that I'm a heartless bastard."

"You don't actually get women to go for that line, do you?"

He grinned. "Do I look like a lonely man?"

If ever there was a contented-looking man, George

fit the ad. "No," I said. "You look like you've just had sex and you're in no hurry for more."

"That just about says it all. I'm a rich man. I can show a young woman a good time both in this city and in bed. I've mastered both arts. Care to give me a spin?"

I didn't know if it was the soft lighting in the upscale coffeehouse, or the fact that the man was simply abnormally handsome, but he was definitely a threat to monogamous women everywhere.

"You caught me on the wrong day, handsome."

"Too bad. We could have had some fun."

"No doubt."

After that exchange, I asked George a few more questions and was out of there. He was waiting to meet Eva Hughes, a twenty-three-year-old runway model who liked theater and late-night dining. The absolute perfect match for a man like George, at least temporarily.

The next two dates weren't quite as interesting, so I rushed right through them, only asking a minimal amount of questions.

Mark Hampton worked in marketing and had teeth whiter than my shower walls. He was looking for a low-maintenance woman, which was his reason for picking me, a writer. He thought I'd be the reclusive type who needed minimum contact. Mark liked to party with his buddies and didn't want a woman interfering with his buddy fun. A great guy if you were a doormat.

Lex Riviera, on the other hand, was a salsa dancer by night and an accountant by day, neither of which gave him access to the kind of woman he wanted. According to Lex, a romantic breakup with his dance partner left him without a dance partner, and dating another accountant was like dating himself. He just wanted a "normal" woman. I assured him *normal* wasn't in my vocabulary, nor was it an adjective to describe the modern woman. He elaborated on the domestic traits of his mother for twenty minutes and I gave him the name of a good psychologist.

After that, I went home and hardly thought about Nico at all. I was proud of myself for not dwelling on who was helping him sleep or how that person was helping him sleep. Instead, I changed into a purple Marc Jacobs dress with a plunging neckline that barely covered my breasts and cupped my cute little ass. I wrapped myself in the fragrance of Chanel, and just as I was putting the final touches on my lipstick, Mr. Perfect rang to get into my building.

"Samantha?" the voice said.

"Yes. Come on up," I told him. I thought perhaps we'd have a glass of wine before we left. Just to get into the right dating mood.

Two minutes later, there was a knock on my door. I took a deep breath, checked myself in the hall mirror…I looked marvelous…and opened the door.

Mr. Perfect was nowhere in sight, instead a strait-laced-looking guy with messy black hair, black rimmed glasses, a day-old beard and very odd clothes stood in my doorway, grinning.

CHAPTER SEVEN

"I HAVE COME," THE STRANGER announced while holding on to a huge bouquet of white roses. He was probably in his mid-thirties, average height, but a hottie with a mischievous sparkle in his amber eyes that made him super cute in that sly-little-boy way.

Unfortunately, I had no idea who he was, and no time to play his game.

"Excuse me?"

His smile changed, almost as if he'd gotten embarrassed. "I have not come in the way *you* mean, I have arrived in the way *I* mean."

He handed me the flowers. "Thank you."

"You are very welcome."

We stood there for an awkward moment, him smiling and me trying think of what this was all about. Then I realized that he was just some quirky delivery guy from a florist and now he was waiting for a tip.

I opened my bag and pulled out five dollars and handed it to him. He took it and looked at me. "Why are you giving me money? The flowers are a present."

"And that is your tip. Thank you." I closed the door and searched for a card, but there wasn't any.

A couple minutes later, while I was putting the roses

in water, wondering who would have sent them to me, there was another knock at the door.

Jason, no doubt.

I swung my door open and a tall middle-aged man dressed in a black suit and a white shirt, with a small pink rosebud stuck in his lapel, stood in my doorway. I should start using the damn peephole. There was no telling who would show up next.

"Ms. Porter?"

"Yes."

"Mr. Rocket is very sorry, but he's running late and asked me to escort you to the restaurant. He will meet you there as soon as he can," he explained with a formal edge to his voice.

"And you are?" I asked.

"Richard. Mr. Rocket's driver."

"Of course."

"Shall we go?"

I was tempted to refuse the ride on principle, but then thought better of it. After all, the roses were probably from Jason trying to make up for the fact that he couldn't pick me up in person. Nico was busy sleeping with some babe and I was dressed for sin, so why waste a perfectly good driver on principles? I grabbed my coat and Richard escorted me out to the Mercedes.

When we stepped outside, the delivery guy was just getting into a cab. Our eyes met for a moment, and he started to say something, but I slipped into the Mercedes, thinking he was some kind of weirdo.

The ride over to Masa was pleasant enough, considering traffic in the city is always bad. When we arrived, Jason was just getting out of a cab in front of us. I almost felt as if he'd planned this whole thing. Like he was testing me or something.

Jason waited while Richard opened my door and I slowly slid out of the seat. I didn't know what game Jason was playing, but I wanted him to know I wouldn't be part of it. He reached for my hand. I gave him a lukewarm smile and took his hand. That's when he leaned in and kissed me.

Not a passionate kiss, just a friendly hello kiss. It took me by complete surprise, and when it was over he acted as if nothing had happened. "Sorry I couldn't pick you up myself, but I ran into a buzz saw at work and had to resolve the problem."

I was still a little confused over the kiss but managed to pull myself together. "No problem. Richard took good care of me." Richard and I exchanged nods and smiles. I liked his style, and I somehow knew the sentiment was mutual.

I took a deep breath and could feel myself relax as Jason and I walked up to the front of the Time Warner Center on Broadway and Fifty-Ninth. The entrance was an expanse of glass and steel, and I could see some of the shops nestled on the inside. I loved the place. It housed some of my favorite stores, Cole Haan being one of them. I was wearing his open-toed Lorenza pumps.

Jason and I were still holding hands as we walked into the building, just like old lovers. I wasn't sure I liked all of this, until I thought of Nico and his babe.

I squeezed Jason's hand tighter. He looked over and smiled. Now we were getting somewhere.

"Have you been to Masa before?" he asked, moving in closer as we walked.

"No, but I've heard it's marvelous." I nudged up to his shoulder a little tighter.

"You're in for a treat."

"I bet I am," I teased in my sexiest voice.

He stopped for a moment, looked at me as if he was about to say something, but then continued on.

"Something wrong?" I asked, all innocent like, but I knew that look he'd just given me. He was probably deciding if we should forgo dinner and go straight to the sex part. However, if I remembered correctly, you simply didn't cancel a reservation at Masa unless you were next to death. It was hard enough getting a reservation in the first place, and if you didn't honor it, who knew what could happen?

Once we stepped inside the crowded restaurant, we were promptly seated at a private table. Of course, I would have preferred being out with everyone else, at the bar, perhaps, but apparently Jason liked the solitude.

Before I could even start a conversation, a peach-colored drink in a martini glass was placed in front of me. "That's a kinkan. You'll love it. Kumquats, vodka, oranges, a splash of cranberry juice and something else."

"Sake," the waiter added, then bowed slightly and walked away.

I would have liked to pick out my own drink, but the man liked to entertain his way. For tonight, I'd let him. "Can't wait to try it," I confirmed. He sat back and watched while I took a sip.

Okay, so it was great. Sweet with a bite. The man knew his drinks. "That's marvelous. Aren't you having one?"

"I only drink wine or sake."

"Then how did you know I'd like this?"

"I didn't."

"You mean you just guessed?"

"Something like that. By the way, you look fantastic."

I smiled. "You didn't expect anything less, did you?"
I was feeling all vampy inside and wanted to flirt.

He reached out across the table. I took his hand.
"Nothing less," he teased, gently brushing his fingers
across my open palm. God, this man was having an
effect on me. I could only imagine what those fingers
could do to me if we were in bed together.

"Mmm. Maybe we should skip dinner and go straight
to dessert." He kept playing with my hands, lightly caressing each finger, occasionally kissing the tips. We
stared at each other, and I decided I liked our private
room after all.

"This is our time to relax. To enjoy our surroundings.
To satisfy our spirit as well as our hunger. Dessert will
come when we're ready."

Okay then. The man had a plan and I was rushing
him, but the hand thing had to stop or I'd never make it
through the first egg roll. I gently pulled my hands away.

The rest of the meal was slow and sensual. He ordered
everything, while I merely smiled at the various waiters.
Of course, the food was amazingly good, served on exquisite lacquerware that had a beautiful look as well as
feel, and the hand-crafted wooden sake cups enhanced
the sake with a subtle aroma of cypress. The entire experience had brought pleasure to almost every sense.

Two hours later, when the meal was finished, I was
ready for the next sensation.

We had talked and laughed and gotten to know each
other, or at least I'd gotten to know him. He was willing

to talk about his personal life even though it had been only twenty-four hours ago that neither one of us wanted to get into the details. I figured that two bottles of sake must have warmed his confessional palate.

Suddenly he was telling me about his company and his family. I learned that he admired his grandfather, worshiped his father and thought his mother was beautiful. Apparently the woman's biggest challenge was to entertain and raise Jason. It made me wonder if the poor woman's brain had atrophied with all the men around her thinking and doing for her. But then I thought of Tess. Spiros had provided the money to get her started, but she ran her own show. I could work it like that. I'd fall in love, or something like it, with Jason, we'd get married, I'd use his money to get my own magazine launched and then run it myself.

Could happen.

"So how long have you worked for *Tess*?" he asked when we were back in the Mercedes on our way to his place for sex, but playing the just-for-a-drink game.

"A few years…wait. I never told you where I worked."

"Rio told me."

"What else did Rio tell you?" I sat forward, turned and looked at him.

"Nothing too personal, just that you broke up with your boyfriend recently."

"He wasn't exactly my boyfriend, and I would say that's fairly personal information."

"I had to know if you were available."

"You make it sound like a room reservation."

"I didn't want to start a relationship with a woman who was still involved with someone else."

"Is that what this is?" Suddenly, after one dinner we'd progressed to a "relationship." The man was moving much too fast. Soon he'd be asking me out for breakfast.

"What?"

He pulled me back to him.

"A relationship?"

He leaned in and kissed me. This time he threw in tongue action, and hugging. I closed my eyes and waited to be swept away, but it must have been low tide because that ocean never pulled me in.

When it was over, he whispered, "What do you think?"

I hesitated for a moment, staring into his gorgeous green eyes, thinking of magazine launches and what Tess would do, and what Nico said about love finding you. Was this love and I just didn't recognize it? Was love something that started out slowly and had to build? I decided for the sake of the moment, I would go with the "slow" explanation. "Yes. We have the beginnings of a relationship."

Then I kissed him, and I got into it this time, going with the tide that was building inside me. And just as I was about to get pulled under he stopped for some reason. I held on, resting my head on his shoulder.

The car stopped in front of a flower shop and I remembered that I hadn't thanked him for the roses.

"I love white roses. Did Rio tell you that, too?"

"No, but now that I know, I'll send you some every day."

We kissed again, but all the while I kept thinking that something wasn't right. I pulled away. "Rio didn't tell you I like white roses?"

He shook his head.

"Then how did you know…"

My mind did an instant replay of the flower-delivery episode and a fantastic thought hit me, one that, as incredible as it seemed, was probably true. I could think of only one thing. "I have to go home."

"Is something wrong?"

"I don't know. I just have to go home."

I wasn't absolutely sure, but I had this crazy feeling that it had been Nico standing in my doorway delivering those white roses, and the more I thought about it the more confused I became.

But, if it had been Nico, why hadn't he told me?

I was probably completely wrong, but I had to know, and know soon before I had sex with a guy who thought we were in a "relationship." Somehow, the way he'd used the word made it sound like some kind of legal thing. Like something I'd need a lawyer to get out of.

"Whatever you want, Samantha." He told Richard to turn the car around and take me home. Then he put his arm around me and I suddenly felt all warm and cozy and wondered why in hell was I going home to chase after a guy who was probably sound asleep in his own bed, with some other chick, three thousand miles away. And what was wrong with a real relationship, anyway?

"I've changed my mind. Let's go to your place."

He held me tighter. I nuzzled in closer. "Are you sure?"

"Very."

CHAPTER EIGHT

JASON LIVED IN A penthouse apartment that was bigger than some airports I've been in. It was decorated in contemporary extravagance, with a view of most of Manhattan. Although the place was outrageous, it still maintained a sense of balance with dark woods, deep golds, reds and warm textures.

We began the second half of our date with a glass of port in front of the fireplace. I wondered if we would do it right there on the hand-loomed carpet, or if we'd ease our way into his master suite. Either way, I wanted to get to it so that the whole Nico thing could fade back into the friendship that it was supposed to be.

"You have an extraordinary home," I remarked right after we sat down together on a bronze-colored silk sofa.

"Thanks, my mother was the decorator. I had nothing to do with it. If it were up to me, this place would still be empty. But let's not talk about that now." We started kissing again, long passionate kisses, with some removal of clothing, mostly his because mine was almost nonexistent to begin with.

Just as we were really getting into it, and heading for somewhere other than the silk sofa, we were rudely interrupted by two monster balls of whining white fur.

One of them jumped right up on Jason's lap, and the other one pawed me from the back of the sofa.

Needless to say, I about jumped right out of my dress. "What the…"

They had those punched-in faces and long brushed hair that looked like it needed its own traveling kitty stylist just to keep it from tangling.

I stood up. I didn't want the little critters anywhere around me. "Damn! You really do have two cats!"

"You didn't believe me?"

"It was our first date."

"What's that supposed to mean?"

"People exaggerate on first dates."

"I didn't."

"I don't like cats."

"I thought you said you always wanted one."

"I'm part of the group who exaggerates. Can you do something with them?"

My skin felt all prickly just watching the slithery little vixens. I'd had a bad experience when I was five with a cat who wouldn't leave me alone. It belonged to one of my cousins. Her name was Connie, and her cat's name was Connie. Connie the cat scratched my hand so deeply I needed five stitches, and Connie the cousin bit me when my mother scolded her cat. That was the only time I ever saw the two Connies, but I did hear that Connie the cat got declawed after it scratched a nun, and Connie the cousin lost her front teeth in a freak play-ground accident.

"They won't bite. Besides, I think they like you."

One of them was pacing back and forth on the back of the sofa, staring right at me.

"How can you tell?"

"Fraidy wants to jump into your arms."

I covered my exposed breasts with the little bit of fabric that made up my dress. There was no way I was letting a cat jump into these arms.

"That's it. I'm done."

I grabbed my coat and bag and headed for the door.

"Wait. You can't leave. I'll put them in another room."

I stopped and considered it for a moment, but the mood was gone and I wanted to get home where there wasn't a sofa lion waiting to attack me. I kept flashing on that dream I'd had the night before and just couldn't take being in the same room with two white beasts.

"Thanks, but I have to get up early tomorrow."

"I'll call Richard."

"Don't bother. I can take a cab."

"I can't let you go like this. I really think you're overreacting. They're actually sweet animals."

One of them was heading right for me with a gleam in her golden eyes. When she got about a foot away, she stopped, arched her back and hissed right at me. "Isabella, no!" Jason swooped her up and tucked her in his arms. "I'm sorry, but sometimes she gets a little jealous. That'll fade once she gets to know you."

"Unless you have a muzzle for that thing, I'm not going to wait around until we can become friends. Thanks for a great evening."

I continued on to the door. Jason followed right behind me.

"Look, they actually belong to my mother. I just brought them over because you said you always wanted a cat."

I turned and glared right at him. "So you went beyond exaggeration and into out and out lying."

"Well, yes. I suppose I did."

Isabella hissed again. He opened what appeared to be a closet, threw her inside and shut the door. She started crying almost instantly.

I opened the front door, stepped out in the hallway and pressed the down button on the elevator. He followed me out. "Please let me make this up to you. A play, maybe, or a bike ride through the park, anything, but let's just try it one more time. No cats. I promise."

He looked so sweet standing there, all sorrowful and pleading. Without that monster cat in his arms I just couldn't refuse.

The elevator door opened. I stepped inside, pulled a business card from my bag, turned and handed him the card. "Tell you what, if you can get me a front-row seat for a catwalk show in Bryant Park, you have a date."

"I'll call you when it's set up."

"Then you've got yourself another date…but no cats."

"I'll drown the little beasts."

"Now you're talking."

I let the doors shut.

ONCE OUT ON THE sidewalk, I decided to walk for a while before I hailed a cab. After all, it was only ten-thirty on a Friday night. Prime time for romance and I wasn't quite ready to go back to my apartment, alone.

Restaurants were crowded with lovers holding hands across tables or waiting out in front talking, laughing, gazing into each other's eyes. More lovers walked hand in hand while window shopping or hurrying to their next event.

I kept my hands in my pockets.

After about five blocks of feeling completely sorry for myself, I decided it was time to hail that cab. I stepped out on the curb and a black stretch limo pulled up in front of me. The window rolled down and Abby's face appeared from behind the gray glass. "What's a hot babe like you doing walking the streets of New York alone on a Friday night?"

I leaned over to answer. "I was just asking myself that same question."

Julia leaned forward. "Get in. We've got this thing until midnight courtesy of Tess."

"How'd that happen?" I asked as I climbed in and sat down next to Abby.

"Tess had a party to go to," Abby announced while she poured Dom Perignon into a glass.

"She didn't want to go alone," Julia added. "Spiros is out of town on business for the weekend."

"So where's Tess?" I asked as Abby handed me a crystal flute of champagne.

"She's at the party."

"I don't get it."

Abby smiled. "Apparently, she hates to sit in the back of a limo all by herself, so she begged us to come with her for the drive."

"We have to pick her up at the stroke of midnight," Julia interjected.

"Or what happens?"

"I think she melts or something," Abby said.

"You have your fairytales confused. This is more of a Cinderella story."

We pulled away from the curb. "I'll drink to that,"

Julia interjected, holding up her flute then taking a few sips of champagne. "Don't be surprised if we all turn into mice at midnight."

I toasted, then drank some of the golden liquid. It fizzed on my tongue and felt cool going down. I loved champagne, especially Dom. "The way my night's been going, it would be a relief."

"Well, sit back, take your shoes off and tell us all about it, because for the next hour or so we have nothing to do but ride around the streets of New York with Fred, that's our driver, and drink champagne." Abby refilled my glass.

"So who's the bum this time?" Julia wanted to know. She had her legs tucked up under herself as she lay on the rich tan leather seat.

I did the same thing, while Abby sat up straight in the middle holding onto the bottle of champagne as if it were the most precious item in the world. I noticed another unopened bottle sitting in an ice bucket, and the bottom of a third bottled peeking out from under the seat. I guessed that one was dead.

"Here's the thing," I said once I was comfortable. "Jason had been a sweetheart up until his cats attacked me."

"Wait. Who's Jason and what kind of cats are we talking about here?" Abby leaned forward, intent on what I had to say.

"Jason is this guy I met during my coffeehouse research." I didn't want to tell them his last name. At least not yet. Abby was bound to know who he was.

"And the cats?" she asked.

"From hell. They hate me."

"Competition," Julia declared. "I know cats. They're

very jealous creatures, but they can be so sweet. You just have to get to know them."

"Not going to happen. Not with these babies. If they hadn't hissed at me, I probably could've been lured into Jason's bedroom."

"Are you sure it was his cats keeping you out of his bed, or was there something else going on?" Abby asked, filling her glass with more champagne, then placing the bottle in the secure bucket.

"I don't know. It's this whole in-town dating thing. If he had been visiting, I wouldn't have met those nasty jealous creatures and we would have had sex. Possibly even wild, crazy sex. He seems like the type."

Julia sat up. "Define wild and crazy."

I looked at her. Her hair was actually pulled back in pigtails. I couldn't define wild and crazy sex to a girl in pigtails. It just wouldn't be right.

"Some other time," I quipped.

She shrugged and fell back into her prone position.

I continued. "Anyway, after sex, he would have gotten on a plane and gone home. What's wrong with that? It seems perfectly ideal to me. We both win and neither one of us has to alter our lives for the other. He could have ten cats for all I'd care."

"But you can't see him every day and that's the best part." Julia got all dewy eyed as if she were thinking of someone special, which I knew she was. The girl had it bad.

"Not always. It depends on the guy."

"Could Jason be that guy?" Abby asked.

I didn't know how to answer that question, so I

changed the subject. "If we have this thing until midnight, let's have some fun!"

Abby and Julia let out a few squeals and started to dance in their seats. Then Julia reached up and opened the sunroof, I found a Tina Turner CD and cranked it up. The three of us squeezed through the sunroof and sang along with Tina as our driver cruised Times Square and drove up and down Broadway.

If we were going to turn into mice at midnight, at least we'd be happy mice.

MY PHONE RANG WAY TOO early the next morning. The number that flashed up across my screen belonged to my older sister, Natalie, married to Brent, the foot doctor. I hadn't called her in more than two weeks, which was unacceptable to Natalie. I had to think of something to distract her anger, but still remain in good standing with my childhood heroes.

"Natalie. I was just thinking about you." Which I was as soon as her number flashed across my phone screen. "Can you ask Brent what he thinks of that new surgery some women are getting to help their feet fit into pointed-toed shoes?"

"I can't."

"Why?"

"Because he left me for a woman with bunions."

I wanted to laugh, but I didn't know if she was serious. Brent was a weird guy, and it sounded reasonable that he would be attracted to bunions, but Natalie was my sister and…

"It's a joke, Sam. He hasn't left me and you don't have to feel guilty for not calling me. I know how busy you are, and I know you would never have surgery on your feet simply for style…would you?"

While she spoke I got out of bed, walked into the kitchen and sat down on a chair, carefully. My head was pounding.

"Of course not." But I'd actually considered it last year, until I realized how much pain was involved in the healing process. Pain and fashion could only go so far with me.

"So what's going on?"

"Nothing much. Same old, same old. But I do have a question for you. How long did it take you to fall in love with Brent?"

"You've met someone, haven't you? This is great. Now, please tell me he lives within fifty miles of you."

"Maybe five."

"There is a God."

"How long did it take you?"

"For what?"

I lit up a cigarette. This could take a while.

"For you to know if you loved Brent?"

"Actually, I knew it the moment we kissed."

That seemed impossible. I must have kissed…well, way too many men to count, and I never once thought I was in love. Not once.

I took a long drag on my cigarette and let it out. "Why? What was different?"

I could hear Natalie sigh, as if she was remembering Brent's kiss as we spoke. "The way he made me feel."

"I need more than that. Cough it up. I'm your sister. I want details. Was it something he did to you? I mean, the man is a doctor. They know more about a woman's body than the average guy."

"Nothing that complicated. It's hard to explain. It's just something you know when you kiss him."

"What, like breathing?"

"Yes. That's it exactly. Like breathing."

I wasn't getting anywhere with her.

"Yeah, well. Okay. So why did you call?"

"Because you sent me the oddest e-mail. I think it was meant for someone named Nico, but I got it instead. Is he the guy you think you're in love with?"

I crushed out my cigarette. It wasn't tasting good anymore. Must have been the patch on my butt.

"Nico? No. Don't be silly. He's just a friend."

"That's not how the e-mail sounded. I think he's more than just a friend."

"I was tired when I wrote it. You were merely reading fatigue." I suddenly remembered writing to him in the middle of the night about the roses. Oh God!

I must have clicked on the wrong e-mail address. How could I have been so stupid? Now my whole family would know about Nico.

"So you think he brought you white roses? The fact that you even told a guy you like white roses says it all."

"You're reading far too much into this. Look, he lives in Italy. I can't be in love with him. Nothing can come of it."

"Then who's the guy who lives five miles away?"

"That's Jason Rocket, but we've only gone out once. Twice. But you can't really count the first time."

"You're dating Jason Rocket? The real-estate tycoon?"

"How does everybody know this but me?" I decided that I must have been living in some kind of bubble not to know about this guy.

"Don't you ever watch the news? He's the next Donald Trump."

"Does the Donald know about this takeover?"

"You know what I mean. So how does Nico play in all of this?" I hated that I'd sent my sister Nico's e-mail. She would never stop bugging me about it, and eventually my other sister would join in on the fun. It could be months before they'd let it go.

"He doesn't. Look, I've got to go to work. I've been late every day this week and Tess is starting to get touchy about it."

"Okay, but call me when you know."

"When I know what?"

"Who you're in love with."

"I'm not in love with anybody."

"Your nose is going to grow."

"I'll talk to you later. Give the kids a hug for me."

I hung up and went right to my laptop to send another e-mail to Nico. As soon as I opened the program an official invitation to the Dolce & Gabbana catwalk show at Bryant Park on Saturday afternoon at four-thirty popped up on my screen.

Love was definitely in the air.

CHAPTER NINE

THERE I SAT, RIGHT NEXT to the catwalk as color and form strolled by as if it had been sent down from couture heaven just for my entertainment. The Dolce & Gabbana runway models floated past me in some of the most fabulous clothes I'd ever seen: garish florals, psychedelic sixties swirls, belted A-lines, minis, slick wool jackets, plunging necklines, frilled cropped blouses, jeweled bodices and polka-dot halters. There were star models and rock singers, dilettantes and famous actresses. There couldn't have been another place on the entire planet that was more exciting, more provocative, more stimulating…an haute couture orgasm.

The earth moved.

"Sexissimo," to quote one of the fashion-trade mags.

This was love, all right. I was falling hard and it had nothing to do with Jason's kiss. It was Jason's power and status.

As the designers took their bows, I was surrounded by all those I most admired in the fashion world and it was all Jason's doing. A rush of adrenaline swept through me like wildfire, and I wanted to kiss everyone for giving me so much pleasure. Of course, I limited myself to gushing smiles and repeating "Bravo" over and over until the show ended.

Afterward, I had to sit back down for a while just to regain my normal condition of controlled skepticism, but for some reason that fashion rush was still doing a number on my mental stability.

It was love, pure and simple, and I had found it right there in Bryant Park with a man who lived only a short cab ride away. I couldn't wait to tell him, or at least affirm that we were indeed in a relationship.

"Did you enjoy the show?" some guy asked. He sat directly behind me.

"Yes," I answered, hardly turning.

I just wanted out of there without having to chat with a stranger, so I tried to ignore him and got up from my seat.

"Those two are the best Italian designers."

"Absolutely," I mumbled, but just kept walking.

I found my way through the crowded park, past more white tents, a couple of fountains and a lively game of pelanqué, the ball game that seemed to attract older men, where one of them threw metal balls along the ground to try to come as close to the wooden ball as possible. Judging by all the cheering and swearing, I'd guessed that one of the men had just scored.

When I got out on Avenue of the Americas, I grabbed a cab and headed for Jason's. Right after I'd received the invitation, I'd phoned him and we made a date for dinner at his place. I couldn't wait for the loving and lovemaking to begin. The she-devil cats were back at his mom's and we had the whole evening to explore this budding romance of ours.

I had one more coffee date on Sunday morning at ten-thirty and couldn't wait for it to be over. It was with an Anthony Somebody at Uptown Perk. I tried to cancel, but Rio had made the date for me and wouldn't let it go. For some reason, she wanted me to meet the guy, which I couldn't understand, considering how hot she'd been for me to hook up with Jason. Sometimes the woman made no sense whatsoever.

I'd had the first of my final dates, right before the Dolce & Gabbana show, with Grace Bernstein, who was seriously disappointed that I was only interested in her story rather than starting a love affair. She was a lovely brunette, with big brown eyes, flawless skin and the right sense of humor. Grace wanted a lover who could match her wit, had a high-paying job, and liked to mud wrestle. Grace owned her own private mud pit. I'd told her if there was ever a woman who could tempt me, she'd be the one, and I left it at that.

All in all, the day and my love life was gearing up for a bodacious finale.

There was only one pesky fly in this seemingly white ointment. One tiny gnat that still buzzed my face.

I had been unable to contact Nico.

It was as if he'd simply disappeared. I even tried calling his number in Milan, but couldn't leave a message because his message box was full. I was actually beginning to worry about the guy. And if he was in New York, which I couldn't be sure of, I really didn't want to miss him.

Of course, the mere fact that I was still thinking about Nico while Jason's love was looming just a few blocks away caught me by surprise. I'd thought perhaps it was just a case of cold feet. Jason meant possible commit-

ment and stability, while Nico meant uncommitment
and instability, both of which I'd grown rather fond of.

The cab driver stopped in front of Jason's building.
A doorman opened my door as I paid the driver. When
I got out, I took a few steps toward Jason's apartment
building, a lovely historic building with an ornate facade
and brass-edged glass doors. The place oozed society
and money. Suddenly, I couldn't make myself go inside,
couldn't force myself to take the necessary steps to get
to the front door. It was as if my feet weighed more than
I could manage and I simply couldn't walk another step.

"Is there anything wrong, miss?" the gentle-looking
doorman asked as he approached the door.

"No," I assured him. But for some reason, I couldn't
move. I was frozen right there on Fifth Avenue while the
city whizzed by me and my future soul mate waited up
in his penthouse.

"Whom did you wish to see?" he asked, concern
showing in the corners of his eyes.

I hesitated for a moment. If I told him, then he'd
announce me and I'd have to go up. I'd have to begin a
"relationship." Begin a love affair with a very handsome, very rich man who seemed kind and generous and
loving and…what more could a girl want?

It started to rain, and although we were standing
under an awning, the rain blew in enough so that my feet
were getting wet. But I still couldn't move. "Well, that's
really the crux of it, isn't it?"

He smiled, shook his head a little and walked toward
me. "If you give me a name, perhaps I can help you."

"I think I'm beyond help."

"There's always a choice."

A man in a black suit got out of a cab and Mr. Doorman greeted him and escorted him inside. The man threw me a look as if I was a little weird, which, in the scheme of degrees of weirdness, I probably ranked right up there at the top.

"But the trick is knowing what to choose," I mumbled when Mr. Doorman came back and stood beside me.

"Just go with your heart," he instructed.

I looked down at his feet. They were getting rained on along with mine. However, he wore thick black boots, where I wore open-toed heels. A pair of my very favorite open-toed heels. The ones I'd taken back four times while deciding on the perfect color—lime-green—and fit—seven and a half. The ones I only wore on special occasions because they cost me four hundred bucks, yet there they were getting totally ruined while I waited for my mind to wrap around the correct choice.

"What if you've never gone with your heart before and you're a little scared of the outcome?"

"Sometimes you just have to jump in with both feet."

We stood there for a few minutes more. Side by side, with the rain blasting our feet. After a while, he went back to opening doors.

I, on the other hand, persisted in my sudden weirdness, staring down at my feet for what seemed like hours, watching as the fine Italian leather soaked through, changing from a lovely shade of lime-green to a rancid yellowish color. Then, when I couldn't take the destruction another moment, I did something that was probably destined to become the biggest mistake of my life.

I hailed a cab and went home.

MY CONFUSION DIDN'T STOP at my apartment, it just continued to haunt me. I didn't change, or get out of my wet shoes. Instead, I began pacing, which didn't amount to much considering my apartment was four hundred square feet. I could cover the entire place in less time than it took to jump from one puzzling thought to another.

I wasn't home for very long when my phone started to ring. It was Jason, and after his third desperate phone message I had no choice but to pick up.

"I'm here," I blurted into the phone.

"Then you're safe." I could hear the frustration in his voice. "What happened? I've been worried about you. You said you would be right over. That was more than two hours ago."

I took a deep breath, sat down in a chair in the living room and proceeded to try to explain my feelings to a man who should be my lover. "I can't do it. I tried, but it's just not going to work out."

"What are you talking about?"

"Us. This relationship we're in…or not in."

"Is it the cats? I told you they're gone. I gave them—"

"It's not the cats. It's you and me. I can't…I just don't…" I gazed at my wet feet, and suddenly I knew what I was feeling. What I had to say. "I think I'm in love with somebody else."

A mixture of relief and anxiety swept over me. Had I really said it out loud? Had I really used the words *love* and *somebody* in the same sentence?

My heart fluttered.

"You met somebody on your coffee dates." He sounded dejected and sad. What was I doing? I wanted to retract my love statement, but I knew I couldn't.

"No. Nothing as rational as that. I've never met this guy…at least I don't think I have. Although, he may have delivered white roses to me, but I can't be sure."

"You're in love with a delivery boy?"

"Yes. No. He's actually a chemist."

"Posing as a delivery boy?"

"I think so. Yes."

The thought made me laugh. How could I possibly be in love with someone I've only known through e-mail, never talked to face-to-face, only caught a glimpse of and even then dismissed him as some weirdo. There was something seriously wrong with me, and I loved it.

"I asked you when we first went out if you were seeing someone. You said you weren't. Was that one of those first-date exaggerations?"

"I told you the truth. I'm not dating anyone."

"Then how can you be in love?"

"I can't explain it. I just am…I think."

My shoes were finally beginning to dry out and return to their intended color. It didn't look as if they were ruined after all.

There was a moment of silence. I could hear him breathing, sighing, actually. "Jason?"

"Yes. I'm here. Just trying to grasp all of this."

"I want to thank you for this afternoon. It was amazing. But how did you know they're my favorite designers? Did Rio tell you?"

More silence. More breathing. Then, heavy sighing. "Oh, God. That's what all of this is about. You're mad because I forgot to get you an invitation to that thing going on in the park. What was it, now?"

I sat up straight. "Fashion Week."

"Yeah, yeah, yeah. I've been busy at work. Had to fly to my L.A. office yesterday. Your little fashion show skipped my mind. So now you're breaking it off with me because of that. I'm sorry. Let me make it up to you… I'll—"

Everything was beginning to make sense. I stood up. "You didn't send me that invitation for Dolce & Gabbana?"

"What's that?"

"It's *who's* that? They're two of the finest fashion designers in the world."

"Okay. We'll go tomorrow."

"They already had their show today. I was there, and I think I know who sent me the invitation."

"But—"

I couldn't talk to him anymore. I had too many thoughts rushing around in my head to concentrate on Jason's excuses.

"Listen, here's some advice to get you on your way to being attached. Get your mother out of your life. Pay attention to what your date wants. Don't try to change her, and find a chick who likes she-devil cats, because I know those two little bitches are yours. Have a nice life, Jason."

I hung up, changed into comfortable nightwear, set my shoes out to dry, pulled out a fresh pack of cigarettes, made myself a pot of coffee, got into bed and set up my laptop to try to find my out-of-town lover, Nico Bertuzzi.

CHAPTER TEN

WHEN I GOT UP THE NEXT morning and realized that the TV hadn't been on once all night, I'd never opened my pack of cigs and the coffeepot in the kitchen was still full, I thought perhaps something was wrong with me. I immediately went back to bed, frightened by my own normal behavior.

Then, what was even more alarming, was the time on my digital clock, 7:05 a.m. I hadn't seen 7:00 a.m. since I left college, and even then it was only in my first year when I hadn't known any better.

And the odd thing about it all was I actually felt great. I mean, I wasn't the least bit tired, and my throat didn't burn from a night of smoking. The morning had been perfect if my attempts to find Nico would have worked, but the message on my screen still read "Nico is away." I could only hope that it meant that Nico was actually in New York somewhere, and not "away" with his Ms. Perfect somewhere in Milan.

I needed to get out of this final coffee date. I had enough information to write my story, and didn't need any more research. All I had to do now was convince Rio.

I stayed right there in my bed and wrote a quick first

draft of my story, then around eight-thirty I took a shower, got dressed and went over to Uptown Perk.

"I'm getting married," Rio said crisply. I nearly choked on my Mocha-Choca-Double-Espresso.

"Get out," I protested. "When did this happen?"

"Last night. Wait. Technically it was early this morning."

"Have you known him long?"

"Not really. We were just friends."

"Then how did you go from 'just friends' to a marriage proposal?"

I was happy for Rio. She always struck me as the married-with-children type.

"It was just one of those things."

"Isn't that a Cole Porter tune?"

"Yep. And he wrote it just for me."

I sat down on a bar stool. Rio stared at me from the other side of the bar, grinning, her hands on the bar, acting as if she had a major secret and she couldn't wait to spill it.

"I don't see a ring."

"We're going to pick it out today. Anything I want."

This was sounding too good to be true. I tried to read her face, but she looked totally sincere.

"Wow! Sounds like you hit the big time. Do I know this guy?"

"You sure do." She was absolutely glowing.

I put my coffee down on the bar and leaned in closer.

"Who is it?"

"Nico Bertuzzi."

She said the name, but it was like my mind couldn't grasp what she'd actually said.

"Could you please repeat that, 'cause I just thought you said Nico Bertuzzi but that can't be. He's in Italy. In Milan, or he's supposed to be, but he may be…you don't even know him."

"He's in New York, honey. Been almost living right here for the past three days trying to get your attention. Whining and moaning over you and Jason. I told him it was a losing battle. That you'd made up your mind. No more long-distance dating. That you and Jason were made for each other. So, when he tried to get your attention at the Dolce & Gabbana show—"

"Wait. He was at the show?"

"Sure. Who do you think got you that invitation?"

"I suspected him, but—"

"He lives in their building. They're good friends. Nico sat right behind you. He tried to talk to you after the show, but you blew him off."

Rio was totally exaggerating now. I had to defend myself against her onslaught.

"I would never do that. I've been looking for him. Trying to contact him. If he tried to talk to me I would have—" I flashed on the guy behind me who'd said something about the show, but I wouldn't turn around. "Right behind me. Didn't he?"

"Directly."

My heart sank. I had been such an idiot.

"I can't talk about this anymore," Rio said. "You have a date in about five minutes. Shouldn't you get ready for it? Fix your makeup or something?"

Of all the times that I really did not want to go on a coffee date, this was absolutely one of them. "My makeup's fine. Can't you cancel this thing?"

"It's too late to cancel. Besides, this guy is the one. Trust me on this. I know men."

Now I was really getting confused. She wasn't making any sense.

"What about Jason? I thought Jason was the one for me."

"Actually, he's more my type. We've got a date for tomorrow night. I hear he's looking for a shoulder to cry on."

That's when she grinned and I knew the whole thing was absolute silliness. I'd been had. Again. But to what degree?

"What's going on?"

A big, warm smile spread across Rio's face as her gaze shifted to someone behind me. I abruptly spun around.

"I believe we have a coffee date, *signorina*." A firestorm swept over me as I focused in on his voice…the same voice from the runway. The same man who had delivered those beautiful roses sitting on my nightstand.

Without even thinking about it, I went right to him, embraced him and we kissed…one of those long, hungry kisses that took my breath away. His arms wrapped around me as if he knew my body. Knew just how to hold me. How to make love to me. I wanted to fall into bed and never leave.

"Nico," I mumbled when it was over.

He took a half step back. "Anthony Nicholas Leonardo Bertuzzi." He moved his right arm across his chest and gave me a slight bow, but he never took his eyes off of me. I felt as if he was making love to me, only no one else could see it. I wanted to kiss him again, but I knew if I did I'd want to rip his clothes off, too.

"Samantha Marie Porter," I sighed.

"Your ten-thirty coffee date, honey," Rio chimed in. "Now, would you two please go somewhere private before my shop burns down? Way too much heat for this coffee kitchen."

I turned back to her. "Why didn't you tell me he was hiding out here?"

"The man wouldn't let me," she whispered. "He's more stubborn than you are. Wanted to do things his way."

"Would you join me in a cup of some of the finest coffee in all of New York City?" Nico asked, reaching out for my hand.

"Love to," I answered. I took his hand and followed him to a table in the back of the coffeehouse where white roses nestled inside a lovely glass vase sat off to the side, and two blue mugs filled with Rio's finest waited in the center.

He pulled out my chair, I sat down and he sat across from me. For a moment, all we did was stare at each other.

Then we both started talking at once, laughed and sat back and stared at each other again.

"What happened to Ms. Perfect?"

"Too perfect. What happened to Mr. Perfect?"

"His cats knew I was lying."

He reached over, put a finger under my chin and studied my face. "Your nose still fits your beautiful face."

We both smiled again. He had one of those fabulously beautiful smiles. Nico looked even better than I could have ever imagined. He was absolutely breathtaking to look at, or was that just my libido showing?

"I confessed before anything catastrophic happened."

"Then you are both beautiful and wise."

Nico always knew just the right things to say to me. I wondered what his childhood had been like to produce such a man. I wanted to find out everything about him.

I took a sip of coffee. The hot, familiar liquid swirled around in my mouth, and when I swallowed, a surprising thought hit me. One that seemed so natural that I simply couldn't hold it in a moment longer. "There's a great little breakfast place right around the corner. I was wondering—"

"You want to have breakfast with me?"

"Yes. More than anything."

"Are you sure?"

"Very."

"Then we should go." He stood up.

"Yes. Let's go." I stood up.

He took my hand and I wanted to melt right there. "But before we have breakfast, my apartment is just up the street."

"I know. I've been there before."

"But the girl who lived there was pretty confused. She's not anymore. She knows exactly what she wants."

He took a step closer. "I love this girl who knows what she wants."

"That's a good thing, because this girl—"

I didn't finish the sentence. Instead, I kissed him again and the same rush of breathlessness came over me and I knew. "I love you, Anthony Nicholas Bertuzzi, and I don't give a damn where you live."

He pulled back and looked at me. His eyes still smoldering. "Are you sure?"

"Very."

"Then this is a good thing because I have just

accepted a job here in New York City. I was hoping you could help me find an apartment."

"Sure, but in the meantime, there's a great little apartment just a few blocks from here, and the girl who lives there really needs a man in her bed. It's the only cure for her insomnia."

"Then she should consider herself cured."

We kissed again and there it was. Just like my sister Natalie had said. No questions. No second-guessing. And just like breathing, I knew I was in love.

EPILOGUE

WHEN THE FEBRUARY issue of *Tess* hit the newsstand, it was a complete success and even Tess herself was a little surprised by the number of sales. Although, she would die first before ever admitting she could have possibly underestimated her own ingeniousness.

With that success tucked into her mental cache of incredible story ideas, it was no wonder she called Abby, Julia and Samantha into her office for an unexpected meeting first thing on a Monday morning. Samantha hadn't had time to finish her third cup of coffee when she found herself sitting alongside the other two women, each trying to prepare themselves for yet another unconventional assignment that was sure to bounce them right out of their nice little comfort zones.

"It came to me while Spiros rinsed my hair with rosemary water," Tess began. "I was gazing up at the lovely cloud formations drifting high above us. We were on our deck at Olympia and it was an absolutely perfect morning." She gazed out of the window as if she were trying to recapture the moment. "The sky was a crisp blue, dappled with clouds so white they reminded me of billowing wedding dresses."

She stopped speaking for a moment, brought a jade cigarette holder with a pink cigarette burning at its tip to her mouth and took a long drag. She blew the smoke out in a great swirl of white that completely encircled her head.

Abby coughed while Julia sat forward, totally engrossed in the vision of wedding dresses dancing in the sky.

Samantha crossed her ankles out in front of her so she could better admire her latest pair of zebra print boots. The Cole Haan boots Nico had picked out. Not only did the man solve her sleeping problems, but he knew shoes.

Tess drew in a breath.

"Here it comes," Abby muttered to Julia, who wore a perpetual smile. Ever since Julia and Daniel Taggart had been practically living together, not only were her clothes more fashionable, but she was even more wholesome than one could imagine. Ironically, her Betty Crocker attitude didn't seem to phase Samantha anymore. In fact, she rather liked it. Especially since Julia started bringing in homemade goodies for Samantha to take home to Nico. He missed Italian desserts and even though Samantha had come from a family of bakers, nothing she ever attempted resembled something edible. That was where Julia stepped in with mounds of Italian cookies and pastries. Could the woman be a better friend?

"Yes, darling, *here it comes,*" Tess mimicked, turning her gaze right on Abby while flicking an ash off the end of her cigarette into her always clean, Venetian glass ashtray. Samantha had given up smoking, finally, but the smell of good tobacco still attracted her like a horny nympho to a naked man.

Tess continued. "I thought of my own wedding gown that Vera had designed exclusively for me, the darling. And of my absolutely incredible intimate wedding that took place on Spiros's four-hundred-foot yacht, with sixty of our closest friends, while we slowly cruised the Meditation at sunset."

"But I though you were married here, at the Castle on the Hudson," Julia commented. She turned to Samantha and Abby. "I love that place. It's so romantic."

"Of course we were. That was for our east coast friends. Our west coast friends enjoyed our wedding at the Koontz estate."

While Tess spoke, Samantha remembered the gossip that had been going around during that time of her perpetual wedding bliss, so she blurted it out. "I heard you couldn't decide on which dress to wear."

Tess let out a stream of smoke, stared at Samantha for a moment, then said, "That's what I love about you, darling. You get to the point. Yes, it *was* an impossible decision. I couldn't just let someone else wear Stella's exclusive design, or Donna's. It wouldn't have been fair of me to disappoint them. So I wore all three...at different times, of course."

"I can relate," Samantha told her in all honesty. Tess was a fashion diva and Samantha loved her for it.

Tess sat up straight and they knew what was coming—their next feature assignment. Abby tightened her grip on her thighs. Julia played with her hair, while Samantha took up more space on her chair.

"Our dating piece was such a huge hit that we've received more positive e-mail and letters from our readers than ever before. The response has broken all our records. There's even a group of readers who are getting married because they tried our dating methods. It was a brilliant idea and you girls outdid yourselves, so—" she hesitated, taking a sip of coffee from a delicate, white china cup.

Abby cringed and changed positions in her chair, anticipating the worst. She and Ned had been going round and round on the type of wedding they wanted and where to have it. The whole thing had become a sore subject and the last thing Abby wanted was to write a piece on weddings. Of course, knowing how Tess worked, the woman probably thought the assignment would solve their wedding planning woes.

"Oh, I love weddings! Everyone is so happy. I think it's my favorite kind of party. Is that our next assignment? Because I'd love to write about a wedding, even an extreme wedding. I wouldn't really care. I just love the whole event." Julia was literally beaming with story anticipation.

Samantha, on the other hand, was beginning to sweat just thinking about the possibilities.

"No, darling, I'm not sending you girls out there to research weddings. I have something better in mind."

Julia's smile faded.

Samantha's body tensed.

Abby kept fidgeting in her chair.

Tess opened her mouth to speak just when her intercom buzzed.

"Yes?" Tess answered.

"Your husband is waiting for you in your limo. You have an appointment in fifteen minutes," Ling Ling relayed. She and Ling Ling had come to an understanding of sorts. Ever since her father had offered Tess a part in his next movie, Tess had lightened up. It was a small part—only one line—but Tess loved the possibility of starting a challenging acting career. At least that was what she'd told everyone.

She played an eccentric American magazine editor.

"I'll be right there," Tess answered, crushing out her cigarette as she stood.

Everyone stood with her, still waiting to hear the exact purpose for the sudden meeting. Tess grabbed her bag, brushed her hair back with her fingers and started for the door.

Abby and Julia gazed at Samantha with a what's-going-on kind of look on their faces. Samantha shrugged.

And just as Tess was about to vanish in one of her usual exit flurries, she stopped and turned to face the women. "It's our sweet Ling Ling. She's getting married. She met her fabulously wealthy fiancé on a speed date. Isn't that marvelous?"

The women nodded, but they each had a sneaking feeling there was more to this.

Tess continued. "It's simply delicious when I can witness the fruits of my hard work. So, in honor of the event, I've offered up Olympia for her wedding and she's accepted. Ling Ling's family will be flying in and she would like you three to be her bridesmaids. The sweet girl looks to us as her American family. We're going to run the story in June as a follow-up on the dating feature. It's going to be such fun. I'm her maid of honor."

"Wouldn't the correct title be matron—?" Julia stopped when she saw Tess glaring at her.

Tess in no way liked the word *matron* when referring

to herself. It reminded her of her age, which she'd spent a good deal of her time and money trying to overcome. "There are several titles for a maid of honor—chief bridesmaid, best bridesmaid et cetera. *Matron* of honor is not a term I wish to entertain."

"Absolutely," Julia said.

Tess immediately donned her happy face. "This wedding is going to be such fun. I'm always on the lookout for the best interest of my staff, especially my girls. That's what keeps us such a happy family. Now I must be off. Spiros loved my little costume party so much he wants to plan one for his surprise birthday party next month."

Julia turned to Tess with that confused look she often got whenever Tess made a contradictory statement… which was about once a day. "But if it's a surprise birthday party, why is *he* planning it?"

"The surprise isn't for Spiros. It's for everyone at the party. You know how people love to think they're in on a secret. It keeps his friends happy and it keeps Spiros from having a heart attack."

Tess sashayed out of her office and the three women followed right behind her like baby ducklings waddling after their mom in a pond. When they were all in a row, Tess stopped and turned back to Abby. "Of course, darling, I can't show favoritism, so if you would like to have your wedding at Olympia, we can work something out. Spiros and I would be honored. Besides, our readers would love it." She leaned back on a cubicle wall, thinking.

"Thanks. I—" Abby started to tell Tess her thoughts on the subject but Tess had found a solution to the story problem.

"Great! Can you imagine the spread we could have if we did both weddings on the same day? Think about it. The perfect follow-up. Two of my staffers getting married at Olympia, all because of one of our very own stories! You can't buy that kind of advertising." She hesitated for a moment. "Of course, with all that foot traffic, I may have to reconsider my white carpeting."

She whirled back around and headed for the bank of elevators. Abby, Julia and Samantha stood in a single file as if they didn't quite know which way to go now that Mom had left the pond.

When Tess was safely out of earshot, Abby asked, "Did I just agree to have my wedding at Olympia for the sake of a good story?"

"I think you did," Samantha said, nodding.

Abby actually liked the idea. It would solve everything. No more arguments with Ned, but still…she was worried about her eager acceptance. "This can't be good. It makes me a story slut."

"It's who we are, dah-ling," Julia said in her best Tess imitation.

They all laughed, but underneath the laughter they each knew Julia was exactly right. And they also knew that Tess, in her own way, was their very best friend.

Everything you love about romance...
and more!

Please turn the page for
Signature Select™ Bonus Features.

Write It Up!

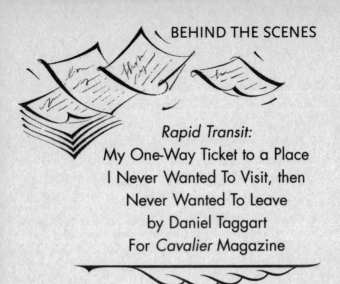

Rapid Transit:
My One-Way Ticket to a Place
I Never Wanted To Visit, then
Never Wanted To Leave
by Daniel Taggart
For *Cavalier* Magazine

4

*The hero in Rapid Transit, Elizabeth Bevarly's
novella, wrote an article after his experience with
speed dating. Did you really think we wouldn't let
you read it? Here it is! Straight from a man's
perspective—and heart!*

New York City. Night. The throbbing blur of the
club scene. Two people—one man, one woman—
sit at a table eyeing each other thoughtfully.
Intently. Maybe even a little predatorily. Both are
dressed in a way they think will best attract the
other. Both are considering every word they say in
an effort to be witty, dazzling, seductive. Both of
them want to score. Unfortunately, neither of

them is playing the same game. To her, scoring will be taming the alpha male and wrapping him—or a diamond ring that symbolizes him—around her finger. To him, scoring will be, well, *scoring*.

The opening of the latest chick flick? you might be wondering. Will there be a happy ending? Maybe the woman in the scene thinks so at this point. She's thinking about inviting him over to her place later in the week so they can cook dinner together. She's thinking about a few impromptu lunches with him at Rockefeller Plaza. She's thinking her bridesmaids will look better in petal-pink than sky-blue. The guy, on the other hand, is thinking about flipping up her skirt, pushing aside her thong—because they're always wearing a thong in the early, wrapping-him-around-the-finger stage—and then bending her over the table and going at her from behind. And he's thinking maybe he'll try the Belgian pale ale for the next round.

This is why it's not good for men and women to be together for any length of time. This is why it's essential for men and women to have sex and go to their corners. Because unless it's to couple like wild animals in heat, men and women just don't seem capable of finding common ground.

Okay, now go back and cast the scene in the bar. The guy is yours truly, the author of this article. The woman is... Hell, I forget her name. She's got red hair, though. I think. I do recall she was wearing a thong. And a skirt, too. Because it was easy to shove both aside and pummel her from behind the minute we closed the hotel room door behind us. And I remember that the pale ale I had down in the bar afterward was excellent. Helles, a new Belgian brew. Nutty flavor, a little spicy, not too bitter.

Oh, right, the woman. She was... Not Belgian. Not spicy. Not bitter, either—which was a first for me, quite frankly. Kind of nutty, yeah. But nowhere near as memorable as the beer.

Okay, now cast the scene a second time. The guy is me again. The same night, in fact, only earlier. The woman is...blond? Maybe. Wanted to couple like a wild animal in heat the minute we closed her front door behind us, as evidenced by how quickly she shoved aside her skirt and thong and invited me in. I had a German pilsner later that night, which was actually something of a disappointment. Much like the woman, come to think of it.

That said, the dating scene in New York City leaves much to be desired, thongs, skirts and pummeling from behind notwithstanding. Which is troubling in the extreme, since this is the hippest, happeningest, biggest, badassest city on the planet. If a man can't find a woman here—

who's good for more than pummeling from behind, I mean—then it can only mean there aren't women anywhere who are good for more than that. Which can be a real problem when a guy wants a little more from a woman.

So when my editor asked me to check out the dating scene in New York for the February (and, inescapably, Valentine's Day) issue, I went into it with a pretty wary view of the whole thing. Good thing, too, since by "dating scene," I knew what my editor actually wanted me to write about was the "scoring scene" in New York. Hell, he's even more jaded about women than I am. And here at *Cavalier*, we don't do the hearts-and-flowers thing, no matter what month or holiday it is.

There were a few more things I knew going into this article, too. I knew I wouldn't have trouble meeting women, since there are so many here and, all modesty aside, I've never had trouble meeting women. And I knew at least a few of them would be attractive enough for me to consider while they were sizing me up for my wedding tux since, all modesty aside, I've never had trouble leading women to believe I was interested in them—for more than just scoring, I mean. I also knew I'd score with at least a few of them because, all modesty aside, I've never had trouble scoring with women. (See above comment about leading them to believe I'm interested.)

And I knew something that *wouldn't* happen, too. I knew I wouldn't meet a woman I'd want to see again, once I'd shoved aside her skirt and thong and... Well. No need to be gratuitous about it. There are other men's magazines for that.

To take on the New York dating scene, I chose for my weapon of mass seduction the somewhat narcotic-sounding practice of "speed dating." And narcotic it was. Parties full of women who are looking to spend only a few minutes in a man's presence to size him up for his potential as a mate. This is an excellent venue for men. We don't want to spend more than a few minutes talking to a woman anyway. We can size up their potential for mating in half that time. Speed dating is like grocery shopping for sexual partners. At the end of the night, a man can literally check off the names of the women he thinks are most likely to put out on the first date. Then he hands in the list and is rewarded with the e-mail addresses of all of the women who think he's sexy, too. No, not all of those women are going to hop into the sack the first time.

But some of them are.

Is this a great country or what? Who else could come up with drive-through, fast-food sex like this? I was a complete convert to speed dating the first night, scoring not once, but with *two* women I met on that occasion. I couldn't sign up fast enough for the second party. Since I'd made it to home plate twice at that first one, my goal for the second was a triple-header—if you can pardon the incredibly crass pun.

So it was with more than a little anticipation that I attended that second speed-dating party. And it was that second speed-dating party where the cast of the movie changed again. This time, for good. Because you see, I met this woman. And for the life of me, I can't remember what I had to drink later that night.

I could physically describe her here down to the last detail, but I'd just as soon keep her to myself if you guys don't mind. (And even if you do mind. Mitts off.) Mostly what you need to know about her is how she made me realize what an arrogant ass I've been when it comes to the dating—all right, *scoring*—scene. This woman is intelligent, quick-witted, beautiful, sexy. (And the fact that I'm naming her attributes in that order should tell you something.) She challenges me on a number of levels. She appeals to me on a number of levels. She's a hell of a lot of fun to be around. She's like no woman I've ever met.

Long story short, I left that second speed-dating party without even turning in my shopping list. And I haven't wanted to go to the grocery store since. The woman I met that night has satisfied every hunger, every craving, every demand for sustenance I have. Not just the needs and appetites I recognized in myself, but the desires and hopes I didn't realize I had. She's made me remember that there's more to life than succeeding in business without really trying, that there's more to male-female interaction and that there's more to sex than getting your rocks off.

Over the course of a couple of weeks, this woman made me remember what it's like to be, not a single man checking out New York's scoring scene, but a human being checking out life on *Spaceship Earth*. What I've found with her is an enjoyment of the most basic pleasures that life—and, hell, New York, too—has to offer. Cooking dinner with someone and leisurely enjoying it afterward. Taking a stroll through Central Park with someone special. Having lunch—and a few laughs—in the sunshine. Making out in the back seat of a cab, not caring what the driver or passersby think.

So now it's February. The month of Valentine's Day. The month of romance. The month of hearts and flowers. The month *Cavalier* normally publishes its annual beer Issue. I was supposed to be writing about speed dating and scoring for Valentine's Day. Instead, I'm writing about something else entirely. Something that can indeed be found in the pulsing blur of the New York dating scene. Something that can be found everywhere you look, if you just forget about scoring and grocery lists and let it happen.

Because mostly what this woman I met at that second speed-dating party made me figure out is that I, as a universal human being with basic needs—and not an arrogant, *Cavalier*-reading male on the prowl—have the capacity to fall in love.

And fall in love I did.

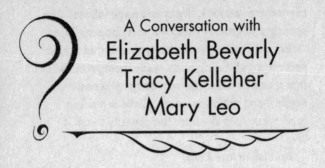

A Conversation with
Elizabeth Bevarly
Tracy Kelleher
Mary Leo

Do you have a worst-date-ever story?

Elizabeth Bevarly (EB): You know, I don't, actually. I was extremely fortunate to meet my husband when I was sixteen and he was seventeen, and I really never dated anyone but him. Unless you count the guy I went out with very briefly before I met my husband. He was a year younger than me, and we both had braces. Not so much the dating, but kissing between two people with braces can be a seriously unpleasant—and sometimes even bloody—experience.

Tracy Kelleher (TK): Unfortunately, yes. When I was a senior in high school, I met a guy when I visited my older sister at college. Later that summer, he came for a weekend visit when my parents were away and only my sister and I were home. He stepped off the bus wearing a leather Carnaby hat—not a good look in any decade.

From there it went further downhill. I insisted that my sister accompany us whenever possible, even sitting between us at the movie theater. As soon as he left, I vacuumed the house thoroughly to eradicate all traces of his presence. I even used all the attachments!

Mary Leo (ML): Do I ever...! I was fresh out of high school and had just been dumped by my first real love for a much-older woman of twenty...heavy sigh! My friend thought I needed some cheering up so she and her fiancé set me up with the "perfect" date. Apparently, her fiancé had chosen this guy especially for me and even though I'd only met her fiancé once, she assured me that "Charlie knew how to pick 'em." The blind date (I've since forgotten his name) was certainly cute enough, had a good sense of humor, but reeked of cigarette smoke. His teeth, lips and fingers were all stained a delightful shade of burnt yellow. At the time I smoked, as well, but I can safely tell you I was not turning yellow. This guy continually had a cigarette, either dangling from his lips or resting between his fingers. Even while we ate dinner, he smoked. He would take a few bites of his steak, then a few drags on his cigarette. When the hazy night was finally over and he leaned in to kiss me, my lips tightened and my face twisted up in some kind of convulsive terror. He immediately pulled back and said, "Relax, baby, I won't bite." I looked up into his smoldering brown eyes and said, "No, but I will." He stared at me for a moment, told me that I had a real problem and left. That was the last time I ever accepted a blind date...and the last night I ever smoked a cigarette.

Of the various kinds of alternative dating, which do you find most interesting?
EB: I think speed dating would be most interesting. I'm very big on first impressions, and I think it would be a real challenge to size someone up in so brief a time, or to be sized up myself in so brief a time. Plus, I love meeting people, and speed dating would provide A LOT of opportunity for that.

TK: Probably speed dating. I'm a firm believer in first impressions, and besides, having a limited time to make contact minimizes all the embarrassing things one invariably says on initial encounters. Besides, you don't have to wonder if you need to kiss goodbye at the door before never seeing your date again.

ML: Actually, I think a date over a cup of coffee is a good way to check somebody out. There's no real pressure, and you can tell a lot about the other person in a fairly short period of time, depending on how fast or slow you can drink hot liquids.

Why did you become a writer?

EB: I can't imagine being anything else, and never wanted to be anything else. I loved books from the moment I was able to hold one, loved having the stories I read unfold in my head and loved creating my own when I wasn't reading. As a child and adolescent, I read everything I could get my hands on. Books took me to places I never would have been able to visit otherwise, and taught me about people I didn't have the opportunity to meet living in my quiet suburban mid-America neighborhood. There was just never any question in my mind that I would someday write books, too. Writing isn't what I do. Being a writer is what I am.

TK: I've been writing stories since fourth grade. My first story was about lizards in the Roman Forum— weird, I know, but that kind of set the pattern. Then, after various jobs in academia, advertising, newspapers and magazines, all involving writing, I decided to avoid meetings (my least favorite thing besides vacuuming) and write fiction full-time.

ML: I've been writing short stories and keeping a journal ever since I was a young girl. When I was a teen, my friends and I would write steamy romances about whichever rock star we were in love with at the time. We'd spend hours telling our stories to each other, then writing them down so we could store them in our mutual hope chest. I still have some of those stories and they're a hoot!

If you weren't a writer, what would you be doing?
EB: Oh, sure, ask me this after I've just said I can't imagine being anything but a writer. Okay, if I wasn't writing books, I think I'd be decorating houses. Interior designer. I love decorating, love furniture stores, love home accessories, love rugs and fabric. Every time I go into a house, I'm either thinking, "Wow, they did a great job with this place," or "Oh, man, do they need my help!"

TK: I'd probably be back as a newspaper editor, trying to avoid meetings (and vacuuming) whenever possible.

ML: I was an integrated circuit layout designer for twenty-some years. I wrote in my free time, and now I do some circuit layout in my free time. It's the artistic side of electronics, and with the way I'm wired, it works well for me. Of course, I was also a bartender in San Jose and a cocktail waitress in Vegas. Of all my jobs, I'd have to say that I'd never go back to being a drink waitress. That has to be the most difficult job of all.

Do you have any tips on how to have a successful relationship?

EB: Speaking as someone who has been with her soul mate for almost three decades, all I can recommend is that you respect each other and love each other and treat each other with decency and understanding and patience. Share everything—including your feelings—both good and bad. It's not always going to be a bed of roses, but you can't walk away just because something isn't working the way you think it should. You have *got* to remember you made a commitment to each other, and work as hard as it takes to fix whatever is wrong. So many people aren't willing to make that effort.

TK: Get involved with someone with whom you like to travel. It's a good barometer of how both of you roll with the punches, share joint interests and follow the same pace. It's also good to have a relationship with someone who likes to go out to eat—even better, someone who likes to vacuum.

ML: Yes, a few. Don't be afraid to argue it out. Tell him/her daily that you love them. Don't put the good things off…. That includes sex. Take the time and find the money to go on that trip together, or enjoy that fancy dinner. Your relationship is your most important asset.

When you're not writing, what do you love to do?
EB: I'm a real homebody, so I love just being at home relaxing with my family, whether it's watching a rented video and eating popcorn, grilling out on the deck, or all of us reading books in the same room. That said, I also love to eat out, go to movies and visit new places. Again, though, with my family. As an individual, I enjoy recreational shopping. I worked in malls for a long time while pursuing my writing career, and I still love being in them.

TK: Travel. I'd travel all the time if I had unlimited funds, no responsibilities and an endless supply of clean underwear.

ML: I love to hang out with my husband, or my kids, or my friends and just laugh. Laugh about silly things and the crazy stuff we've gotten ourselves into. It's what keeps me centered and it helps prepare me for yet another dose of reality.

Do you believe in love at first sight?
EB: I believe in recognition at first sight. I don't think you can truly love someone until you

know something of his or her character and personality. But I do firmly believe you can lay eyes on someone and think, "Wow. There's something there. Something that I really need to investigate." I felt it with my own husband.

TK: I believe in lust at first sight.

ML: Absolutely. I fell in love with my husband the moment I met him. Only one problem, he was married to another woman. Seven years later, he was free and so was I...the good things in life sometimes take a little longer to get.

Is there one book that changed your life somehow?
EB: Yeah, there is. When I was about thirteen, I read *Your Erroneous Zones*, by Dr. Wayne Dyer, a big lifestyle guru of the seventies. It made me realize how much I cared about what others thought of me, even people I didn't much like, and how I was trying to live my life to conform to others' opinions and expectations. I've felt "different" from other people for as long as I can remember. I think all writers, all very creative people, do. And after reading that book, I realized it was okay to be different. Maybe a lot of people wouldn't like me for being a nonconformist, but what did I care? I wasn't trying to please them. I just wanted to be happy with who I was. This

book helped me do that. And I haven't looked back since.

TK: More like a series of books—the Laura Ingalls Wilder books. My fourth-grade teacher used to read portions of the books at the end of each day, and it was just magical. Is it any wonder that I started writing stories that same year?

ML: Yes...*To Kill a Mockingbird*, by Harper Lee. When I read it, I knew I wanted to be a writer.

What are your top three favorite books?

EB: Oooo. Very hard question. I'm going to have to go by the books I reread most often. The first would be *The Tao of Pooh,* by Benjamin Hoff. Whenever I start feeling stressed-out or anxious or angry or depressed, that book pulls me out of it. The second would have to be *It Had To Be You,* by Susan Elizabeth Phillips. And the third would have to be *Lord of Scoundrels,* by Loretta Chase. Those last two because they just make me feel so good when I'm finished with them.

TK: That's a tough one. Among my favorites are Jane Austen's *Pride and Prejudice*, Charles Dickens's *David Copperfield* and *Lucky Jim,* by Kingsley Amis.

ML: Shane, by Jack Schaefer, *Follow Your Heart,* by Susanna Tamaro and *Shopaholic Takes Manhattan,* by Sophie Kinsella...simply because it made me laugh out loud, several times! And of course, *To Kill a Mockingbird,* by Harper Lee.

What are you working on right now?

EB: As I answer these questions, I'm finishing up my second book for HQN, *Express Male,* a sequel to my October release for HQN, *You've Got Male.* It's due to be published in June 2006, I think. The stories in both books revolve around a fictional spy organization called OPUS, and both feature heroines who are reluctantly drawn into adventures that change their lives...and bring them true love. (But then, that's hardly surprising, is it?)

TK: I'm working on a mystery/chick lit that takes place in southwest France. Think quaint villages perched vertiginously atop mountains, fields of sunflowers and poppies and endless, sun-drenched days. Kind of a Tour de France, only without bicycles.

ML: I'm working on a couple of stories. One is about a spitfire of a diction coach trying to get Italy's latest heartthrob to speak clearly enough for a movie he's making so she can keep her job. The other is about a woman who has spent her life taking care of her ailing mother, but on her mother's passing she inherits the family's abandoned winery in Southern Italy. Against her brothers' wishes, she decides to keep the winery and bring it back to life.

I have a thing for Italy and Italian men...can you tell?

TIPS & TRICKS

Six Tips for Ordering the Perfect Cup of Coffee

A few nights ago, I walked into my favorite coffeehouse in my neighborhood with a new friend. She ordered first while I practiced my order silently. She spoke slowly, distinctly and looked the cashier right in the eye. "I'd like a medium decaf cappuccino. Dry. Single. Decaf. With sugar-free vanilla and two-percent milk. Please make it a decaf." The cashier repeated the order and handed the marked cup to the barista. I couldn't speak for a moment because I was in awe of this woman. I had no idea what "dry" meant, and when I order a cup of coffee, I sputter and stammer until the cashier and I come to some sort of agreement on what she thinks I actually want. Usually, it's totally wrong. Like the time I ordered one cup of coffee with three different ingredients and picked up three different cups of coffee. I've gotten caffeinated coffee when I ordered decaf and my friends had to peel me off the ceiling. And the best one was when I ordered what I thought was a double decaf espresso with steamed milk and a lot of foam. I picked up a shot of espresso in one paper cup, steamed milk in another and an entire paper cup filled with nothing but foam.

If you're like me and you've had similar misadventures in coffee ordering, don't be discouraged. I am here to sharpen your skills so you can order with absolute confidence knowing full well that your coffee will come out perfect every time...unless you want to add a dusting of cocoa powder and cinnamon. You're on your own with that stuff.

Rule # 1: *Decaf* is a word that most coffee cashiers don't hear the first time you say it, and sometimes not even the second time. You must repeat it several times throughout your order and make sure the cashier repeats the word *decaf* back to you, just to be sure.

Rule #2: When ordering size, just use simple terms: small, medium or large. For espresso, use single, double, or for those caffeine junkies who can't get enough of a buzz, triple.

Rule #3: Always specify milk type: nonfat, low-fat, whole, soy or for billows of white foam, 2%.

Rule #3A: The all-important milk information. This is a must-learn if you want your espresso bliss to match your vision. A macchiato is a dash of milk and a hint of foam. A cappuccino is a little milk and a lot of foam. A lot of foam and a dash of milk is a "dry" cappuccino, and an extra-dry cappuccino is no milk and a lot of foam. A latte is a lot of milk and a little foam, and a flat latte has no foam. Coffee with steamed milk can have several names depending on the house. However, "café au lait" sometimes works or "Misto," when ordering at Starbucks.

Rule #4: Be wild! Try adding a flavoring to your coffee. Just make sure you add it to your order in between the type of coffee and the decaf information.

Rule #5: *Always* tip. It's what keeps everybody behind the counter happy, and in turn these happy people will try their best to make you happy. It's one of those win-win situations we all strive for.

Rule #6: If ordering brewed coffee from a doughnut house or other establishments that add your sugar and cream for you, remember these basic tips: black = no cream, no sugar; regular=average amount of cream and sugar; sweet=extra sugar; dark=a little cream; light=more cream; extralight or extrasweet. If you don't want sugar but you want sweetener you'll have to be specific as to what kind: pink, blue or yellow.

And remember: Coffee is very hot...treat it accordingly.

TIPS:

E-mail Etiquette from Tracy Kelleher

Dear All,

So you wish to write e-mails that impress your boss, slay your sweetheart or make the Chief Justice of the Supreme Court take notice? No worries. Just follow these eight simple rules and you will shine in cyberspace...or at least avoid those embarrassing faux pas that have a way of living on...and on... and on.

1. To-ing and Fro-ing

You would think it wouldn't be that complicated to address an e-mail. Unfortunately, not everyone is enlightened regarding "To", "Cc" and "Bcc". Let me explain. "To" exists for those you need to take action. "C" is for someone you are indirectly addressing. You are basically sending them an FYI. "Bcc" refers to a blind copy; you are sending it covertly without the "To's" and "C'ers" knowing you've done so.

A word of caution regarding replying: Don't forget that hitting the Reply All button means everyone on the "To" list hears back. Did you really want everyone to know that you spent a wild night drinking champagne out of a shoe with Harry? Especially Harry's wife? Not to mention the person from whom you borrowed the shoes?

2. It's Not the Great American Novel

So many messages, so little time—especially if the e-mails go on longer than Homer's *The Odyssey*. To quote a politician I know, who is not incarcerated, "Be brief, be brief, be brief."

3. CAPITALIZATION and punctuation??!!

WHAT'S WRONG WITH SHOUTING, I ASK YOU??? Apparently, quite a lot, according to many e-mailers. Capitalization in cyberspace equals raising your voice. And a string of punctuation exacerbates the problem, besides conveying a certain Valley Girl diction. (Is that really how you want to address the board of directors?) My advice: Understatement, like a strand of pearls, is always appropriate. If you truly need to emphasize a word, surround it with asterisks.

As for punctuation, less is more again.
Think Japanese gardens, little black dresses
and scotch drunk neat.

4. Abbrev.

In the quest for brevity (See Rule 2) and
presumably in an attempt to avoid carpal tunnel
syndrome, e-mailers extensively use
abbreviations or acronyms.

A sampling includes such standards as:

BTW by the way

FYI for your information

More esoteric acronyms are becoming
commonplace. For example, for those who
want to convey a Hugh Grant-like modesty,
there is:

IMHO in my humble opinion

Or for the clowns among us, don't forget:

ROTFL rolling on the floor laughing

RTFM read the funny manual

And for the cynics:

TNSTAAFL there's no such thing as
a free lunch

Lastly, for those e-mailers who can relate
to the House of Windsor:

TTFN ta ta for now

FN final note:

Be judicious in the use of abbreviations. **OICLYFSTHARFA**. (Otherwise it can leave your friends scratching their heads and reaching for aspirin.)

5. ☺

Remember when girls who used watermelon-flavored Bonnie Bell lip gloss signed their notes with smiley faces? Well, teenyboppers no longer have the monopoly on these cheery little signs. Smileys or emoticons—to use the technical term—are now part of the regular e-mailer's vocabulary. :-)

Emoticons employ a combination of punctuation marks that supposedly portray a particular emotion, ranging from amusement to disgust to sorrow. They usually appear at the end of sentences. The argument for their proliferation is that these symbols are handy communicators of a mood, particularly humor, which often gets lost in the impersonal world of cyberspace.

One caveat: a few smileys go a long way, especially if the person to whom you are writing is graphically challenged. After too many smileys, the reader just wants to

:-@ (scream) and :-o (yell).

6. John Hancock

Back in the olden days, one used to while away the hours practicing a grown-up signature. Now you can fashion an unique electronic "you" by appending what's called a "signature" to all your e-mails. It identifies the sender with his or her particular profession, affiliation or address. After all, you never know. There could be more than one George W. Bush, not to mention, Pope Benedict XVI.

Something to keep in mind, however: your signature should be shorter than your message. Moreover, if you choose to add a "signature" quotation as an emblematic way of closing all your messages, keep it pithy and appropriate. Think of it this way: Does the claims representative from your health insurance company really need to know you cherish all the lyrics to "Blue Suede Shoes"?

7. To > or not to >

In replying to an e-mail with specific questions, it is customary to quote back the initial inquiries. These quotations should be indicated, using ">" at the beginning of each line of quoted text. This format is particularly handy, since it allows the replier to cherry-pick the relevant lines rather than repeat the whole message. Furthermore, in a more lengthy correspondence, more >s can be added to differentiate the order of e-mails.

For example, Mary asks Jane in an e-mail:
I have just received word from Reginald at the Smithsonian Institute that you have decided to abandon your career studying two-toed sloths. Is it true that you have run away to the south of France and are making lavender-flavored chocolates instead?

To which Jane replies:
>Is it true that you have run away to the south of France and are making lavender> flavored chocolates instead?
It is true I have moved to the Riviera, but I am sitting in the sun and eating chocolates, not making them.

To which Mary replies back:
>>Is it true that you have run away to the south of France and are making >> lavender-flavored chocolates instead?
>It is true I have moved to the Riviera, where I am sitting in the sun and eating > chocolates, not making them.
OK, that sounds more reasonable. I never could see you in the kitchen.

Of course, adding >s ad infinitum as the conversation progresses can get a bit ridiculous. One ends up more concerned with counting the >s to figure out who said what rather than deliberating over the actual substance of the e-mails. My words of wisdom on the topic: at a certain point, stop all the >s. In fact, stop the conversation entirely. Turn off your computer and smell the roses. Maybe go seek out Reginald, who now appears to be alone with the sloths.

8. Up in flames

What was it Thumper the Rabbit said? Something along the lines of "If you have nothing nice to say about someone, don't say anything at all?" The same holds true for e-mails. A hasty reply in anger has a way of hanging around in cyberspace. And don't kid yourself; *nothing* in cyberspace is private.

Lambasting someone via e-mail is called flaming. It is rude and will undoubtedly come back to burn you, especially when you least expect it—such as when you've forgotten that others were on the "Reply" list of the original e-mail. (See Rule 1.) In addition, responding to someone who has flamed you with a like-minded reply merely evolves into a flame war. Life is too short to go up in smoke. Instead, look on the bright side. Now there is one less person to whom you need to send holiday greetings.

In conclusion, while this list of dos and don'ts is hardly inclusive, it will help keep you on the straight and narrow in the world of e-mail. Remember, e-mailing is a form of communication in which clarity and courtesy are paramount.

All the best,
Tracy K.
E-mail Etiquette Adviser to the Cyberstars